JOBS FOR THE BOYS

BY

HERBIE NEIL

for Stephanie

love from

Grandad.

Enjoy

Acknowledgements

Although I wrote this book single handed, I couldn't have completed it without help and encouragement from good friends who commented on early partial drafts and made valuable stylistic and plot suggestions. Most of all they convinced me I should keep going! In particular I should mention Rick and Marilyn, David and Heather, and Carrie

A book is never finished until it's finished and the final task of proof reading proved to be an onerous one for poor Kath, who discovered dozens of instances of misplaced full stops and quotation marks, not to mention numerous places where my auto correcting spell checker had decided I meant "We'll"and not "Well". If only I could touch type, I could watch the screen and pick those up as I go along.

Lastly I would like to thank those kind folk who sent in such encouraging reviews when this book first appeared as an ebook on the Kindle platform. They may not have made me rich but they have made me feel it was all worth it.

Foreword

Readers of this book would be forgiven for wondering if any of it is true. Well the plot certainly isn't. However, many of the scenes featuring Eric's clients are based on actual cases, although the clients concerned are of course heavily disguised to protect their anonymity and it was all a very long time ago. Don't even assume they are necessarily the same gender! All of the naughty people in this book are totally fictitious.

The one group of characters that are a hundred percent genuine, even having their real names, are the Blues and Folk musicians featured. They are all well worth following up. If by some chance a couple of readers should make the effort to find and listen to their music, then they would be well rewarded. Most of them can be found on YouTube.

Finally, you may suspect that the character of our hero Eric is based on the early adult persona of the author. All I can say is, you might think that, but I couldn't possibly comment.

CHAPTER 1 - A TASTE OF PORRIDGE

Clang.

The slamming of the metal gate echoed round the brick walls of the block. Eric gazed upwards at the iron staircases and the balconies with safety nets stretched across to prevent suicides or worse. It was just like he had imagined. Victorian he supposed. It was almost cathedral like with its high ceiling topped by a lantern window letting the daylight stream in, so that the shadows of the iron work made patterns on the cream painted brick walls.

"So this is it. Bloody hell, this is really it. Porridge. He felt the hairs stand up on the back of his neck.

It was indeed just like the new Porridge sitcom on telly. All it needed was that Mr Mackay strutting round with his nose in the air and that would be it. The officer leading Eric though was nothing like Mr Mackay, or Mr Barraclough for that matter. His fat bum rolled in his shiny trouser seat as he waddled rather than marched, his feet splayed and his knees rubbing together. He might have looked better if his trousers and blue jumper hadn't been a size too small.

A rattle of keys. Clang. Through another iron gate and then, clang, another. Eric winced. All this clanging did nothing to settle his nerves. He spotted some characters leaning over the balcony looking at him. They didn't seem particularly bothered. One shouted "Oi Smiffy where's this one going?".

"Never you mind Bennett, and it's Mr Smith to you." More rattling of keys and the officer opened the steel door into the courtyard. "Take no notice of them sir, nosey lot of buggers all of 'em. There's the education block over there." Eric looked at the prefabricated huts across the yard. They might have been the temporary classroom blocks in any of the local schools apart from the twenty foot high wall looming behind them. Quite a contrast from the Victorian cell block they had just passed through.

"OK, thanks." He started off across the yard.

"Hang on sir, you can't just go walking about on your own, and in any case, you need me to unlock and let you in." Yet more rattling keys. Eric was beginning to get the picture. Every single door in the whole complex was locked. He began to realise that getting in and out of here was going to be a tedious process.

Once inside the education block Smiffy (for Eric had already decided the name suited him) showed him into the tutor's office, offered him a seat, then left after saying that someone would be along in a minute to look after him. Sure enough, it was only half a minute before a mousy little man in prisoner's blue trousers and striped shirt popped his head round the door.

"Cup of tea sir? Mr Cooper'll be along in a couple of minutes, he's just sorting out your lads." The mousy little man looked to be well into his sixties, his sallow complexion and thinning hair adding to his general air of frailty. Eric supposed he was an old lag, a trusty. Probably been inside a long time. The cup of tea when it came was weak and milky, just like Eric didn't like it. "Thanks," he said, "that looks lovely."

"No trouble," said the little man, "I'll remember to make it the same next time you come."

"Bugger." thought Eric

"Ah there you are. Jack looking after you alright is he?"

Eric looked up and blinked in shock. It was Andy Warhol! Well of course not, but it looked amazingly like him. The spit. Like Warhol always did, he looked ill. He had the same mop of white hair and those horn rimmed glasses. The man held out his hand.

"Cecil Cooper. You must be Dolan."

"Dillon. Eric Dillon." Eric took shook the man's hand and wasn't a bit surprised to find it limp and clammy.

"Aah yes, Dillon. Well the lads are all in the room for you. If they give you any trouble, I'll be in here. Just pop your head round the door and I'll sort the buggers out. Show 'em who's boss and they're usually manageable but give 'em an inch and the little sods will take a mile. Did security tell you about not bringing stuff in? It's a criminal offence if you do and these lads haven't learned yet to keep their trap shut. You'd be found out in no time."

"It's OK, I've had the lecture and signed the forms."

"Well I can tell you now, they'll try it on. You don't smoke do you?"

"No, never have."

"We'll that's start. They can't nick your tobacco then. Oh gawd it's half past two already. Time to get you in. Do you know what you're doing with them?"

"Yes," Eric lied, " I've got a programme worked out."

"Not that it matters." said Cooper, "They won't take a blind bit of notice. Waste of time if you ask me, but it'll keep 'em quiet for an hour." They walked out of the little office and up the short corridor past one empty classroom and then Eric saw his charges through the window of the next room. Young offenders they called them. Hard nuts probably. These lads would already have been through Borstal and various other punishments. You didn't get into prison at the first attempt. He took a deep breath as Cooper opened the classroom door.

"Shut up!!!"

Cecil Cooper might have looked like Andy Warhol, but he had the voice of a sergeant major. Sixteen youths, a motley looking crew, stopped their chattering and looked up. Their eyes met Cooper's in an open display of mutual disdain. Eric got the distinct impression that Cecil was not flavour of the month with the lads.

"This here's Mr Dolan."

"Dillon." muttered Eric apologetically.

Cooper looked irritated at Eric's interruption. "Mr Dillon from the Careers Office. You'll be having him every Monday afternoon for the next few weeks. If I was you I'd take notice of what he says. You're gonna need his help when you get out of here. Give him any trouble and you'll be on report. Understand? "

The lads just looked back at him. One of them, a tall skinny youth with buck teeth muttered loudly, "I ain't gettin no bleeding job. I'm goin' on the dole." The rest of the youths stifled a laugh. "Too bloody right."

"Alright, alright, settle down." said Cecil, "Over to you Dolan."

Before Eric had time to say "Dillon", the door slammed and Cecil was gone.

Eric surveyed the room. Just another classroom, much like any other. Posters on the wall warned of the dangers of drug taking and peer pressure. "JUST SAY NO!"

All was strangely quiet. Eric looked at sixteen lads and sixteen lads looked at him. Somehow he had expected them to look like criminals, but as far as he could tell at the moment they just looked like lads. Some were black. Most were white. Some looked twenty years old, some looked twelve. Eric knew that they were all sixteen or seventeen. Any younger and they wouldn't be here. Any older and they would be outside his jurisdiction. He wondered what they were in for, what offences they had committed. He assumed you weren't supposed to ask. They were all dressed the same. Blue and white striped shirts and denim trousers. Each lad sat behind one of those little single desks you get in exam rooms.

Eric thought he had better break the silence before they did. He cleared his throat and attempted a smile.

"Well 'er hello. I'm Eric Dillon and as Mr er Cooper says, I'm a careers officer."

He paused. The look on their faces said "And?. . .."

Eric had thought about what he would say. He'd thought about it all week. He instinctively realised now he had wasted his time. The reality of looking at these sixteen youths lolling about in their chairs brought the certain knowledge that his planned speech would have gone down like a lead balloon. He would have to wing it.

"Er, well, over the next few sessions I want to see if we can get you set up for when you leave here. Tell you how I can help you get fixed with a job or some training."

Was this the right thing to say? Blank faces stared back. The big ginger boy at the back of the room yawned loudly.

Eric pressed on, his mouth taking over from where his brain should have been. "But as well as that I don't see why we can't make it enjoyable!" He smiled inanely. "I've got some quizzes and games that we can have a go at. They'll help you to think about what's right for you and you can find out about how to choose a job." God, what did he say that for? Eric winced as he heard what he was saying. His quizzes and games were the ones he used for fourteen year olds in schools. They weren't designed to amuse seventeen year old criminals.

"Can we play one now?" It was one of the black lads. Except he didn't look like a lad. A deep voice, dreadlocks and a stubbled chin. "Games is good. I likes games man. I mostly wins."

"That's 'cos you always cheats Wesley" It was the big ginger lad.

"Shut up Clive. You always loses 'cos you's fick as two short planks."

The rest of the class thought Wesley was right about Clive. There was even a little ripple of applause. Eric thought he had better move on quickly. Maybe he could get away with it after all. "Well I can bring a game in next week but today I thought we might talk about what you'd like to do on the rest of the course. You can ask me any questions you like about jobs, local firms, qualifications, er," He paused for breath

"Have you got any sweets?"

"Sorry?"

"Have you got any sweets? Mints, sherbet lemons." It was a rather scary looking skinhead lad in the front row, a scar on his forehead. "Can you bring some in?"

"Ah, well, no I, um, can't. They told me I mustn't bring anything in or out. Apparently it's a criminal offence." Eric was getting blown off course.

"How about out some wine gums? Come on, you could hand them round in the lesson and they'd all be gone by the end of the lesson. No evidence."

"Leave him alone Nigel, you'll get us all into trouble." This was a surprisingly smart looking lad sitting in the middle. Hair Brylcreemed back, white fingernails, shiny boots.

"And you are?" Asked Eric.

"A creep" Wesley got in first, "watch out for Thunderclap sir, he's always brown nosing but as soon as your back's turned.."

Sir? Did Wesley call him sir? Only kids in school did that.

"Shut it Wesley," interjected Brylcreem/ Thunderclap. "My name is Henry Newman, Mr Dillon, and when I leave here I'm setting up my own business. So I won't be needing your services, but I'm interested all the same and I strongly urge the others to give you their full attention."

Eric was beginning to feel unsettled. It wasn't supposed to be like this. He had expected a load of hard cases, perhaps trying to get him to bring in hashish and thinking only of careers in crime. In his mind he had prepared for possible intimidation, or attempts at bribery and corruption. Instead, what he seemed to have was a skinhead called Nigel asking for sweets, a black man with a stubbly chin calling him "sir", and now a young entrepreneur. He'd obviously guessed wrong about what these lads would be like.

Eric decided on a change of tack. "OK before we totally lose the plot here, can we get back to the subject of jobs? Can anybody suggest what it is that makes a good job? Why you would choose one job rather than another."

An old favourite this. Something Eric had done loads of times in schools. After a bit of coaxing the lads started coming up with answers. Money, holidays, not having to dress up, indoors, outdoors, perks, interest, driving, travel, getting a trade, . .. Eric wrote them on the whiteboard, ignoring the ones about chances to nick stuff and measuring ladies for underwear. Then he got a few volunteers up to write ranking numbers up against each topic. It never failed to surprise him how money never came out top. This was actually OK, he was getting away with it even though it was something he usually did with fourteen year olds. There were even spontaneous debates springing up at times. Wesley and another big lad called Clive got quite animated on a discussion of the relative merits of skills training and higher pay. Amazing. Time flew. In fact they all seemed surprised when the bell rang to indicate the end of the session.

Cecil Cooper put his head round the door. "Time's up. Stay put you lot while I get Mr Dolan taken out." He ushered Eric back into the tutor's office. "I've rung for an officer to escort you out. I'll get Jack to do us a brew while we're waiting. A bit noisy in there wasn't it? Don't forget I can come in with the heavy hand if they get too stroppy."

"Oh it was Ok., just healthy debate. I'll be alright I think."

Eric sat with his luke warm milky tea and pondered over the last hour. It could have been worse.

Then there was the topic of the other reason he had been sent to do the job. He'd bide his time on that.

CHAPTER 2 - UNDERTAKINGS

Getting out of jail wasn't easy, even though they had given Eric a get out of jail free card, well a pass anyway. It seemed that escorting visitors through the prison was low on the list of staff priorities. He sat waiting in Coopers stuffy little office for what felt like an age. He surveyed the shelves and the bookcase. A few sets of course books, French, basic maths, and an adult reading course were joined by an assortment of literary classics which looked as though they had never been opened. The other shelves were an untidy jumble of pots of pencils, odd bits of stationery and a couple of photos of sports cars. On the one clear wall was a torn and faded poster of a Picasso painting with eyes and noses pointing in various random directions. This was not a cosy or homely little den, the haunt of someone who enjoyed being there. It was just an office.

When Smiffy eventually showed up to take him out through security it was clear that he thought seeing people in and out was a bloody nuisance. If visitors had to wait, it was their lookout. It looked like Eric's weekly hour would take up a whole afternoon.

Back across town, Eric entered the front door of the office building. The front entrance always depressed him. How anybody worked up the nerve to come in was a mystery. A less welcoming impression would have been hard to design. The team had been chucked out of their previous warm and pleasant offices in the town centre when a local councillor saw the rent bill. This one was about a third of the price, and no wonder. He sniffed and sighed. The kids had pee'ed in the lift again. He took the stairs. Struggling up four flights was better than enduring the pong in the lift.

"Ah they let you out then. What was it like? "It was Wendy the receptionist. "There's a girl waiting to see you. Hazel Tanner, says she has an appointment."

"Oh it went OK I suppose. Hazel who? Oh I remember. Rang yesterday. Has she been waiting long?"

"Not too long, I told her we were waiting for you to get out of jail. She looked a bit taken aback. Quite white faced actually."

Hazel was indeed very white faced, but somehow Eric thought it might be her normal colour. Hmmm smart suit, black hair brushed back in a bun, pale make up and bright red lipstick. Not yer average 17 year old at all.

"Hello Hazel, come through to my office and have a seat. Sorry you had to wait. I've been in prison all afternoon."

"Yes, they said. Nothing serious I hope." She smiled.

"Well they let me out anyway. Sorry for the long walk."

It was truly a long walk up the corridor to Eric's office. He had often counted the number of paces it took to walk to reception and back. Sixty two. Sometimes he did that little journey fifty times a day, because all of the record cards of young people and the job vacancy cards were kept there.

The young person's record was called a Y1, probably a hangover from the old days when the service was called the Youth Employment Service. The Y1 was a manila card envelope containing school report forms, questionnaires filled out by the young person, careers officer interview notes and a copy of the "prescription" handed out to the young person post interview. On the outside of the card were name, address and date of birth, the name of the school attended, and most importantly the general type of career recommended by the careers officer. On the back of the Y1 was the list of jobs that the young person had had, together with start and finish dates.

Now how can I help you?" Eric ignored his untidy desk and sat with Hazel in easy chairs by a little coffee table.

Interviews across a desk might have been OK for formal interrogation, but for guidance work you needed to adopt a more co-operative layout.

"I was hoping you could give me some information about becoming an embalmer."

"Excuse me?"

"An embalmer."

"An embalmer?"

"You know, in a funeral parlour."

She looked perfectly serious, although still smiling politely. She was obviously not having him on. Before Eric could ask her why, she continued.

"I went to see my Gran at the undertakers after she passed away and she looked so nice, all made up and that, and I thought it'd be nice to do that for people. I thought you might be able tell me what it involved."

Eric glanced at Hazel's Y1, the recommendation said personal service/medical, based on an interview by his colleague Linda nearly two years ago. Not a bad guess then. He cleared his throat. He was fairly sure embalming didn't feature in the green bible. The green bible was the standard issue loose leaf binder with details of career entry requirements. He stumbled on.

"Well, er, Hazel, I don't get asked about embalming a whole lot. In fact you're the first. Do you have a job at the moment?"

"I'm doing A levels at the college. English, art, and law. I'd thought about medicine, but I'm really not that clever. Embalming is sort of medical isn't it, and I want to do something helping people."

"Helping people." Eric repeated the phrase as if to help his brain to absorb the concept.

"Yes and I'm good at art, so this way I could put both things together couldn't I?

"Art. Well, er I guess so. Have you discussed this with your parents?"

"They just say to do whatever makes me happy, and it's a steady job."

"Well I suppose there is that. Look Hazel, I have to confess I don't know a lot about careers in the funeral industry." That was a lie. He knew bugger all. "I'll just check the book, but I doubt there's an entry in there, but stranger things have happened." That was another lie. He couldn't off hand think of a stranger thing. He leafed through the heavy book trying funeral director, undertaker, and embalmer, but all to no avail.

"Hmm just as I thought Hazel, you've beaten the system. I'll tell you what I'll do. If you can make an appointment for next week, I'll do some research for you. Maybe I can fix it for you to meet with someone from the funeral industry. How would that be?"

"That'd be lovely thanks. I can't say I'm surprised it wasn't in your book, I drew a blank too down at the library. Your idea sounds good. I'll see you next week then." She rose, smoothed down her skirt and smiled. Eric showed her the way back to reception to book a time. He couldn't help thinking what a pleasant mature girl she was. Employable anywhere. But a funeral parlour? At her age that was just weird.

Back at his desk, the phone buzzed. "Mr Kitchen on the line for you Eric."

"OK Wendy, put him on. Oh, and Wendy can you make me an appointment to see the boss of a funeral parlour?"

"Beg pardon?" It wasn't surprising that Wendy thought she had misheard.

"I know it's odd, but can you just fix it for me. I'll explain later. Now can you switch the big chief through please." Arthur Kitchen was the PCO, Principal Careers Officer for the County.

"Hello Mr Kitchen"

"Afternoon Eric. Just calling to find out how you got on at the Young Offenders Unit at the prison. Was it alright?"

"Errm, yes I suppose it was. It might take a session or two to find my feet but I dare say we might do a bit of good for one or two of them."

"Good, I knew you'd be the right man for the job. What about the other business?"

"Ooh, much too early to say, but there might be something in it. I'll keep you posted."

"Good man, I'll expect to hear from you later then."

The right man for the job. Eric never started out to consort with criminals, but it did seem that it was becoming his speciality. All the earnest middle class, young, psychology graduate females in the service spent their days talking to A level students, helping them choose which Uni to apply to for Sociology or European History, while Eric, a technology graduate, did the rounds of the school refusers units and trying to find work for lads who had "had a bit of trouble with the law". Not that he minded. He was never comfortable dealing with the well to do echelons of society. Not with his upbringing. With the working class, you knew where you were. Getting a trade was what they aspired to. A skill. He recalled the wise words of his mentor Morag Hamilton in his first year. "They might be rough diamonds Eric, but they are nonetheless diamonds."

Eric did of course have proper schools to look after. Two of them. Chalk and cheese. First Oakfield Boys, hub of the largest council estate in the county. One report he had on a pupil before interview said simply "Probably the brightest pupil the school has ever had. Might get three O levels." Strangely though, getting jobs for Oakfield lads was rarely a problem. The building trade in particular seemed to prefer them. They knew these lads had a good solid no nonsense education. Only a couple of years ago, until 1972, these lads would have left school at fifteen. Now they were required to stay until sixteen, they were that bit more grown up. They might not make the professions, but they knew one end of a hammer from the other and liked working with their hands. They would be the essential makers and doers of the community, and many would acquire valuable skills.

Contrast with Eric's other school, The Red House. At first he couldn't fathom why they had allocated a private school to him, but he soon worked it out when he went there. Although they would never admit it in writing, this was an independent academy for the sons of the nouveau riche. Lads whose dads had made a few bob selling used cars, or developing property. They even had the offspring of a couple of minor celebs, a TV comic and a snooker player. Dad might not have had much of an education but mum wanted her little baby to be something respectable. The trouble was that most of the lads had no more academic leanings than their dads. Worse still, a good many of them were clearly browbeaten by their overbearing parents. Meeting the expectations of these families was not nearly so easy as getting an Oakfield boy a plumbing apprenticeship.

"Oi ain't you got no home to go to?"

Lovely Rita the ever cheerful office cleaner stood at the door, a fag hanging out of the side of her mouth. "Come on you, it's nearly six o'clock. Bugger off home."

CHAPTER 3 - HAPPY BLUES

Mississippi John Hurt should never have been the success he was. Alright he had the qualifications. He was from Mississippi, and he was poor, black, and quite old when they rediscovered him in the 1960's. That put his blues legend score up no end. But MJH was really the odd one out. Blind Lemon Jefferson, Blind Willie McTell, Blind Blake, Blind Gary Davis, - John Hurt didn't even wear glasses except for reading. What was much worse, he was happy. With his domed hat pulled down so hard that the wide brim squashed down the tops of his ears, and with his wide grin and his big working man's hands he looked every inch the kindly old grandpa. A happy blues singer. It didn't seem right.

Then there was his voice, soft, warm, and gentle. Old country blues singers were supposed to grunt and moan. You had to listen to their records dozens of times to figure out the words. That was the way it was supposed to be. MJH had it all wrong, you could make out every word and even songs like "I got the blues and I can't feel satisfied" sounded cheerful. Lastly, there was his guitar playing. MJH appeared to have entirely missed out on the obligatory bottleneck slide and the pentatonic blues scales. His bouncy foot tapping accompaniments were melodic and much more folksy than bluesy.

Eric worked hard to play guitar like Mississippi John Hurt. The reason was simple. Women liked it. Eric was a normal red blooded male. Almost everything he did in life boiled down to his need to find a mate, preferably a soul mate, but in the absence of that, a bit of ordinary mating would be good. However, in dealings with the opposite sex he didn't have the self confidence to adopt the direct approach. So he did things which he hoped might tempt prospective mates to approach him. Sometimes it actually worked. Mississippi John Hurt's songs were especially good in this regard. The songs were cute and cuddly and if he got them right it made him look equally cute and cuddly.

The favourite, the one that worked best, was a song about a young bounty hunter, Louis Collins, shot dead by his quarry. The record sleeve described it as '"a threnody after death by violence." Threnody?? Eric looked it up in the dictionary. It said "a lamentation after death by violence". So, thought Eric, Louis Collins is a lamentation after death by violence, after death by violence. He liked that. He always used it in his introduction to the song. Of course in the MJH version, the threnody became not so much a lamentation, more a song of comfort to the bereaved.

Tonight Eric would sing it at the Science Lab social club. They had a folk club there on Mondays. The local folk scene was thriving. Tuesdays was the White Lion, Thursdays the Queens Arms, Fridays The Lord Palmerston and Saturdays the Arts Centre. Eric went to them all. It was practically his entire social life.

Playing a bit of guitar and learning the odd song had been a godsend to Eric. Moving into a new area for work, he had not known a soul. After doing a floor spot at a folk club, complete strangers felt they knew him a bit and acquaintances were easy to make, even unattached females, who under other circumstances Eric never seemed to meet.

Floor singers got about ten to fifteen minutes up front, or three songs. That was the deal. Eric nearly always over ran, because he tended to rabbit on in his song introductions. Nobody seemed to mind because for some reason Eric could never work out, people thought he was funny. Maybe it was the air of desperation he put into his performances. He'd get very keyed up before his spot. A bit of adrenaline was always a good thing, except it tended to raise the pitch of his voice. He always had to set his guitar capo two frets up for a live performance. Once he was out in front of the audience, the adrenaline took over and the nerves turned to pure energy. It was only when he returned to his seat that he realised he was soaked in sweat.

Tonight went well in terms of Eric's performance, but in his main aim of attracting sexy women like moths to a flame, he drew the usual blank. There was a slim blonde girl in the third row. Eric noticed her as he was playing. She was watching him intently. He tried hard not to look stupid as people giggled at his performing antics, but it was hard to look cool when you were doing a song about a hippie crying about having his hair cut. At the break, Eric was looking out for her when he was accosted by Gerald.

Gerald wore a cravat. Say no more.

"Enjoyed your set Eric, especially the bit where you missed that B minor chord and played an F sharp instead. Priceless." Gerald snorted a laugh.

"Ah well, good to keep you on your toes Gerald. Glad you were paying attention." Eric was looking over Gerald's shoulder try to see the girl, but she was nowhere.

CHAPTER 4 MILKMEN AND CHRONIC JOB CHANGERS

Tuesdays was Oakfield day. They had a nice little careers suite with a library and a cosy interview room. They also had that great rarity, a full time careers teacher, Lennie, a likeable bloke with a heart of gold and a remarkable resemblance to Harold Steptoe on telly. Eric and Lennie got on well, they were kindred spirits and they made a good team.

"What you got for me today Lennie? Please tell me they don't all want to be carpenters and painter decorators." It was hard doing a day's guidance interviews when all the kids were interested in the same jobs. Keeping concentration was a struggle. Eric kept losing track and was never sure if he was asking the same question to the same kid twice, or was it in the previous interview?

" 'Fraid so Eric, but I've fixed up a treat in the lunch break. I've got four lads who all want to be milk men, and I got in touch with Davis's dairy to find out what sort of test they give to applicants, so we'll see how these lads cope with it. You can sit in for a bit of entertainment."

The dairy hadn't revealed their test questions of course, but they had told Lennie the kind of things they asked. If a customer has had seven pints of milk this week at six pence and three loaves of bread at fifteen pence, how much should they be charged?

"Sounds fair enough, how d'you think they'll manage?"

"No idea," said Lennie, "but I'm not getting my hopes up. Lovely lads, but this lot was at the back of the queue when the brains were handed out. Being a milkman is pretty aspirational for them I would think. Oi up, here's your first interviewee."

True to form, the five interviews before lunch were all with lads who aspired to building apprenticeships. Eric longed for a nice would be gardener or sign writer to break the monotony, but it rarely happened at Oakfield.

The milkman test was, as Lennie predicted, quite an eye opener. The lads appeared to be as keen as mustard. Eric sat with Lennie in his office eating sandwiches while the lads wrestled with the four questions Lennie had set. Luckily the sound of pencils being chewed was drowned out by the school's brilliant steel band practicing next door. Eric began to feel refreshed to face the rigours of the afternoon.

Lennie marked the test sheets in a couple of minutes while the lads waited outside. "Well, how have they done?" Eric was curious.

"Hmmm. Well, put it this way." said Lennie scratching his head "If they got the job, these lads would be the only milkmen whose customers were fiddling *them*. I'll go and break the news."

Aah, sad really. Eric looked through the glass partition as Lennie broke the bad news. Four pairs of eyes blinked. Then four sets of shoulders shrugged and as though nothing had happened, the lads charged out into the playground to join in what was left of the lunchtime footy match. None of them looked above twelve, but they were all fifteen. Poor little buggers. Probably under nourished. Eric knew he would be dealing with them himself before term was out. He might find them something, or more likely they'd wind up working for an uncle on a market stall or washing cars.

The afternoon was a bit more entertaining than the morning. One lad was actually not interested in a building trade. Hallelujah. Deep joy. Even better, he wanted to be a chef. Right up Eric's street. He had done a project on it in his training year. Seizing the moment, he warmed to his subject, spilling out his deep knowledge of City and Guilds courses and training opportunities in the hotel trade. The lad's mum was dead impressed. Variety was indeed the spice of life.

Often when school finished, Eric would go straight home to write up his notes, but today was the last day to hand in his travel expense form so he popped back to the office. That was a mistake. The waiting room was heaving with kids and Wendy was looking stressed.

"Oh Eric, be a love and see one of these kids will you, we'll never clear them before closing time at this rate."

Eric sighed. "Ok who've you got?"

"Sep's in again, how about him?"

"Sep? Again? What's he done this time?"

Septimus Augustus Boswell was a regular. With a name like that, you might expect him to be the product of an aristocratic family and a public school, but far from it. Sep was in fact from Romany stock and his dad was a scrap metal dealer before he died of a heart attack at fifty two. The family was hard up now and Sep was supposed to be the main bread winner although he was only just seventeen. However, despite the responsibility thrust upon him, Sep was no good at holding down a job. He was what the Careers Service referred to as a chronic job changer.

Eric had done a statistical survey of chronic job changers when he was in training. Typically, these young people would have in excess of a dozen jobs a year, sometimes as many as twenty. Eric had gone through the records of all of the ones registered at his office. There were about twenty five of them. The similarities were depressingly familiar. Large low income families, poor or non existent academic achievement, and a high proportion were known to the police. Sometimes they left their jobs because they couldn't stick it, sometimes they got the sack because they were regularly late for work, or quite often they failed to show up at all. Eric got to know a number of them only too well because they were such regular customers. Despite the fact that they were a bloody pain, Eric actually got to like a number of them. They weren't bad kids, they mostly just had never had a role model to show them how to get on in life.

And so it was with Sep. Eric took him into his office and sat him down.

"What was it this time Sep? Late for work? Breaking things?"

"Nah. It wasn't my fault, honest. I just kept getting sawdust down the bloke's neck. He shouted at me. I didn't like it there anyway, so I walked out. Ain't you got anything outdoors Mr Dillon? I feels cooped up inside."

Eric didn't bother to further investigate the sawdust incident, he knew it wouldn't get him anywhere. "You know you won't get any unemployment benefit Sep; you left voluntarily."

Sep knew alright, he'd been there before. He sat there looking down at his hands while Eric gave him a talking to about keeping his temper. He was a nice lad but he had a very short fuse. On the positive side, his mum always sent Sep out looking scrubbed clean although his clothes were often pretty threadbare.

Eric looked at the back of Sep's Y1. "You're getting more and more difficult to help Sep, that's seven jobs you've had this year."

"Yeh, I know. Just find me a job outdoors and I'll stick it, honest."

Eric took his usual sixty two pace stroll down to the vacancy files and back. A miracle. There was one that just might be alright.

"Sep, there's a job here. Little firm your end of town. Fencing contractors. You'd be digging holes and putting up posts and rails. Ten quid a week. It says they want a strong willing lad. Urgently required so you might get lucky."

"That'll do me. Can you ring 'em up?"

"Only if you promise you won't let me down this time Sep. I can't have you back in here next week saying you walked out again or got the sack."

"I won't, honest. That'd be a good job for me. I done a bit of that wiv me uncle once. I liked it."

Eric phoned the employer explaining that Sep was a good strong lad but needed a firm hand and that he'd lost his dad and needed someone to look out for him a bit. The employer sounded like he was a bit of a rough diamond himself. "Send him down. As long as he can do the physical work he'll be fine. We'll look after him as long as he works hard. If he don't, well a sharp clip round the ear might put 'im straight."

It was Hobson's choice really, and Sep and his family needed every penny, so the deal was done. Eric just hoped that it would work out this time and Sep would heed the advice he had given him. He filled in yet another line in Sep's Y1 and noticed he was running out of blank lines.

Time to go home, shopping on the way for ingredients for a bacon and mushroom risotto. Eric had learned a bit of cooking when he was a student, but he didn't go much beyond meals he could cook in one pan. He had a dislike of washing up.

That night was the White Lion club. Perhaps that blonde girl might be there.

She wasn't.

CHAPTER 5 - ONE MAN'S MEAT

Wednesday was Eric's industrial visit day. One day a week he was supposed to visit at least one local company to learn about employment opportunities, about what the jobs involved, and more often than not, to fail to convince the employer that it would be worth taking on and training a school leaver. Once he could find an employer willing to take a visit, Eric would always learn something. He especially liked the tours round factories, seeing how they made biscuit tins, or filled beer bottles.

Today was a special treat although this time he wasn't hoping for a back room tour. Quite the opposite in fact. His interview with the funeral director had been set up. Finding the place would be easy on a normal day, Eric had passed it every morning for the last two years on his way to work. Today was however, not a normal day. Freezing fog and black ice. What would normally be a ten minute drive took him nearly an hour. He parked on the hard standing outside and went into reception. The homely lady at the desk wore a fuzzy black cardigan and a twinkling smile.

"Cup of tea? Poor love, you look frozen. Mr Burnapp will be with you in a few minutes. He is expecting you. Quite looking forward to it I think. We don't ever get enquiries about careers in our line of work. A pity really, I love it."

Bang. The office door swung open against the stop and a large red faced man stood on one leg, clutching his other foot. "Ow, Ow. That door 'll be the death of me. I told Harry to fix it." He looked up. "Aah hello. Don't mind me I'm always stubbing my toe on that damn door. Are you the chap from Careers? Very pleased to see you."

He held out a huge hand and Eric winced when he felt its iron grip. "Come away into the office young fella me lad. I expect Olga has offered you a cup of tea has she? Or would you like a nip of something stronger?" In the little office he opened the bottom drawer of the grey metal filing cabinet revealing a bottle of malt whisky and some rather expensive looking crystal tumblers. "It's bloody freezing out there today. Proper brass monkey weather."

"Well, er, " Eric was partial to a nice malt but he was sure he wasn't supposed to drink on duty.

"Well I'm having one so you wouldn't want me to drink on my own would you?" Mr Burnapp smiled broadly and gave Eric a wink.

Eric nodded in assent and accepted the proffered glass. It was alarmingly full.

Mr Burnapp raised his glass. "Happy days." He downed it in one. "Now then, to business. What's your name son?"

"Dillon. Eric Dillon."

"Pleased to meet you Eric, call me Jim. We like first names here. One big 'appy family we are. I must say it's nice to have one of you chaps come to see us. Quite a treat. People generally steer clear of us until they become customers, but they don't need to. One big 'appy family." Jim was indeed a jolly character. You couldn't help warming to him.

Eric sipped his malt. He blinked. Jesus, it was a belter.

"Drink up lad and we'll have a refill and get down to business. You've got some young lass with an interest they said."

"Yes, she's asking about embalming. I have to confess I don't know anything about it. Do you do that here?"

"Oh yes, every day. I got a lovely lady, Freda, been doing it for us for years. Hygienic Services we call it these days. A work of art if you do it right. Lovely job. You have to learn a lot mind. There's proper qualifications for it these days, got the college brochure here somewhere. Drink up lad before I put this bottle away."

Eric drained his glass and accepted another huge refill. "College?"

"Yes, the industry runs one. Belongs to one of the big firms, but they let us independents send folks there. At a price of course. Quite scientific the course is, I don't even understand the subject titles. People can die of anything you see, there's a lot to know about infectious diseases and all that. And safe handling of chemicals and disposal of fluids. Not making you feel queer am I?"

Eric was OK if a little discomforted. He took another gulp of his malt.

"That's the spirit young Eric. Anyway, where was I? Oh yes, then there's the make up side, getting the deceased ready to be viewed by relatives. We can cover up all sorts of damage, you'd never know. It's a lovely job really. Very satisfying."

Eric skim read the college brochure and asked a few pertinent questions. He was sure he had enough to feed back to the girl who had enquired, so he moved on to ask about other jobs in the firm.

"Of course, there's your's truly," explained Jim, "I meet the clients and explain everything and then I do the business at the ceremony. Olga does all the paperwork, booking vicars and the crematorium and all that. Then there's the lads that polish and drive the vehicles and carry the coffins. They're on piecework, it's not a full time job, we just call 'em in when we need 'em."

"Can they earn a living that way?" asked Eric.

"Oh I should say so," Jim laughed, "if we get a few more of these lovely cold snaps they'll make a good living this winter."

Eric spluttered, he nearly choked on his malt.

"Oh"

Lovely cold snaps. After that he somehow didn't take any more in. He just kept thinking of hypothermia.

After he left, Eric went for a walk. He was sure if he went back to the office they'd smell the booze on his breath. He bought a big bag of extra strong mints and sat in the car writing up his notes as he sucked. When he eventually decided to move, he drove the back way round by the railway arches to avoid the queues of traffic. There were lots of little industrial units there, one man outfits mostly. Just occasionally he placed a school leaver with one of them, usually a manual job, but sometimes they could pick up a skilled trade. Glancing up the end of a row of units Eric saw a new sign. Cathcart Motors. He decided to take a look.

Opening the sliding door of the building he was struck by the smell of paint thinners. Aah, a car body repair shop. "Morning sir, can we help?" A man was kneeling by the wheel arch of a Rover. "Had a knock have we?"

"Morning. Ooh it's nice and warm in here. What terrible weather, I'll be glad when this month's out."

"You might be guvnor, but for some of us this freezing fog is manna from heaven. Give it an hour or two and they'll all be in here with their dings and scrapes. Lovely jubbly." The man rubbed his hands. "Your's outside is it? Let's go and have a butchers at it."

Eric explained that his car was so old it was what the insurance companies referred to as uneconomical to repair and that he was merely prospecting for jobs for his clients. The man was not unsympathetic, he had lads of his own, but he had only just moved into the premises and didn't have enough work yet to consider a helper or an apprentice. Maybe if this bad weather kept up, he might be in a stronger position after Christmas.

And so Eric made his way back to the office with a new found appreciation that one man's meat is another man's poison. Maybe there was such a thing as a lovely cold snap after all.

As for Hazel, the girl who enquired about embalming, he met again with her the following week and passed on all the info. Two years later, she called in at the office to thank him. Now qualified and employed, she was one of only three people in his whole career who came back to say thanks.

"Don't take your coat off, Kitchen's been after you again. Wants you to call in at the Kremlin at twelve."

Eric looked at Wendy and sighed. "It just took me fifteen minutes to find a spot to park the car, and now you're pushing me out in the freezing fog again."

"Poor old you. Look, just sit in the warm for five minutes and I'll make you a cuppa. You'll still have time. Here," she sniffed the air, "can you smell spirits? You haven't been at the bottle have you?"

"Eh? Oh no, I've just been talking to a bloke in a car paint shop, trying to find jobs. You can probably smell the thinners." Eric congratulated himself on his neat escape.

The Kremlin was the colloquial name for County Hall, about ten minutes drive out to the edge of the town. Eric, now feeling weary and not yet entirely sober, made his way up to the PCO's office.

"Aah, hello Eric. Mr Kitchen will be with you soon, he's just waiting for another gentleman to join you." Daphne the

PA sniffed. You been varnishing your nails or something? I can smell thinners."

"No that's the whisky." Eric smiled, "I had a couple of large ones to stave off the cold."

Daphne laughed. "Good job I know you better or I might have believed that. Oh here's the other gentleman now. Would you both like to go through?"

Despite him being head of the service, Kitchen's office wasn't any bigger than Eric's little box of a room. The Careers Service was one of three or four departments that liked to refer to themselves as the Cinderella service.

"Come in, come in and have a seat. What terrible weather. I expect you'll want a hot drink. Can't afford anything stronger I'm afraid." Kitchen grinned, although Eric knew he was a teetotaller. "Now then Eric, meet Ian McNeish, Head of Audit."

McNeish offered his hand. "Hello Eric, call me Jock, everyone else does." Eric recognised the accent as Glaswegian so his moniker was hardly surprising.

"Audit?" Eric was nonplussed.

"Don't worry, you're in the clear." said Kitchen, "Ian, er Jock, just needs your help. You remember we asked you to observe the work of Cecil Cooper while you were in prison doing your sessions?"

"Yes of course," Eric interrupted, "but I thought that was only because people had reported that he was er,"

"Not delivering a good education. Yes," Kitchen broke in, "but it seems that there might be more to it."

It was Jock's turn to speak. "Naturally I can't divulge too much Eric, but it has come to our notice that our Mr Cooper may be involved in something more serious than mere incompetence."

"Well, I don't see what that has to do with me." Eric was a bit taken aback. Why was he being told this stuff?

"It's like this Eric." Jock leaned forward "Being as it's inside the prison there isn't really anybody we can trust, and we don't have any jurisdiction in there apart from the employment of Mr Cooper. All we need you to do is keep an eye open and report back on anything odd that you see."

"What about the prison officers? Can't they do it?"

Jock smiled. "Aah if only. They're not County staff. Plus, I'm afraid Eric, that the way of the world is that prison officers are not unknown to be involved in shady dealings. We need someone we can be sure of."

"How do you know you can be sure of me?" Eric was beginning to feel indignant.

For a brief moment, Jock looked uncomfortable then he smiled a somewhat patronising smile. "Let's just say we are happy that you're an honest citizen."

"You mean you've been checking me out?" Now Eric really was indignant.

Kitchen butted in. "Perhaps I should just explain that we have been able to assure Jock that you are a known and trusted member of staff and leave it at that. Now can we move on? What exactly is Eric supposed to be looking out for?"

"Well," said Jock, "it's come to our notice that Cecil Cooper's lifestyle is somewhat more extravagant than his salary band would permit. People have been muttering about it. Then we got a call from the Prison Governor asking us what was all the fuss about Conversational French."

"Excuse me?" Eric was naturally puzzled by what he was hearing.

Jock went on. "Cooper's Conversational French course for the adult prisoners has suddenly become very popular." He looked over his shoulder conspiratorially to check that the office door was closed. "Very popular indeed. And not only that, the people attending are not your ordinary cons, but the big boys. The ones the little guys run in fear of. Know what I mean?"

"I'm sorry Mr Kitchen, but I'm not getting mixed up with spying on hardened criminals. It's not in my job description. You can't ask me to do something like this. I might be in danger. Anyway I only have contact with the young offenders." Eric felt no shame in his zeal for self preservation. "And another thing, I don't see what right County Audit have asking us to do their work."

Kitchen leaned forward. "It's like this Eric. The prison education unit is part of the County's Education Department just like the Careers Service, but if Audit are seen to be taking an overt interest then everything is likely to get covered up. In any case, it might just all be speculation. We need a softly softly approach. Now, you don't have to take any risks or take any specific action. All we need is for you to tell us anything you notice in your normal line of work."

Eric sat in awkward silence for a full half minute, then said, "Well OK but don't expect me to go asking suspicious questions or poking my nose into places I don't belong. Actually, I very much doubt I'll be in a position to see anything."

"Well if you don't, you don't." said Jock, "But I'd like to give you a call after your next visit. When's that?"

"Next Monday."

"Ok, I'll call you Tuesday. One thing you might do is to keep an eye out for any French stuff left on the blackboard. It might just give us a clue. Mr Kitchen tells me you have French O level"

"Yes, yes. OK."   Eric was weary of argument and capitulated. The others didn't notice that it was the whisky that had finally sapped his will power.

CHAPTER 6 - RED HOUSE

Eric's battered old jalopy rattled down the long winding drive, suspension graunching over the speed humps as the ivy clad school building hove into view. There was something musty about the Red House. A private boys' school it might be but it was pretty down at heel. The cars in the staff car park were mostly better than Eric's, but that was not difficult to achieve. His car was falling to pieces with rust. The tyres were thin and the engine was on its last legs. It had cost him seventy five quid, and he had been ripped off. The teachers' cars were mostly Minis and Volkswagen Beetles. They might have been old, but they were in much better nick than Eric's. Not that the pupils in the school were impressed by any of them. Once, he entered a classroom and a couple of pupils were idly gazing out of the window. One said, "Look at all them VW Beetles in the car park." and the other replied, "Well, it's all this class of person can afford."

Of course they were right. Not that Eric would have minded a Beetle. It was a cut above his old wreck of a motor. His old banger might have been one of the great car designs of the twentieth century, but the ravages of time and rust got the better of all cars in the end and Eric's was well past its expected life.

Eric parked the old banger in as hidden a spot as he could find and made his way to Charlie Tanner's room. Charlie was the teacher with responsibilities for Careers. A nice old buffer, a pipe smoker with one of those tweed jackets with the leather elbow patches, and then over the top, a faded academic gown covered in chalk dust. He didn't actually do any careers teaching or advising, Latin and German were his subjects, but he was Eric's point of liaison. He sorted out which boys needed to see Eric. Largely these were the ones without any hope of getting significant academic qualifications. The brighter ones were kept well away from Eric, presumably for fear he would talk them into leaving. Sixth form students were a valuable source of income for the school.

"Just got four for you this morning Eric." He struck a match and puffed at his briar pipe to light the tobacco. "God knows what we can do with them; they don't have a bloody clue, any of 'em. One of them has his mother coming in. Mrs Marshall. Expecting miracles no doubt. They think because they're paying for an education that their kids will turn out to be brain surgeons or captains of industry."

Eric was, as ever, more confident that he could make progress with these young people than others expected.

"Leave 'em to me Charlie. We'll make a start today and then perhaps we'll see them again next term when they've had a chance to ponder over what we discuss today." He knew that the problem with a lot of these kids was that they had yet to work out who they were. A lack of self-awareness. His job at this stage was to get them to think about themselves and to begin to recognise their own capabilities, likes, dislikes, circumstances and all that. Thinking about specific careers would have to follow later.

They had sorted out an interview space in the corner of the library. A sort of three sided cubicle formed by the arrangement of the tall oak book cases. Three easy chairs and a coffee table made it quite cosy. It was a good arrangement in theory, as it made for relaxed conversation, but it meant Eric had to make his notes on a pad on his knee. The penalty came later when he tried to read what he had scrawled.

The first three were straightforward enough although none of them had a clue what they wanted to do. Expecting a careers officer to make up their minds for them was beyond the realms of common sense. So Eric started at the beginning, patiently going through the youngster's attributes stage by stage trying to get them to form a self-image, not only of what they were able to do, but to question their own needs and values and to recognise any special opportunities their circumstances might present. That was about as far as you could go on a first interview in such cases.

Number four was Philip Marshall, a tall, thin, shy boy accompanied by mum, a petite lady in very high heels and one of those wrap around macs with a belt you tied rather than buckled.

"Pleased to meet you." She shook Eric's hand and he noticed her look him up and down, appraising him from head to toe. She must have approved because she then continued, making rather more eye contact than he was comfortable with. "I've been so looking forward to this interview. Philip needs all the advice he can get, but you know what boys are like, they never listen to their mum, you can't tell them anything. Do you mind if I smoke?" She sat down and started rummaging in her handbag.

"Well, er I don't think smo..,"

"Do you want one? Gitanes, my husband picks them up when he's working abroad. Never at home he isn't. Have you got my phone number on that card? You might need to call me." She lit up her cigarette, took a long slow drag, and smiled as she looked at Eric. "You know, to discuss Philip and that. Do you do home visits?"

"Well er, we don't normally ..."

"It's very warm in here. Do you mind if I take my coat off?"

Eric blinked. Would he ever get a word in edge ways with this woman? Where was Philip in all this? Actually, there was no need to worry. Gazing out of the window with a blank expression on his face is where he was.

Mrs. Marshall took off her coat revealing an archetypal little black dress and a very trim figure. Nice legs too, thought Eric.

Whoops, he noticed her noticing him looking at her. She smiled again and sat back down. She tapped her cigarette ash on his empty tea cup. "Well, shall we start?"

Eric was disconcerted. In less than a minute this lady had put him right off his stroke. She was certainly over familiar, and he didn't altogether like it. Well, actually he did, but he knew he shouldn't, so it made him uncomfortable. He gathered himself and tried to focus on Philip.

"Now Philip, let's talk about your interests."

And so the interview proceeded, with Eric doing his utmost not to catch the mother's eye. This was not at all easy, as she was leaning forwards looking into his. Philip was an unprepossessing boy, and progress was slow. The pauses were difficult. Mrs Marshall, her legs crossed, kept smiling and making encouraging comments. She seemed to be hanging on his every word. It was all very intimidating. As for Eric, his palms were sweating and he was trying not to blush. All he could think of was that she was silently flirting with him. A bit blatant to say the least, and right in front of her son and all. Somehow he got through to the end. Well, to the end of the allotted time anyway.

Eric summed up and gave Philip some reading matter. Mum shook his hand and stood uncomfortably close to him as she looked purposefully into his eyes. "Thank you so much, you've given us a lot to think about. Perhaps we could continue the discussion later. Can I call you at your office?"

"Of course. Ring for an appointment when you're ready." What else could he say?

They got up to leave and as she passed out of the door, Mrs. Marshall turned. She looked Eric up and down again and said "Until later then." Eric flushed and mumbled something about sending an interview report.

Once on his own he sat and gathered himself. "Jesus Christ, did that really happen? Coming on to me like that, and in front of her son!" What was worse was that she was very sexy. It was hard to remain professional in circumstances like that. He didn't know whether he ought to be pleased or to run a mile. He let out an ironic sigh. Bloody typical. He had spent half his life wishing he could get off with women, then when he encountered one that fancied him she was off limits. It always seemed to happen, the ones that were attracted to him were not his type and the ones he fancied were unobtainable. He looked down at the record card for Philip. No phone number. Eric didn't know whether to be relieved or disappointed.

A knock, and Charlie came in, lighting his pipe. "That's your lot Eric old chap. Hope they weren't too ghastly. How did you get on with Mrs. Marshall? She's a bit of a man eater by all accounts. Did she say what her old man did? 'Something in entertainment' is all our records say."

"Er, no. She didn't say." He changed the subject. "Got your diary? We need to book in those group sessions.

CHAPTER 6 - THE STREET SINGER AND THE CADDIE

The Reverend Gary Davis was one of the greats. The old blind guitarist and singer started out in North Carolina but he eventually settled in New York where he made a living singing and playing on street corners. He was another of Eric's unlikely blues guitar heroes. I mean, how could a blind man with a badly set broken wrist play guitar with such virtuosity? Actually it was a miracle he had survived at all. A blind man busking on the mean streets of Harlem was an easy target for thieves. He had lost a couple of guitars that way, not to mention his meagre takings. Someone wrote that the Rev Gary had eventually got a gun to defend himself. It occurred to Eric that a mean street with a blind man wielding a pistol was not a place he would like to be, guitar virtuosity or no.

A lot of Gary's songs were too hard for Eric to play, and as for the singing, well, Gary was a real street singer with a loud rasp like a gospel preacher. "Bad company brought me here" was Eric's favourite. It was a song relating the lament of a boy waiting to go to the electric chair. One of Eric's few musical strengths was that he knew his limits, and that particular song was way beyond them. He stuck to one he could do, "All my friends are gone" in which someone at a card game shoots a lady called Delia with a forty four calibre pistol. Eric preferred a modified version by Stefan Grossman in which the weapon becomes a "great big Gatling gun" Quite how anyone could go into a bar carrying a Gatling gun was a bit of a mystery, but there it was. How could Eric not sing a song like that?

It was Thursday night. The Queens Arms at the top of the steep hill out of town was always packed. The folk club had a room upstairs with creaky floors and the window curtains behind the singer would light up as the buses passed outside. Downstairs the public bar was pretty rough, reflecting the general population of the area, and on the wall outside the back door which led to the outside Gents urinals was a sign made up of individual capital letters each on its own glazed tile. It simply said "COMMIT NO NUISANCE". Eric feared that nuisance was indeed committed here most Saturday nights, which was probably why the folk club was on Thursdays.

He liked the Queens Arms club. The room was always packed and full of energy. The audience didn't come just to listen, they came to join in. They sang, laughed, cheered and barracked. It made for a great atmosphere, no doubt helped by the fact that the beer was cheap and well kept. Tonight he did his Gary Davis song and one by Loudon Wainwright, another of his musical heroes. Wainwright's songs, desperate and funny at the same time, always hit the spot if you were brave enough to commit to them.

Desperation suited Eric. He was good at it. The more desperate his performance, the bigger cheer he got when he finished. Some of the more talented and serious performers seemed to resent Eric's popularity, muttering about his admittedly dubious singing voice and the triviality of his material, but he didn't bother about that. What he was a bit anxious about was whether the ladies thought he was a bit of a fool. That was why he generally included something more poignant in his set.

Two studenty girls with long hair watched him intently as he sang, and afterwards came up to ask about the Rev Davis. Being a normal red blooded young male, he switched straight into chat up mode. It was hard to say which of them he liked more and he did his level best to keep the conversation going until two blokes in rugby shirts came up with the girl's drinks and gave him a distinctly disapproving look. The girls smiled and returned to their seats with their boyfriends. Ah well, another defeat snatched from the jaws of victory. One day . . . .

Eric spent most of Friday preparing a talk he had to give at Oakfield parents evening next week. Most people dreaded the thought of public speaking, but not him. The showman in him made it fun, and he liked making up the coloured pie charts and little cartoons with speech bubbles on overhead projector acetates. He made use of anything to amuse the audience whilst he got over his points about academic subject choices for types of careers and all that stuff. The desk top was full of coloured pens and scraps of acetate, and finished sheets festooned the walls of the office.

Wendy poked her head round the door as Eric was scribbling and humming to himself. "Sorry to disturb your revelry Eric, but it's mayhem in reception. Do you think you could see one or two people to cut the waiting time?" He sighed. No rest for the wicked. Much as Eric liked working with his young clients it was really nice to have a day off. "OK. Give me a minute and I'll come and get somebody."

Next on the list was a boy they had no record of, just a name, James Hall, and a date of birth showing he was just sixteen. Normally virtually every young person had been seen by the time they were fifteen when they were still at school, and so a Y1 would be made up ready for the day they might come into the office looking for help or advice. Eric walked him up the corridor to his office. "Excuse the mess James, or is it Jim? I'm preparing a talk."

"Call me Albert, everybody else does."

Eric thought that was a bit odd, but he continued. "We don't have any records for you, um Albert. Which school have you been at?"

"Oh I haven't been at school for quite a while. Nearly a year. The head got fed up with me getting into trouble and so when I didn't show up, they never really chased me. I been doing bits of work." The boy showed no embarrassment or remorse at his failure to complete his education; in fact he seemed remarkably comfortable in his own skin.

Eric sat back and studied the boy. He didn't look like a school leaver, more like an eighteen year old. He'd easily get served in a pub. Mature looking lads were often at an advantage when they went for job interviews. Employers had more confidence in them.

"Bits of work?" Albert would have been too young to be legally employed in school time, but Eric knew it happened more often than people liked to admit. "What kind of work?"

"Caddying down at the Grange." The Grange was an exclusive golf course a mile or so from town. "They've got a hut where us caddies wait, and the players come along and ask one of us to carry for them, and they pay us whatever they like at the finish. Sometimes, if they like you, you get to carry for them regular. I done it for some famous people sometimes. Most players down there have got plenty of money. There's nobody in charge, you just turn up and wait to see if anyone picks you. Anyway now I'm sixteen I can get a proper job can't I? So that's why I'm here."

"To get a proper job eh? What sort of job?"

"Something outdoors: good pay. I can work hard. Them golf clubs is heavy."

Eric didn't see a lot of point in asking the usual questions about best school subjects and all that, so he just asked the boy to wait a minute while he went to consult the vacancy files. Albert was in luck, there were half a dozen jobs vacant that he might be alright for, one with a roofing contractor, a landscape gardening labourer, yard work at a builders merchants and a couple of others of a similar ilk.

With his mature looks and strong physique he would stand a good chance of being taken on. He took the vacancy cards back to the office and spread them out across the desk.

Albert peered at them. He nodded his head in approval. "Some of these look alright. Which one pays best?"

"They're all much of a muchness. The going rate is around ten or twelve pounds a week to start with. Normal sort of pay for these kinds of jobs at your age. Not bad really."

"What?" Young Albert seemed taken aback. "Not bad? Ten quid a week? You're jokin' ain't yer? If you don't mind me saying so, that's terrible. I've been earning twice that down the golf course." The boy rose to his feet. "Thanks all the same mate, but if that's really the going rate, I'm going back down the Grange."

Before Eric could gather himself, the boy had gone. He could hear him whistle as he half ran down the corridor. When he "came to", Eric pondered what had happened and realised that he didn't blame him. In his position he would have done the same. Some kids didn't need to follow the system to make a good living. He suspected Albert would be driving round in a nice car by the time he was eighteen. In twenty years' time his kids would probably be at the Red House school.

Eric turned to the record card to write a note of the interview. He amended the front of the wallet to reflect the fact that the boy called James Hall preferred to be called Albert. Eric laughed as he realised why. Nice one.

The weekend was good. A quick trip down to the market for some fruit and veg, an hour or so reading the paper in the launderette, a lunchtime pint in the Bull and back to the flat to get on with some guitar practice. Eric needed new material to sing; he couldn't do the same old stuff week after week. He was a quick learner when it came to lyrics, but it took him ages to work out guitar chords by ear. By the end of the day his finger tips were really sore, but he had nailed another good Loudon Wainwright song, so he was well satisfied. He knocked up a meal of fried tomatoes and egg and bacon, grabbed a quick shower, coaxed the old motor into action and headed off to the Arts Centre.

He was a bit late, so the place was humming by the time he got there. He added his guitar case to the pile of similar cases in the corner and headed off to the bar.

"Hello Eric, lovely to see you. Are you doing your drowned lovers song tonight, it's so gorgeous." It was Alice, she was gorgeous too but off limits. The story of Eric's life. Alice was engaged to Gary, the club organiser. She had a nice friend though, Elaine who always set Eric's pulse racing. Elaine played a nylon strung guitar and sang Joan Baez songs. He had been gently chatting her up for some weeks.

"Is Elaine in tonight?"

"No, gone home to Cheltenham. Her Gran's eightieth birthday. Big family party."

Just Eric's luck, he was beginning to think he'd never get lucky with women. Never mind, it was time to get psyched up for his performance. He bought his pint and went back upstairs to wait his turn. When it came, he did pretty well. He over ran as usual but seemed to be forgiven. The crowd of thirty-odd folkies laughed at the Loudon Wainwright song, which was a good thing because they were supposed to. However there was one person who didn't seem to get it.

"Rather odd choice of material Eric, are you sure it qualifies as folk?"

"Oh hello Gerald."

There's always one.

After the club, Eric tagged along when a few of the others went round to Alice's flat. Even Gerald came. Bottles of cheap red wine were dug out from dark cupboards and people performed some of their party pieces. Sometimes two or three would form an instant group and attempt a familiar song, with pretty mixed success it had to be admitted. It seemed the only time he hung around with these people was when they were singing and playing. He had no idea what the rest of their lives were like. Neither, he supposed, did they know anything about him. People's personalities and character were judged by what and how they sang. Maybe that was as good an indicator as anything else. One thing he did know was that a lot of them liked a drink.

It was well into the early hours when the music finally ground to a halt. Some of the gang had left. Others had just fallen asleep. Next morning Eric woke up to find himself in one of Alice's armchairs. Others were draped over various chairs and the sofa. It seemed they had had a good night but his head hurt too much to try to remember the details. After a slice of toast and jam, he sloped off home to sleep off his hangover. Got to be alert tomorrow. Prison day.

CHAPTER 8 - FRENCH LESSONS

Eric was a bit late getting to the Education block. He had had to wait ages for an escort. They put him in the waiting room with the young mums and toddlers waiting for their periodic visits to their inmate loved ones. He came to realise that the visitors waiting room was the saddest place in the prison. A toddler played with wooden bricks on the floor while his mother, pale, drawn, and shabbily dressed, sat chewing her nails. No mistaking what sector of society they came from. Crime obviously wasn't paying. Eric would bet they didn't come here in a BMW. Life for a prisoner was no tea party but for the wife or partner it was worse.

While they all waited, Eric sat thinking about his secret mission, telling himself to act normally. Whatever normal was. By the time he actually got to the Education block, it was ten minutes after his class start time, but Jack the trusty showed him into Cecil Cooper's office.

"'Aah Dolan, they got you in at last did they. Lazy sods those escort officers. It's a wonder anything ever gets done in this place. Anyway sit and have your tea, the lads can wait."

Jack came in with the teas. "There's yours sir, I remembered how you like it. Plenty of milk."

Yuck. Eric thanked him and said, "Lovely". He hadn't the heart to tell him otherwise.

"How many classrooms have you got here Mr Cooper? It's not a very big facility is it?"

"Only the two you just walked past, plus a little library, and a small group discussion room and that's it. The discussion room gets used by the so called therapists. Huh." Eric gathered from the way that Cooper spat out the word "therapists" that he didn't think much of them.

"So you can have up to two proper class sessions at a time then? Is that enough?"

"Yeah. Just about. Not too many of the inmates have a yearning for learning. One or two classes are popular."

"Like what?" Eric feigned a casual interest but he felt his hands clench as he asked.

"Oh literacy, basic maths, and one or two others"

"Your French class is doing well sir."

Jack was watering the pot plants on the window sill. Cooper gave him a sharp look and said "Shouldn't you be sorting out the library Jack? Off you go." Turning to Eric and looking somewhat rattled he said "Time you got your class started Dolan. Oh and while you're in there, use the whiteboard would you? The stuff on the blackboard is saved for my next class."

"Yes, yes, right. I'll, er, get on then."

Eric went into the classroom. The boys actually looked pleased to see him.

"Afternoon gentlemen, how are we all?"

"Oh bleedin' marvellous, it's like an 'oliday camp in 'ere".

"Thank you Wesley." Eric was pleased with how he could remember names, not that Wesley was too difficult a name to recall when the lad was West Indian. He looked round the room. "Where's what'sisname this week, um, Clive the ginger lad?"

"Banged up in the chokey."

"Excuse me?"

"Banged up in the chokey mate."

"Would somebody care to translate that into English?"

"Confined to solitary sir. He stole a broken hacksaw blade from the metalwork shop." It was the Brylcreem boy who answered. "He reckons he was going to saw through the bars of his cell window. The only trouble is, his cell's on the fourth floor. If he'd have got out he'd have broken his neck. I told you he was a dumbo."

"Yeah," said skinhead Nigel, "after he'd been sentenced in court, he tried to make a break for it. Tripped over an usher's foot and knocked himself clean out. What a plonker."

Well, that lightened the mood. Most of the lads were now laughing and cheering. Eric thought he had better bring the room to order before Cooper poked his nose in.

"Did you bring in any sweets then?" Nigel, despite his hard looking exterior was obviously a big kid.

"No Nigel, I told you before, they won't let me. Now can we settle down and make a start. I've brought in a handy little questionnaire for you all to have a go at. Just a bit of fun, but it'll sort out what types of jobs you might enjoy most."

After explaining the rules of the exercise, he let the lads get on with ticking the boxes on the answer sheets. Once again he was surprised how co-operative they were. He supposed anything which broke the boredom of prison routine was a pleasant diversion. While they were busy ticking boxes, Eric gazed round the room. His eyes fell upon the blackboard. French! He sat up. It was all in French. Maybe there's a clue for Jock the auditor. What did it say?

"Est ce que vous aves une chambre pour une nuit?"

"C'est combien?"

"Je le prends."

Each line in different handwriting. It looked innocent enough. A room booking dialogue. He supposed the students had been called up to write up their bits. Still, he noted it down on a scrap of paper and tucked it in his folder. Jock might want to see it. Eric felt a bit of a buzz. Maybe this was a bit exciting after all. Cloak and dagger stuff.

The lads soon completed their questionnaires and Eric showed them how to score their answers. It was a clever little sheet really. Respondents were asked state a preference between two occupations in each square of a grid. "Would you rather shear a sheep or help a disabled child to walk. Would you rather install wiring in a house or add up the cost of a customer's bill?" and so on. All kinds of jobs were compared with all other kinds in this way. The cunning thing was that occupations in a particular category, say outdoor, were arranged in diagonal rows of the grid squares. You wouldn't notice this when filling in the form, but afterwards it was easy to see if you got a lot of ticks in a particular diagonal.

Before they could discuss the results a klaxon sounded and Cooper put his head round the door. "Time to finish, Dolan. These lads have to get back to the main block." Eric's late start had not left enough time, so he'd have to continue next week.

Surprisingly, Smiffy the escort showed up almost immediately and Eric was marched out along with the lads, saying cheerio to them as they reached the metal staircase in the main block. He wondered where the chokey was. Poor Clive. What a plonker.

That night, Eric tossed and turned. He'd never dreamt in French before.

CHAPTER 9 - MR LLEWELYN

Next day at Oakfield, Lennie had a special favour to ask of Eric.

"Eric me old mate, do you think you could come along to a meeting with a parent at half past three? You don't need to rush off do you? We've got this tiny little lad called Gwynfor Llewelyn."

"Irish is he?"

"Oh very funny. Anyway as I was going to say, he's very immature, and not doing well at anything much. His dad can't admit to Gwynfor's limitations and he's insisting we put him in for science 'O' levels so he can study to be a doctor. He's got more chance of being Dr Who if you ask me. Margaret Harris, head of year will be heading up our side, but we might need you as backup in case careers come up."

"Gawd, you do give me some treats don't you Len. OK, but you owe me one."

Half past three came and Eric and Lennie walked across to the main block where Margaret Harris was waiting. "Hello Eric, pleased to meet you, and thanks for coming. This is liable to be a bit difficult to put it mildly. Our Mr Llewelyn is not much of a listener. We might need to gang up on him for Gwynfor's sake."

"What does Llewelyn do, for a job I mean?"

"Oh he's an accountant or something like that down at Highfield House Hospital. You know, for mental patients. He acts more like a fire and brimstone preacher. You wait till you meet him. It'll be entertaining if nothing else."

The meeting was held in Margaret's office. It was too small really, but in schools that was normal. Eric was used to interviewing in stationery cupboards, cloakrooms and the like. Mr Llewelyn duly arrived and was offered tea, which he refused. Actually, dismissed might have been a better word. He was a remarkably small man, but fiercely imposing. He was meticulously dressed, his thinning grey hair was slicked back against his scalp, he sported a neatly trimmed moustache and little gold rimmed specs. He carried with him a sheaf of notes, which was obviously his prepared speech.

Llewelyn jumped straight into the driving seat. Before any of the teachers could get a word in edgeways, he launched into his prepared diatribe, a tirade about the lack of ambition the teachers had for Gwynfor. They were, he insisted, selling him short and holding him back. Margaret, a model of restraint, responded patiently, talking through the boy's dismal exam results and homework marks and tried to get over the fact that the poor lad was struggling to follow courses for which he wasn't mentally equipped.

Llewelyn looked angry and affronted. "I don't think you fully comprehend the situation." he began in his rich Welsh accent, "My son has abundant natural intelligence, and I will now demonstrate that he must do. In my role at the hospital I have become thoroughly acquainted with the science of intelligence. It is, you see, influenced by two factors, heredity and environment. Now, you infer that Gwynfor is lacking in intelligence, but this cannot logically be so. I shall explain." This was turning into a lecture. Llewellyn went on.

"His heredity of course comes directly from me and clearly I am a highly intelligent person as I am the holder of numerous professional qualifications. As for Gwynfor's environment, he lives alone with me and I can assure you all that I personally ensure that he has every opportunity to learn. Every opportunity."

Llewelyn was in his stride now. It was obvious he was approaching the climax of his speech. He rose to his feet, clutching his coat lapels, his back straightened and his chin pointed skyward like David Lloyd George addressing parliament, his voice trembling with emotion. He looked around the assembled company, then with all the power and gravity of that great orator he announced "I will have you all know, that in his room, Gwynfor has the Complete Works of Charles Dickens."

There was a brief shocked silence. Margaret sat open mouthed. Dumbstruck. "But Mr Llewelyn," Lennie pleaded, "Gwynfor can't read!"

Eric didn't know whether to laugh or cry. This poor little lad. What chance did he have with this father breathing down his neck? Perhaps there was a way through to the father. He was clearly a man to be impressed by psychological theory. He cleared his throat. "Mr Llewelyn, would it help if I offered to give Gwynfor a special opportunity to undergo some psychometric tests which might indicate his leanings towards particular careers? These tests are not generally available as they can be misinterpreted," he lied, "but as you clearly have some knowledge of psychology I'm prepared to make an exception. Once we have those results then we could set up another meeting with the school to discuss the most appropriate subject and level choices."

Llewelyn narrowed his eyes as he looked at Eric. He tapped his fingers on the table. After what seemed like an age, he nodded. "This gentleman has just made the first sensible suggestion I have heard on this matter and after due consideration, I am prepared to go along with it. I will allow Gwynfor to undergo these tests, which will reveal I assure you, his true capabilities."

The relief amongst the school staff was palpable. Margaret wrapped up the meeting with a few placatory words and Eric and Lennie walked back across the yard.

"Cheers mate, I really do owe you one." Lennie said.

"Hmm, well it might have placated him for now, but I don't hold out too much hope that he'll be pleased with the test results when we're done. Is Gwynfor really illiterate?"

"Virtually. At any rate, I don't reckon he'll be finishing the Complete Works of Charles Dickens any time soon."

By the time Eric got back to the office, it was nearly closing time. Wendy was tidying up the waiting room. The kids always left it in a mess, Coke cans under the seats, chocolate wrappers stuffed down the back of the radiators, and screwed up balls of paper lying round the waste bin where throws had missed.

"Aah, Eric. I thought you weren't coming back tonight. Some bloke's been on the phone for you three or four times this afternoon. A Mr McNeish. Wouldn't say what he wanted. Very cagey he was."

"Oh, ah, yes, um, a mate of mine. Probably didn't want to let on it was a private call. You didn't happen to get his number did you? I might give him a call now before I shoot off home."

"Yeah, I left it on your desk. I'm off now. Turn the lights out when you leave will you?"

Eric walked along to the end of the corridor to where his office was. All the other rooms were now empty. Good, he would be free to talk to Jock without being overheard.

The call went straight through to Jock's private number. Eric told him about Cecil Cooper's touchiness about mentioning the French class and read out the French phrases he had copied from the blackboard.

Jock was intrigued. "Do you know what they mean? My school French is pretty rusty."

Eric explained that they were merely lines about enquiring about a hotel room booking.

"You don't suppose they're planning a job in France do you? Cooper might be helping them organise it." Eric was really getting into this detective business. "Do you think Interpol ought to be alerted?"

"Hang on Sherlock, I think you might be jumping to conclusions a bit old son. Och, it's very probably nothing at all. Nothing at all. Just keep your eyes and ears open next week and call me again. And don't go doing anything to arouse their suspicions, do you hear? We don't want them getting wind of our interest. We're keeping a very low profile on this one. Did you see any papers on his desk?"

"Piles of 'em, his in tray looks a mess, but he wouldn't keep anything incriminating in his office would he? What about in his car?"

"We're only audit, not the police. We can't go round searching private property, that's a police job, and they won't be interested unless we find that a crime has been committed. By the way, have you seen his car?"

"No, why?"

"Silver blue Mercedes convertible. Brand new. That's part of what drew him to our attention. Not the sort of car a bloke on his salary can normally afford. Although in fairness, he might have inherited enough to buy it. His Mum died a couple of months ago. County Councillor on the youth offending committee. She was alright actually. Met her a few times. Anyway, enough of all this, I'm off to the match in an hour or so. Do you follow the Blues?"

"Not that sort of blues." said Eric. "G'night"

CHAPTER 10 - INVITATIONS

Nehemia "Skip" James was mind blowing. A one off. Nobody sang like him and nobody played like him. He had a smoky falsetto singing voice and tuned his guitar in his own weird way, often to an E minor chord. How did he think that one up? Nobody did that! This ethereal mixture of voice and guitar made up some of the most haunting blues music ever recorded.

Like a lot of the great old blues men, he made records in the 1930s, then sank into obscurity until the new generation of blues guitar freaks dug him out in the 1960s. Thirty years older, but as good as ever, he re recorded a lot of his back catalogue and stunned people with his appearances at the Newport Folk Festival. Truly a living legend was old Skip.

Eric could never hope to sing like Skip, no-one could, but he had mastered one accompaniment which sounded great even without the words. Hypnotic and bluesy, it had a real power. The song was called Special Rider in which the singer laments the receipt of a letter telling him his sweetheart has died.

Eric's guitar playing rarely impressed other guitarists, but this one actually did the trick. Sometimes he showed them how to play it, but it was so different from conventional folky playing that they never took it up. Likewise if anyone tried to learn the tune purely from written guitar tablature, they would never get it to sound right. You had to hear and feel Skip's recordings for the music to make sense. It was the feel and not the technique that mattered.

Eric liked the White Lion Folk Club. There seemed to be different crowd there from the others. People played different stuff and there was a lot of mutual support amongst the performers. The room was long and narrow and people were crammed in along the walls. The performers had to clamber over half the audience when it was their turn to go to the front.

That night as usual, Eric fell a bit in love with the female guest artist, an urbane city girl singing her witty songs about female angst. He was used to falling in love with lady singers. To him it was perfectly routine, and of course it never led to anything.

In the interval, she came up to Eric, saying she liked his playing of Special Rider. He said he liked her stuff too. Then they ran out of things to say. Somebody announced it was time for the raffle and another of Eric's fantasy females faded away.

Another Wednesday, another industrial visit. Eric was trying to put together a list of good places to take school groups on industrial visits. Somewhere they could see for themselves what work places were like, and where they could see young workers at work. Sometimes this was to inspire them to work hard at school. Sometimes it was to show them what they might have to do if they didn't work hard at school. Today was one of the latter.

Spray Industries was a place where aerosol cans were filled. Filled with all manner of stuff, perfumes, paints, insect repellent, you name it. The stuff came in in big drums, and they doled measured amounts into empty aerosol cans before adding the propellant and fitting the spray nozzle and cap.

Apart from the engineers who maintained the production line machinery, there were virtually no skilled jobs there. Staff turnover was high and wages were low. At the Careers Office there was nearly always a vacancy card for Spray Industries. It wasn't a complicated selection procedure. If you could stand up and count to ten then you had an excellent chance of being accepted.

The strange thing was, if you could find the right sort of person, they would sometimes stay there for years. It needed to be someone for whom the stresses of having to think for a living were too great. A high IQ was definitely a disadvantage. Eric tried not to be judgmental about this. He knew only too well that there were people who struggled with numeracy and literacy, who might be withdrawn and over awed by complex situations, and would find comfort and even pride in being able to manage a very simple routine task.

Ray, the production manager showed Eric around the factory. It was clean and bright and had the most amazing range of odours according to whatever they were filling the aerosols with at that time. Workers were loading empty cans onto moving belts from cardboard boxes or taking the full ones off at the end and putting them into more cardboard boxes. In one special room, workers wore protective clothing and masks. This was where the more noxious products were handled; nothing really dangerous, but things that might be irritant.

Ray relied on Eric to keep him supplied with staff and Eric was glad of it when he had a client that might otherwise be difficult to place. "That girl you sent me last week Eric, Karen Thomas, only stayed two days. Rang in sick on the third day and we haven't seen her since."

Karen was another of Eric's chronic job changers. "Mm, that'll be about her eighth job in the last two months." said Eric, "Sorry about that, but it was worth a try."

Eric relied on a few employers who understood these kids. They might lose a good many, but they really tried with them and just occasionally they would make something of one of them. Ray was a bit like that. He would bend over backwards to give kids a chance, sorting out their transport problems, teaching them how to manage their money and all sorts. He took Eric along to see Lindsay, a girl Eric had placed there six months ago. "She was always late at first, and had terrible concentration, but we coaxed her along and now I reckon she's here for good. Come and see her at her workstation." Eric remembered Lindsay well. She was a very slow girl, always getting rejected at job interviews because her personal hygiene was awful. Also it didn't help that she was virtually illiterate. She had often come to Eric asking him to read official letters she had received and getting him to fill in forms for her. Sending her to Spray Industries had been a last act of desperation on Eric's part.

They walked along the production line until they came to the part where the filled and pressurised aerosol cans were leak tested. The conveyor belt carrying the cans sloped down and into a water bath about ten feet long and a foot deep. Lindsay stood alongside the water bath peering into the water and watching the endless stream of cans moving steadily past. She seemed immobile for several minutes, just listening to the pop music blaring out from the shop floor loudspeakers, occasionally mouthing the words of a familiar song. Then suddenly she would plunge her hands into the water and pull out a can. "A leaker." said Ray, "She sees a can emitting air bubbles and oiks it out. That's a reject. Never misses one as far as we can tell. Hello Lindsay, do you remember Mr Dillon from the Careers Office?"

"Course I do. Hello Mr Dillon, how ya doin'?" Lindsay never took her eyes off the water bath for a second. "I'm fine Lindsay, glad to see you settled at last. Do you like it here?"

"Yeah," she seemed surprised at her own answer, "I do! I can listen to the radio and think about anything I like. The canteen food is good as well. I don't need to have a dinner at 'ome; I gets what I wants here. I been savin' for an 'oliday and me and my boy friend's goin' to Butlins next month."

"A boy friend eh! Well done you." Eric noticed that Lindsay was indeed looking a lot more presentable these days." He turned to Ray, "And well done you."

Back in the Ray's office over a cuppa, they worked out a couple of dates for school parties to visit. Ray didn't really expect it to produce anything in the way of recruits but as far as he was concerned, Spray Industries was a part of the local community and ought to do their bit. As far as Eric was concerned they did as much good, if not more, than social services sometimes did.

Back at the office all was quiet. The weather was too damned cold it seems for the unemployed youth of the town to venture out looking for jobs. Actually it was too damned cold in the office too. The heating system was pathetic and there were draughts from all the doors and windows. Eric was sure the temperature in there was below that stipulated by the Shops, Offices and Railway Premises Act. If he could be bothered, he should make a formal complaint, but it was too cold to bother. He nipped downstairs and out into the town to get some lunch to warm him up. The bakery next door did some nice little mini pizzas and you could get them hot. He bought two and took them back to the office where Wendy made him a cup of hot coffee.

He was scribbling a few notes on his factory visit when the phone rang. "Yep" he couldn't say a lot more, his mouth was full of pizza.

"Got a lady on the phone asking for you Eric, a Mrs Marshall. Says you saw her at school recently."

Jesus, it was her! Eric nearly scalded his mouth trying to wash down the pizza with the hot coffee. "Mrs Marshall, Eric Dillon here, how can I help?"

"Hello there. Do you mind if I call you Eric? You can call me Doreen by the way. After our meeting the other day, which I found very helpful, I was wondering if we could set up another meeting so my husband could join the discussion."

That sounded safe enough, surely she would behave more discretely with hubby there. "Yes, of course. Let me look at my diary, I'm pretty booked up for the next week but there might be a couple of slots."

"Ah well the thing is, George, that's my husband, is away for work such a lot that we can't really make any appointments in office hours next week. Could we do something after hours? If your office is closed, you could come to us."

"Well, that's not something we normally . . ."

"I'd be ever so grateful. Would seven o'clock tomorrow evening be alright? It needn't take long. You could stay for a drink and a bite to eat after."

Eric rarely did home visits, but this one sounded alright if it would get her off his back, so he capitulated.

"Ok then, seven o'clock. I've got your address here, and I'll bring you some reading material you might find helpful."

"Bless you." she said, "I'll look forward to it. 'Bye Eric."

That last sentence unsettled Eric. She was putting on that sexy voice that women know how to do. No, it was OK, hubby would be there.

No folk club on Wednesday night, so Eric picked up a couple of bottles of beer on the way home and decided on a night in. He had bought a copy of *The Transfiguration of Blind Joe Death* by John Fahey. With a title like that he thought the album couldn't fail to be interesting, and anyway John Peel had played bits of it on the radio

Eric's two roomed flat was really pretty good. It had been allocated to him by the council as his job designated him as a key worker. When he first came to town he had to go and see the housing officer to show them his job offer and sign the forms. "The rent is seven pounds a week," she said, "paid monthly in advance. Is that something you can afford? How much will you be earning?"

"Eighteen hundred a year." said Eric.

"Oh," she said, appearing quite satisfied, "you'll be fine then."

Although the flat was modern and light and airy with a huge picture window overlooking a grassy open space, it was bloody cold. The only heating was a two bar electric fire in the living room. Staying in on these cold evenings was not such a good idea as it sounded. The pubs were a lot warmer. If you took into account the cost of electricity for the fire, the pub might even have been cheaper.

Eric cobbled together an omelette of sorts from bits and pieces in the fridge and sat in front of the electric fire with a blanket across his lap. He was enjoying the record even though the track titles seemed to bear no relationship to the musical content. He suspected that John Fahey was playing a joke with his tune titles. Eric was sitting listening and musing over the very odd album sleeve art when the phone rang. He threw off the blanket and reached over for the phone. "Hello, Eric speaking."

"Oh hi Eric, this is Elaine from the folk club. I hope you don't mind me calling. Alice gave me your phone number."

Blimey. Elaine. Ringing him! This was his lucky day.

"Hello Elaine, of course I don't mind. Lovely to hear from you. Is there something I can do for you?"

"Well, yes if you don't mind. I was going to the Queen's Arms club tomorrow, they've got Peter Bellamy coming and my car has failed its MoT. Do you think you could give me a lift? If you're going that is."

Whoopee. Eric certainly did not mind. Not one little bit.

"Of course. Be glad to. Peter Bellamy's great isn't he." Eric was warming to his subject, then . . Bugger. Bugger. Bugger. That appointment with Mrs Marshall.

"Oh Elaine, I'm so sorry. I just remembered I've got an evening appointment at work, I don't think I'll be back here until eight or half past at the earliest. Is that too late? I'm so sorry."

"Oh never mind. Yes that would be too late, we'd never get in. It'll be packed by eight. Sorry to have bothered you. I'll try one of the others from the club."

When Eric put the phone down he let out a shriek of pure frustration. "Aaaaaghhh. That bloody Mrs Marshall." A golden chance to get it together with Elaine gone down the tubes. He was in a bad mood for the rest of the evening.

CHAPTER 11 - PANIC IN THE RHODODENDRONS

Thursday was ok to start with. No school today, Red House was having a school theatre trip, so Eric was able to spend the day catching up on paperwork. Each school interviewee had to have an advice summary written out and sent to them. Some of his more organised colleagues did them on the spot and handed them out at the end of the interview, but Eric always ran out of time and had to do them later. The trouble was, some days after the interview he often forgot what went on in it. His scribbled notes taken during the session often seemed too cryptic in hindsight. It was late afternoon before he cleared the backlog. As he had his evening meeting to go to later, he had a clear conscience in going home early to get a bite to eat.

He wasn't a bad cook. He could knock up a mean mushroom risotto which when washed down with a glass of cheap supermarket plonk he regarded as quite civilised. A far cry from the meat and two veg and a cup of tea he had been brought up with. Sometimes he felt quite bohemian. In their previous office building they had had a proper canteen, although the menu seemed to consist largely of variants of Spam and chips. Eric's favourite trick was to enquire if they had any lobster thermidor, but Maisie the serving lady just looked blankly at him and his humour was wasted. To be fair though, Eric wasn't really sure himself what lobster thermidor actually was.

Time to get off to the Marshall's house. He knew the road, Lacketts Lane, one of those un-made-up roads with gravel and pot holes but big posh houses. Funny how the people with all the money had the worst road surfaces outside their pads.

Fearing for his car's fragile front suspension, he left his car at the end of the lane and walked down past the tall hedges and the wrought iron gates. Foinavon, that was the one. Strange name for a house. Wasn't there a racehorse called that? Probably where the money came from. There was a keypad on the brick gate post. Eric pressed what he hoped was the buzzer. It was. "Hello." He recognised the voice, it was Mrs. Marshall alright.

"Eric Dillon from the careers office Mrs. Marshall. Sorry I'm a bit late." Actually he was only a couple of minutes over.

"Oh hi. Come through." There was a click and a buzz and the double gates swung slowly open. Eric's steps crunched on the gravel as he walked up the driveway, rhododendron bushes on either side. There was the house, mock Georgian porch with big tubs of flowers either side, a double garage at the end with what looked like a new extension above. These folks obviously weren't short of a bob or two.

The door opened and there she was, beckoning him in. She looked pretty dolled up considering she was at home. High heels, a figure hugging skirt and a black silk blouse with rather more buttons left undone than there should be. Eric made an effort to avert his eyes from her bosom. Mr Marshall was a lucky man. It was a good job he would be there.

"Hello Eric, so glad you could come." There, she did it again. She leaned with her back against the door post obviously trying, not without success, to look sexy. "Let's go through to the lounge."

She took his arm and as she guided him through the hall Eric noticed a side room, an office or something with a trophy cabinet and billboard posters on the wall.

"Whose trophies? They look impressive."

"Oh they're George's, my husband."

"What does he do? He must be good at it."

"Oh he is. One of the best. He's a wrestler."

Eric started in surprise. "A wrestler?"

"Yes, look at the posters."

Eric took a step into the room and looked at the first poster.

BEDFORD CORN EXCHANGE

JULY 14th 8pm

MARK "THE MANIAC" HAMMOND

v

MAX "MANGLER" MARSHALL

HEAVYWEIGHT CHAMPIONSHIP FINAL

Full supporting programme.

"Is that him? The Mangler?" Eric was surprised and not a little impressed. "I thought you said his name was George."

"Oh it is, but Max is his professional name. He's a pussycat really." she paused, "Unless you cross him that is. Come on let's go through to the lounge and get comfortable."

The lounge was big. Cream carpet, sheepskin rugs, floral sofas and matching curtains. Quite tasteful really except for the rather kitsch looking cocktail bar in the corner of the room. It had one of those quilted fronts in imitation white leather. On top was an equally tacky plastic ice bucket shaped like a pineapple. Through a gap in the curtains Eric could see French doors looking out presumably into the garden, although it was dark outside so he couldn't see.

"Drink? What'll you have?" She was pouring herself a monster gin and tonic. That is to say the gin was huge, but there didn't seem to be a lot of tonic in it. Eric didn't know whether he should, but hey, it was outside of office hours. Why not?

"Oh just a small, er," he didn't know what to ask for. He put his briefcase down next to one of the sofas.

"Here, have a G&T? I make a good one" she looked at Eric and winked. He shrugged his shoulders in submission and she poured him a huge gin and a splash of tonic. Handing it to him she chinked glasses and stood close, looking into his eyes. "Cheers." She sipped her drink. "Well this is nice."

Eric backed off a pace and gazed around the room to think of something to say.

"Very nice house, Mrs Marshall. Nice, um, nice wallpaper."

"Doreen. Call me Doreen, I'm calling you Eric aren't I? Much more friendly don't you think?"

"Um, is Mr er, George going to join us?"

"Ah," she took a step closer. "Well no. He's got a couple of gigs in Antwerp. Someone else dropped out." She took another step closer. Now she was right up close. She ran her fingers down Eric's lapel. She pouted. "So I've got you all to myself."

Eric gulped at his drink. "Oh dear. I mean , um . ., What about Philip? Isn't he joining us?" He looked round the room as though expecting Philip to pop out from behind the sofa. He discerned a creeping sensation of panic in himself.

"No, he's having a sleep over at a friend's house. It's just us really." Her fingers were running down Eric's chest. He was breathing heavily. He had no experience in this kind of thing. What was he supposed to do? It was no use kidding himself any more. She was in the act of seduction and he was the target.

"Oh. I see."

Doreen put down her drink and took Eric's from him, placing it on the cocktail bar. Turning back, she slid her hands up round the back of Eric's neck and pulled him closer.

"Oh God," he thought, "this is it." He could feel her breath, hot on his cheek. No sense resisting now. He put his arms around her waist. Their noses touched as she looked close into his eyes.

"Ever since I walked in that room I've been dreaming of this." Her lips brushed his, at first gently until,

Bzzzz Bzzzz.

"What the hell?" She turned and looked at the intercom by the lounge door.

Bzzzz Bzzzz. "Have you been changing the gate number again? Open up will you babe?"

"Bloody hell, it's George, what's he doing home?"

She pressed the intercom button. "George? I thought you was in Antwerp."

"Cancelled after I got there. Bloody Legionnaires disease in the building. Would you believe it? Come on babe, open up."

She pressed the button for the gate and turned to Eric with a look of panic. "Jesus, if George catches you here he'll kill us both. Quick, out the French windows. Get in them bushes and get round to the front. When I get a chance I'll push the gate button and let you out. For Pete's sake keep out of sight."

The front window lit up with the lights of a car approaching up the drive. Eric didn't need telling twice. She opened the French door and he leapt out and scrabbled into the shrubbery across the lawn.

"Oh Jesus, my briefcase, it's by the sofa." Eric was in shock and panic. He could hear the car engine stop and the door slam on the other side of the house. Suddenly the French window opened and his briefcase was flung out of the door, the contents spilling out onto the lawn. The ring binders on his green book burst open and pages flew out in all directions. Eric flinched at the bang as the door opened again and his jacket landed on the muddy lawn.

"Oh God, Oh God." Frantically he scrambled round the lawn grabbing the pieces of paper, all the time looking back at the lounge window. Inside he could see Doreen and this huge man. The Mangler.

Grabbing his muddy jacket and as many loose pages as he could in three seconds he flung himself back into the bushes tripping over and barking his shin on the process. He looked back inside the house through the gap in the curtains. Doreen was giving the Mangler Eric's drink. "Christ, yes, the drink." Smart thinking. Otherwise the two glasses would have given the game away.

It took a few minutes to work his way round the side of the house nearly falling over the rubbish bins behind the garage. He was still hyperventilating and his grazed shin was stinging. Slowly, he crept from shrub to shrub, all the time looking at the house until he was near the gate. It was cold and dark and the bushes were wet. Eric was frightened, panicked and miserable. His papers were all wet and muddy. How long would it be before he could get out of this bloody garden?

His mind was racing. Suppose things had gone a bit further and the Mangler had caught them at it. What was it she said? He's a pussy cat until someone crosses him. Then what? Eric had no doubt it would involve physical violence. Three falls, a submission or a knockout, that was the wrestling rule. He doubted the Mangler would be adhering to any rules.

Click, buzz.

The gates! She'd opened the gates. Eric gathered up his briefcase and crept up to the edge of the sopping wet rhododendron bush ready to make a dash when the gates were far enough open. Then, a light from the house. He looked back and in the doorway silhouetted against the hall light, stood the Mangler.

"Oh God, oh God." Eric tottered backwards into the bushes, pulling his coat over his head. Had he been seen? Was the Mangler coming for him? He could hear the heavy footsteps crunching on the gravel, getting closer and closer. Eric froze.

Peering through the leaves he got his first good look at the wrestler. My God, he was huge. What was that in his hand? A package wrapped in orange paper, not much bigger than a few packets of cigarettes. Not a knuckle duster or a gun anyway. Eric closed his eyes and hoped for the best.

The footsteps paused at the now open gate and then he heard them out in the road. Did the man think Eric had escaped? Then, opening his eyes and looking through the gateway, he saw a flash of light. Headlights. Flash flash. Someone in a car was signalling. The Mangler looked right and left as if to check no-one was watching, and walked over to the car. The car window rolled down and the big man passed in the package. Not a word was spoken. From inside the car an envelope was passed to the wrestler and the window rolled shut.

The gate was open. Should he make a dash for it? He decided not, he would be bound to be seen. The big man walked back through the gate, no more than eighteen inches from the quivering Eric and crunched back up the drive. Once he was inside the door the gate mechanism clicked and he made his bid for freedom before the wrought iron closed once again. Out on the pavement he caught sight of a car driving away. The car in which the occupant had received the Mangler's package. As it passed the street light Eric could see it was a convertible. A silver blue Mercedes convertible.

CHAPTER 12 - HELLHOUND ON HIS TRAIL

There was no sleep for Eric that night. His head was in a whirl of panic and confusion. The sexy Doreen and what might have been, the close shave with the Mangler, and then that package and the Mercedes. His mind was overwhelmed with questions. What would he do if Doreen rang him again? Had he left any papers in the garden? What was in the orange package? And that Mercedes. That silver blue Mercedes convertible. Could it be? Could it really be Cecil Cooper in that car? No that was too much coincidence.

Eric was exhausted when morning came, he open the curtains and looked out at the miserable weather. What day was it? Friday. That was his day in the office, so no appointments. He rang in sick, mumbling something about coming down with a cold. Actually he was sneezing a lot; he'd probably got a chill from cowering in those damn bushes.

He picked up his guitar and tried a few chords, but he couldn't concentrate. Maybe listening to a record would help. He put on his favourite John Mayall LP, A Hard Road, impossible not to listen to. Eric paced up and down chewing his nails. What was he going to do? He was in danger of getting into something deep here. What about Cooper? Should he mention something to that auditor? No, how would he explain being in the bushes in Marshall's garden when he saw the Mercedes? Anyway it probably wasn't Cooper's car. But if it was, if it was . . , might it be connected to whatever was going on in the French classes?

Eric tried to calm himself down. Think of things one at a time. First the car, was it Cooper's? He hadn't seen the registration plate, and anyway he didn't know Cooper's car number either. He had to do something before it all drove him crazy, so he decided to drive past the prison to see if he could see Cooper's car in the car park outside the main gate. He grabbed his coat and keys and stepped outside. His old car was in a right state, all spattered with sandy coloured mud from the potholed lane where the Marshall's lived, perhaps he would treat it to its annual car wash later.

He had to drive half way round the town to reach the prison because of the one way system and the traffic was slow as usual. Eric manoeuvred into the inside lane so as to get a good look at the prison car park, and luckily the traffic was at a crawl when he reached the spot. Where was Cooper's car? Don't say he'd driven all that way for nothing. Wait, there it was, in the corner. Eric strained his neck to see over the little wall. He wanted to get the number plate. He couldn't quite see it all but it ended in 275L. He was just making a mental note of that when he realised something far more significant. The bottom of the Mercedes was spattered with a fresh coating of sandy coloured mud!

How Eric didn't run into the car in front, he'd never know. Pure instinct made him slam on the brakes when he turned back to look at the road. He winced as three or four other drivers honked their horns at him. So it really was Cooper. This needed thinking about. Eric drove down to the car park in the meadows by the river, stopped the car, and got out for a walk. He must have walked for well over a mile before he surfaced from his thoughts. He decided he couldn't go to that bloke Jock the auditor, or the police, but he had to find out about that package and that meant finding out more about Mangler Marshall. And that meant he had to meet up again with Doreen.

What was he going to do about Doreen? Sure, he found her attractive, sure she wanted him, an ideal scenario in normal circumstances and precisely what Eric spent half his life dreaming about. But there was the small matter of her marriage to a championship wrestler. A bit of nooky was all very well, but not if it led to the later administration of a double footed drop kick or a fore arm smash. He was going to have to string her along to see what he could find out about hubby, but not get into a compromising situation.

He had no idea how.

When Eric bought his Robert Johnson LP he had to go all the way to London to get it, and even then, to Collet's specialist record shop in New Oxford Street. Back home, no one had heard of The King of the Delta Blues Singers and none of the record shops could obtain it. Going into the specialist shop had been quite an experience. Eric enquired about the Robert Johnson record and the counter guy said "Sure" and turned round and pulled a copy from over a dozen similar in the rack behind him. Just like that. It was as if Maisie in the works canteen had suddenly produced a plate of lobster thermidor. That same evening, Eric stayed on in London to go to a blues club to see the legendary british blues man Alexis Korner and afterwards asked Alexis to put his autograph on the Johnson LP. "On this? Are you sure?" Above his signature, Alexis wrote "This is indeed an honour".

Robert Johnson would never fall into an easy listening category. Definitely hard listening at first, but that's what made it great. Johnson famously disappeared for a year or so in his youth and returned playing guitar like no one ever heard. The legend claims he had sold his soul to the devil at a meeting at a lonely crossroads in the Mississippi Delta. In return he was granted his amazing technique. Not that it did him much good, because he died in 1938 at the age of twenty seven. Some said he was poisoned by the jealous husband of a woman he had flirted with.

Maybe Johnson knew he was doomed. Maybe that was the reason for his song Hellhound On My Trail.

Eric struggled with Robert Johnson pieces, and couldn't get to the stage where he could perform them at folk clubs. Just as well perhaps. There might be too many parallels with someone murdered by a jealous husband. Wouldn't that be an ironic way for a Johnson fan to meet his end.

That night at The Lord Palmerston Eric steered well clear of blues with scary omens and sang cheery songs about herring fishing and hunting the hare. The room was packed as usual and he couldn't help scanning the faces in the back row in case a wrestler should appear. On the way home afterwards he drove by a deliberately circuitous route and then set the deadlock on the door once he was inside the flat. Paranoia rules OK.

Eric had the rest of the weekend to worry about his predicament and that's just what he did. He couldn't settle to anything. If he had paced up and down any more, he would have worn a track across his carpet. By Sunday night the sofa was littered with biscuit crumbs and empty crisp packets. A clutch of empty beer cans lay on the floor. Little balls of scrunched up paper sat around the waste paper bin, the result of missed throws, on each piece of paper a list of scribbled out actions and ideas. Tomorrow was Monday. Prison in the afternoon. He needed another look around Cooper's office. Maybe that package was there now.

CHAPTER 13 - NOT JUST ANOTHER MONDAY

Eric was late getting to work. Finding somewhere to park was getting to be a nightmare. If he had to park any further out it would be quicker to walk to work. The waiting room was busy by the time he arrived.

"Ah Eric, good of you to show up; can you help out Terry and Bob, they're snowed under."

Terry and Bob were the office's Employment Assistants; they did the day to day work of helping young people to find jobs. Placement they called it. If you got a kid into a job, he was placed. Provided the young person was after the kind of work indicated by the Careers Officers recommendations on the Y1, they could go ahead. If the young person wanted something very different, or needed guidance, then the Careers Officer had to see them. Terry and Bob were overworked and underpaid. They were officially a grade below the Careers Officers because they hadn't taken the Diploma course. Eric thought they were worth their weight in gold. They did what they did for the love of it and the kids seemed to know it.

"Sure. Who've you got Wendy?"

"How about this lad? The Y1 says you saw him at Oakfield last year. Trevor Johns."

Eric flipped through the notes. "Oh I remember him. Dyslexic supposedly. Isn't he fixed up yet?"

Dyslexia was a bit of a mystery to Eric, he wasn't really sure if it even really existed. Word blindness they used to call it in earlier times. Maybe the kids were just plain bad at reading. Now was his chance to find out for himself. He decided this might be a good opportunity to carry out his own investigations to get a grip on what the problems actually were for a boy like Trevor.

He put his head round the waiting room door and recognised Trevor sitting in the corner.

"Hello Trevor, will you come this way please?"

They walked up the long corridor together exchanging pleasantries. Trevor was a nice lad, and obviously quite bright, but held back by his reading and writing. Once in the office Eric asked Trevor to go through what had happened in the months since leaving school. He had applied without success for this and that, but was still unsure of what he should be doing.

"To tell you the truth Trevor, I don't understand a lot about dyslexia. Would you mind if I explored your capabilities a bit by asking you to do a couple of simple exercises for me?"

Trevor looked wary. "What kind of exercises?"

"Oh really basic stuff, just so I can understand how much of a problem it is for you, and how we can get round the problems by finding the right jobs to apply for." Eric was starting from first principles here. "Can you write me your name on this bit of paper?"

Trevor held the pen well enough and wrote out his name, but oh so slowly. The letter e was back to front.

"Hmmm, see if you can write out a verse of God Save the Queen for me would you?" Trevor looked embarrassed. "Go on have a go, I don't mind if you get it wrong."

Trevor sighed and put pen to paper. Two minutes went by and Eric thought he had better put the poor lad out of his misery. The handwriting was actually surprisingly neat, but some of the letters were the wrong shape and the line was unfinished. So this was dyslexia was it? Or maybe something else. Were there different types of dyslexia? Eric had no idea.

"How about reading? Can you read alright?"

"Yes, I'm not too bad at reading. I can read anything really, but I'm a little bit slow."

Eric gave him a page from the local FE college brochure and asked him to read out loud. Trevor wasn't lying, he could read anything, even difficult words like 'sociology', and whilst not fast, at a tolerable speed.

"OK, now one last test. Using the same brochure, can you copy out the text for me on a fresh sheet of paper?"

Trevor set to, and working fairly quickly, copied out three paragraphs from the brochure. He handed it over. Eric gave a whistle of amazement. "Trevor that's amazing." The copy was neat and perfect. Not a letter wrong or out of place. He didn't know much about dyslexia, but Trevor's version of it was not at all what he expected.

"So, just to recap, you can read slowly, and copy accurately and neatly, but not write independently."

Trevor nodded. "Yes, that's about it, especially the neatness thing, I like to have things tidy and in order and I can do nice writing once I can see how the letters go. Can't spell for toffee though."

Eric looked at Trevor with fresh eyes, suddenly noticing his near immaculate appearance.

"Well spelling aside, that's a real asset Trevor. We ought to be able to capitalise on that oughtn't we? Tell you what, I'm a bit pressed for time just now but given time I'd like to see if we can find a job that needs those strengths. I'm pretty sure we haven't got any vacancies like that in right now, but leave it with me for a few days and I'll see if I can get any leads for you. I'll give you a call early next week."

What Eric really meant was, he was a bit out of his depth on this one and would have to talk to colleagues to get some ideas.

Lunch time came all too soon and it was time to get ready for the afternoon session at the prison.

Eric had prepared a big freehand map showing the town's main industrial areas and big employers. In his experience local lads had precious little idea of the firms in their area and what they did. These lads could walk past a factory or a warehouse a hundred times and not notice or wonder what went on inside. He could easily while away an hour with the group asking if they knew which firms did what, and what kinds of people they employed. Fourteen year olds in school always enjoyed the session, and Eric was beginning to know that that meant these young offenders would too.

What was more on his mind however, was what he could do to find out more about what Cooper was up to and what that package was. He decided to show up early and hope that he would have some time to wait in Cooper's office before the lesson started.

He was in luck. He got escorted in quite quickly today, and caught Cooper on his lunch break. He was eating a sandwich and reading the newspaper. He seemed somewhat irritated to see Eric so early.

"Oh Dolan, you're early. Better come in and sit down I suppose. Don't know where Jack is so you'll have to wait for your tea."

Eric sat where he could get the best view of the office. His eyes scanned the bookshelves and what he could see of an opened cupboard. Cooper's desk was a mess, but it bore no packages. Neither did the shelves or the cupboard. Then he had an idea. He drew Cooper's attention to the map he had drawn on a large piece of card.

"I've brought in this map to use in this afternoon's session. I don't suppose you've got an easel I could borrow."

Cooper sighed and put down his paper. "Got one somewhere. Jack. JACK." His shouts were in vain "Where has that bloody bloke got to? Never here when you want him. JACK. The easel's probably in the seminar room, I'll go and have a look." He got up and left the room still shouting for Jack.

Quick, Eric had a few precious seconds alone in Cooper's office. He had a better look in the cupboard, then as fast as he could he opened and closed each of the four drawers in Cooper's desk. Drat. Nothing. There was a clattering and banging out in the corridor. Cursing and swearing Cooper was dragging the easel towards the classroom where Eric would be working.

One last chance, Eric could see Cooper's briefcase behind the desk. Looking over his shoulder he snapped it open, the turning his head to look inside saw . . nothing special. A paperback book, some report forms, a banana, and a packet of felt tip pens. Quick, Cooper was coming back. Eric snapped the briefcase shut and stood up, pretending to be looking out of the window.

"Here's Jack now, coming across the yard. I might get a cup of tea after all."

The little old trusty duly appeared whistling tunelessly and put the kettle on. Then out of his pocket he pulled a black plastic rubbish sack. "I'll just empty these bins while the kettle's boiling sir." Eric by now was back in his easy chair. He reached over to grab the bin and pass it to Jack and that was when he saw it. Granted it was empty, but it was a package wrapper, and it was orange. Surely, he thought, the one that he had seen Marshall hand into the Mercedes. So that was proof enough. Proof that Cooper was the recipient. Bloody hell, this was getting serious. What the contents of the packet were, of course, was still a total mystery.

Eric tried to think of how he could fool Cooper into talking about it, but he could hardly say 'Have you received any interesting packages lately?' could he? Maybe he could ask Jack about post deliveries, he probably handled them. No, that was no good, Cooper would have brought the package in himself. Hmm that gave him a line of questioning.

"They looked through my briefcase when I came in today. Do they do that to the regular staff?"

Cooper looked up. "Spot checks mostly, random days. Sometimes it's just your bag, occasionally you get patted down, that sort of thing. I wouldn't worry about it as long as you're clean."

Eric smiled, "No sweeties for the lads eh?"

Cooper grunted and returned to his Daily Express.

Eric mused on the fact that, if Cooper was carrying in some sort of elicit package, how come he would risk being searched and found out? It didn't make sense. Maybe the package was innocent after all, but if it was, why all the cloak and dagger stuff in the lane at night?

The session with the lads was a lot of fun. Once he had dealt with Nigel's traditional request for sweets, he put up his map and set to work identifying local companies and talking about what they did. The lads knew all the areas on the map and had seen the signs on the office blocks, warehouses and factories, but they had no notion at all of what the firms did or what kinds of job their workers did. Eric suspected that one or two of them were making mental notes about which places to burgle when they got out, but most of them were clearly taken by the idea of the sheer variety of jobs on their doorstep; everything from making electric motors to importing timber and from clipping poodles to growing pot plants.

Wesley was obviously impressed. He raised his hand. "Here, how long have you lived round here?"

Eric told him about eighteen months. "Jesus! I lived here all my life and I knew f___ all of that."

Eric was beginning to feel he was getting somewhere. These kids were now starting to think about work as something that might actually be interesting. One giant step for Eric kind.

After the lads were released to be marched back to the main block, Eric lingered in the classroom and pondered the new French phrases on the blackboard. Once again in various handwritings there was

Est-ce que tu viens ici souvent?

Tu as des beaux yeux

Puis-je vous offrire a boire?

and other lines of a similar ilk

Chat up lines! He was teaching them French chat up lines. This didn't smack of criminal intent. He supposed it might suggest why the classes were popular. He looked at it again. Strange how as far as he could tell, the grammar and spelling were perfect, not what you might expect if members of the class had been called forward to have a go.

Jack put his head round the door. "Your escort is here Mr Dillon."

"OK, thanks Jack. Oh by the way, do you do the French classes?"

"Me? No. Very popular with what you might call the senior inmates, the rest of us don't get a look in. They all come out looking cheerful though. Don't know why they like it so much, I doubt many of 'em will ever go to France. I can't see what they get out of it apart from nicking a bit of chalk for the shove halfpenny board."

Eric sang the same songs at the Science Lab that night that he had done at The Lord Palmerston the week before. That was one of the benefits of frequenting a number of clubs. He could make his repertoire stretch to a wider audience. Not only that, by the time he had performed a song at three or four venues in the same week, he was getting pretty good at it.

Boil in the bag kippers and crusty bread is not a very good dinner to eat if you are out on the pull that evening. Sadly Eric had overlooked that fact and he felt obliged not to get too close to female company at the club that night.

Some girl up the front was singing Streets of London. Why did they still do that? It was a fine song the first twenty times you heard it, but by the time you've heard it fifty times you'd had more than enough. Eric sat at the back chatting to Mitch the club organiser.

Mitch was a food chemist working on packet soups. He apparently had got his PhD while investigating something to do with monosodium glutamate and dehydrated vegetables. Anyway, the point was that as he worked for the chemical company he could book the lab's social club at a token charge every Monday night for the folk club.

"Do you know anything about wrestling?" Eric asked Mitch.

"Not a lot. Why?"

"Oh, I was interviewing the kid of a wrestler last week. Some guy called Mangler Marshall apparently."

"Isn't that the guy who was in the paper for breaking a burglar's arm?"

"What?" Eric sat up, startled.

"Yeh, some bloke broke into his house or his garage or something and he caught him in an arm lock and broke his arm. He's got quite a short fuse supposedly. Got off with a suspended sentence as I recall. He had a lot of supporters. Quite the local hero."

Eric's face went white. That could easily have been him. Ideas he had had about snooping round Marshall's house were rapidly losing their appeal.

CHAPTER 14 – COFFEE WITH DOREEEN

"You alright? You seem a bit distracted. Tea up." Lennie put Eric's mug on the desk.

"Me? Oh, yes I'm OK. Bit knackered that's all. Quite hard going some of your lads this morning."

Eric took a chunk out of his cheese sandwich. "Do you remember Trevor Johns?"

"Yeh. Dyslexic lad, left last summer. What about him?"

"Oh I saw him again the other day. Still looking for a job. Nice kid. Not daft. He's not the type for manual work and too shy really for retail or anything like that. It's just his problem with writing. Did you know he could copy writing brilliantly? I tested him and I was gobsmacked. It's just that he can't write letters from memory. Amazing."

"Oh yeah, we discovered that. You're right, it is amazing. I don't think it's classic dyslexia, he's a bit special that lad. Eventually we found something for him to do at school and he was brilliant at it. In the library, cataloguing stuff. Devised a new system and kept it very ordered and tidy. To tell you the truth, it's going downhill since he left."

"Mmm I remember now his mum talking about how he kept his room at home tidy. Books and records all in order. I don't think the public library would take him though. I wonder if there are any firms with archives."

"Must be."

Eric began to see a dim light at the end of the tunnel. "Lennie, you've cheered me up."

Eric finished his tea and sandwich and looked though the forms for the three interviews after lunch. "Oh lovely. Yet another three who want building trades. Now don't get me wrong Lennie, building trades are brilliant for your lads, but can't you send me someone who wants to be a designer or a politician or something interesting. Just for a change."

"Come on Eric, this is Oakfield, not Eton."

Too right it was.

At the end of the afternoon, Eric popped back to the office. He wanted to go through the vacancy cards to see if anything might give a lead on solving the Trevor problem. Vacancies came and went every day of course, but sometimes it was possible to present an employer with an unusually talented or special candidate and get them to reconfigure the job to suit. Just occasionally an employer could be persuaded to make a risky appointment by appealing to their social conscience. Either way, Eric could see that he might have to make a special case for Trevor to get him into a job.

He took the whole drawer out of the vacancy cabinet and retired with it to his office with a cup of coffee. The office was quiet; the others had all departed for home. He pulled out the meagre handful of cards for clerical jobs and started reading through. First one, no, next one, no, next, no, and on it went. No, no, no. He dropped the pile of cards and leaned back in his chair. This was going to require a different approach. He gazed of the window across the roof tops lost in thought.

Gradually he became aware that a phone was ringing somewhere. Sighing, he stepped out into the corridor and listened. Of course, it was the switchboard. Better see who it is. He walked down the corridor and flicked the answer switch. "Careers Service, can I help you?"

"Can I speak to Mr Dillon please?"

"Speaking"

"Hello Eric"

"Doreen?" Eric recognised the voice only too well.

"I just, um, wanted to say sorry about the other night. Did you get home alright? I hope George didn't scare you too much."

"Yes. I mean no. I mean.."

"Look, don't worry about it. George didn't notice a thing. I found some of your papers in the garden, under the bushes. I've got them here, I'm in town, can I bring them to you?"

"Oh, er, I'm just leaving." Eric didn't want her coming to the office. In fact after the debacle at her house he wasn't inclined to see her ever again, but he did need to find out more about her husband and that package. A thought occurred.

"Can we meet up for a coffee; you could give them to me then? How about that cafe next to the library, they'll still be open." Neutral ground. He'd be safer that way.

Doreen agreed and in less than ten minutes they were sitting face to face across the little cafe table. She handed over the papers and smiled.

"Fun wasn't it? We're still friends aren't we? I mean we can still," she reached forward and put her hand on his. Her charm bracelet rattled on the table surface. "You know. We can still.."

Eric flushed and tried to change the subject. He looked round the room and over his shoulder, anxious not to be overheard. "About your husband."

"What about him?"

"What do you mean, what about him. He's a dangerous man. I don't think I should..."

"Look, don't worry about George, he never notices anything, and anyway, he's away ever such a lot." She squeezed his hand. "And I get ever so lonely."

Eric sat back and looked at the floor. What should he do? He needed to work on Doreen to find out what her husband was up to, and let's face it, she was sexy and available. Nevertheless her husband was a champion wrestler who would have every reason to mangle Eric's body if he found out what he was up to. His mind told him what he should do. Walk away. Have nothing more to do with all this.

"Look Doreen, I really don't think, I mean this is too . . , I mean you're very nice but, . ."

"Oh Eric, you're so sweet." She squeezed his hand again. "Look, I don't want this to get serious any more than you do," Under the table she brushed her leg against his. "but that doesn't mean we can't have a little fun does it? There's no harm in it. What George doesn't know can't hurt him can it? He's away again next week and Philip is on the school skiing trip." She pouted. "Come and see me. Please. You won't regret it, I promise."

Eric felt his resolve drain away. "Which night?"

She smiled, then leaning across the table planted a warm kiss on his lips. "Monday at seven. I'll cook you dinner." She looked at her watch. "I've got to go. Monday, don't forget."

Before Eric could reply she was gone.

"Oh God, I've done it now." Eric felt a thrill of excitement, then as if to justify his capitulation he reminded himself that this was about finding out what the Mangler was passing over in that orange coloured package. He'd just have to make sure that Doreen's table was the only thing that got laid.

CHAPTER 15 - UNIVERSITY CHALLENGE

Another Wednesday meant another employer visit. Someone had arranged a group visit to the university. While the A level specialist careers officers were discussing degree course opportunities, Eric and a couple of the others did a tour of the labs, libraries and back offices to learn about employment opportunities. In the league table of employers in town the Uni was near the top. Clerical staff, technicians, maintenance workers, gardeners, retail staff, audio visual technicians, all sorts really.

Eric's aim for the day was a familiar one. Employers seemed to have a blind spot when it came to taking on young people. His task was to wake the Uni personnel staff to the pool of junior talent in the town. Over lunch in the refectory he was pressing his point to Janet the head of personnel.

"Mind if I join you?"

Eric looked up to see a grey haired lady in a jumper and tweed skirt. She sat down with her plate of pasta.

"Eric this is Lydia Fellows, she runs our local history archive. Lydia this is Eric Dillon from the careers office in town, he's browbeating me into finding jobs for local youth."

"Mmm, not much in my department for the school leaver, youngsters these days don't seem to have the sticking ability to do the sort of painstaking work we do. No concentration span, that's the trouble. It's hard enough finding adults who can do it. I've got a job now I can't fill, and can I find anyone who'll do it? Well I get some who think they can until I show them the size of the task and the little basement room they'd have to work in, then they realise it's a routine job requiring patience and concentration and they don't want to know. People don't want to do the routine jobs these days. Youngsters especially I should think."

"Here we go again." thought Eric. He was fed up with people making assumptions about what youngsters would and wouldn't do. "Don't automatically rule out young people, they do come in all shapes and sizes you know. What's the job anyway?"

"Oh we've got this archive of old engineering drawings and manufacturing documents, nearly ten thousand of them. From firms that used to be local but have closed down. A very valuable historical resource actually, but it's just boxes and boxes of papers in no particular order. Virtually useless like that, so we need someone who can sit down and patiently work through the lot, entering them into a catalogue and setting up a filing and retrieval system."

He put down his fork. "Sorting and cataloging you say. How much writing is involved?"

"Writing? Well only making entries in the index and making out labels. Why do you ask?"

"How does the person know what name to give the document?"

"Well they mostly have a title on the front, or you can work something out from the text."

Well there you go. Just when you think you can't find a solution to a problem, up it pops. This sounded suspiciously like something young Trevor could do.

"Well Lydia, I think I could prove you wrong about young people. I can think of someone who might be right up your street."

He went onto explain all about Trevor and his unusual form of dyslexia. Lydia looked doubtful. "Seems a bit strange to me, you say he can copy anything, but not even write his name?"

"Yep. Look, I know he sounds problematic but I reckon he might fit your job a treat. Just wind him up and set him off and he would do a neat, thorough job. And I reckon he'd enjoy it." He turned to Janet. "I think this could be a good opportunity for the university to show how it supports the local community. You might even get some good PR out of it if it succeeded."

"Mmm, if it succeeded. But how do we know it would? This boy sounds very nice but this an important archive, we don't want it messed up."

"How about a trial period? Give him a chance for a week and see what he can do. To be frank, he would be a lot cheaper than employing an adult. How about I send him to you for an interview? You can test his copying skills."

Janet looked at Lydia, who just shrugged in unspoken reply as if to say "Why not?"

"Eric, you should have been a salesman. OK we'll see him. No promises mind." She looked at her watch. "Just time to grab a pudding before they pull down the shutters. Come on, let's see what's left."

Eric was indeed a salesman. Selling young people to a sceptical older generation. Selling ideas and ambition to kids who had been brought up with narrow horizons. Selling was 'a good half of what he did.

It had been a good morning's work. Not only that, it had taken his mind off Doreen and the Mangler and Cooper for a few hours. Lately, he could think of little else. What was he to do? He knew he was getting mixed up in something he couldn't sell his way out of.

Back in the office he got a call from Jock McNeish

"Anything new at the prison this week? Anything on the blackboard again?"

Eric read out the new French phrases he had copied down.

"Chat up lines? Is that all? Och, I'm getting nowhere with this. Have you noticed anything at all? Heard any comments? Anything." Jock sounded depressed and not a little desperate.

Eric was in a spot. There was a good deal more he could tell Jock but not without disclosing his visit to the Marshall's house. He decided to keep schtumm for now.

"No, as far as I can make out, the other guys in the prison can't understand all that business of the French lessons either. I had a bit of a poke round Cooper's office but didn't see anything. I do get the feeling though that he is up to something." Eric thought he should try to keep Jock on board.

"What makes you say that?"

"Dunno really. He's a creepy guy and he does seem touchy about mention of the French class, and he keeps warning me off using the blackboard."

"The blackboard? Why would he do that? Can't mean anything surely."

"Well, he's very particular about keeping me off it."

"Is it a normal blackboard? Is there anything unusual about it?"

"I don't think so. It's just a blackboard like any other. As for the French phrases on it, I can't see that they tell you anything. Maybe you're right. We're probably barking up the wrong tree on this tack."

Jock just humphed and rang off. Eric got the distinct impression that his observations were falling below expectations. What should he do? How could he feed McNeish the info about the package transfer in the street?

Perhaps he should send in an anonymous tip off. Give the police the information and leave them to get on with it. Yes, that's what he would do, but only after he had had one more visit to the Marshall house.

Next day it was hard to concentrate during his interviews at Red House even though the boys there were some of the most challenging types he had had to deal with. He was having to deal with boys who would find it hard to live up to the expectations of their 'self-made men' fathers. Perhaps the hardest was the boy whose dad was a successful stand up comic. Not unnaturally the boy expressed a desire to follow in his father's footsteps, but how do you do that when you are a sixteen year old? As far as Eric knew there was no college course for comedians or an apprenticeship scheme. This boy was typical of so many others in that they were inclined to favour a particular career because they thought it was good one. Nothing wrong with that you might say, but a job is only good for you if you are good for the job.

It was back to the old first principle of self awareness. First learn who you are, then and only then can you decide what might be the right path for you to follow. Eric had only thirty five minutes for each interview. Thirty five minutes in which to try to understand a young person, his strengths and weaknesses, likes and dislikes, circumstances, needs, values and his opportunities. Actually that was only half the session. It was no good just understanding all that, the young person expected ideas, information, contacts even. Often it needed Eric to try to broaden the boy's mind, recognise his limitations or expand them, ask him to think in a different way. That was why Eric always tried to get the school to put some careers education lessons into the timetable so that he could start this work in class groups before he got to the one to ones. Just one term could make a big difference. Effectively this could multiply the contact time with the young person by a factor of ten. In Red House school they allowed no such time. The boys were too busy cramming for exams. No time for careers when there were Latin declensions to learn. Eric had on more than one occasion made himself unpopular in the staff room by arguing that these kids weren't going to live in Ancient Rome, but they were going out into the world of work.

He was pretty exhausted by the end of school and had picked up quite a lot of follow up work to do back at the office next day. By the time he had finished his drive home, he had no energy left to shop and cook himself a meal so he gave in and submitted to the lure of the chippy down the road. He plonked himself wearily on the sofa, fish and chip paper on his lap, and switched on the telly.

".... A spokesman for the prison said the escaped man, Herbert Quentin 46, had a history of violence. Anyone seeing him should not approach him but should inform the police immediately."

Eric sat up. He had never seen the man in the mug shot before, but he recognised the picture of the prison sure enough. It was the one in town. His prison.

CHAPTER 16 - POLICE DOGS AND BOLOGNESE

Blind Blake had all the credentials of a blues legend. Well he was black and blind for a start. That's eighty percent of the requirement right there. Not only that, he was born in the deep South of the USA, and he died at the age of thirty eight after years of heavy drinking. How could he fail to become a blues legend?

However Blake, whose first name was Arthur, did have a couple of drawbacks. In particular, his guitar playing was a bit too good, too technical for a blues legend. His music was more ragtime than blues. Not once did he wake up this morning feeling for his shoes or have the blues real bad 'cos he lost the best gal he ever had. He had no hellhounds on his trail. He was more interested in singing about his diddy wah diddy. All of his best known songs were 'novelty numbers'.

Nevertheless, the books on legendary blues heroes all mentioned Blake, and Eric had studied to learn Blake's Police Dog Blues.

Eric never actually learned the words, it was the guitar part that was fun. Tune the guitar to an open D chord, fling in a few harmonics and learn the neat little runs, and you had a really impressive sounding piece. There was however one big disadvantage, he had to remain stone cold sober until it was his turn to play, otherwise it was all a bit too technical. Many's the evening Eric had intended to play Police Dog Blues but had to back off because he couldn't wait for a pint before he went on. Anyway, without his pint he would be too nervous. You can't play Police Dog Blues with shaking hands. He would arrive at the pub or club, unpack his guitar and rehearse the song perfectly in the corner before the others arrived, then end up doing something far less impressive by the time he was called upon to perform.

And so it was that Thursday night, his head full of a risky liaison and his belly full of IPA, Eric once again failed to perform Police Dog Blues and made do with an old song he had learned off a Ry Cooder album. *The Taxes on the Farmer Feed us all.*

"That was great Eric. I love it when you do stuff like that." It was Elaine, she had come to stand next to him at the back of the room.

"Well thank you kindly ma'am but contrary to what they tell you, it's the song not the singer." Eric was good at casual humility. He had noticed people warmed to it. "Are you singing tonight?"

"I don't believe a word of it, and yes I am. On next as it happens, just before the raffle."

"Ah, that makes you a pre raffle-ite."

She laughed. "You're too clever by half. Are you going to the Palmerston tomorrow? They've got Robin and Barry Dransfield on."

"Wow, have they really? Oh yeh I definitely don't want to miss them. Do you want a lift?" Good thinking Eric. He wasn't sure if that would make it a 'date' with Eileen but it would be a step in the right direction.

"Oh yes please. Tell you what, why don't you come round early and I'll cook you some dinner to pay for the lift."

Hallelujah. Oh wow. Oh yes! Brilliant. Suffice it to say that Eric thought that this was an offer he couldn't refuse. And so he didn't.

Next day he went out into the town at lunch time and invested in a new bottle of deodorant and a rather striking, he thought, yellow tee shirt. Then he stood for ages in front of the wine counter in Sainsbury's trying to choose a bottle of wine to take to Elaine's. He knew nothing about wine, but he'd heard of Claret so he bought a bottle of that. It cost over a pound but hang the expense.

After work, he hurried home so as to have time for a bath and then a quick practice of a couple of songs in case he was able to get a floor spot at The Lord Palmerston. He looked out of his kitchen window and caught sight of his scruffy old motor in the car park. God it was a mess, empty crisp packets and Coke tins on the floor, bits of old sketch maps and scraps of paper with directions to places he hadn't been to for months. He dashed out with a plastic carrier bag and stuffed the rubbish into it. There. Not too bad.

He was careful to get to Elaine's pretty much on the dot of the agreed time. Too early might catch her not ready and too late would be just rude. Of course, she wasn't ready anyway, she was a woman. She opened the door still in her bath robe, her hair all wet. Eric proffered the Claret and stepped inside.

"Can you watch the stove while I get dressed? Spag Bol, is that alright? Love the tee shirt by the way." She ushered Eric into the tiny kitchen and disappeared.

He looked around at the jumble of jars and packets on the side. Pasta, pulses, dried porcini, brown rice. Hmmm, obviously someone who likes food. He gave the spaghetti a poke and the Bolognese sauce a stir. Nearly ready but not yet.

"How is it?" He turned to see Elaine now dressed in loose flowery trousers and a white blouse with a pinafore type top over it. Eric had no idea if it was fashionable but she looked fresh and nice.

"Needs another four or five minutes I would say Shall I open the wine?"

"Only a small one for me, I might want to play tonight." She picked up her guitar from the sitting room and with one foot on a chair started tuning it.

"Ooh I always need a little bit of Dutch courage." He took a sip.

"Ah, to do well your stuff needs rather more bottle than mine. That's why I like it." She smiled. "Somebody said you're some kind of social worker, is that right?"

"Nearly. I'm a careers officer specialising in the, . . in the . ., well, socially disadvantaged I suppose. Bit of a conversation stopper usually. What do you do?"

"Me? A nurse, A&E at St Margaret's. Why do you say being a careers officer is a conversation stopper?"

"Dunno. I guess people think it isn't interesting."

"And is it?"

"A lot of the time. I get a bit cheesed off when kids don't use their imagination or when employers don't want to treat young workers properly, but it has its moments."

"Aah, cheese. Glad you said that. Where's the Parmesan?"

The meal went well. Elaine was easy to talk to and she had a gentle self-deprecating sense of humour. Eric collected up the dishes while she packed her guitar."

"Oh bugger!" Eric's voice came from the kitchen. Elaine put her head round the door,.

"What's up?"

"I got a bit of your nice Bolognese sauce on my new tee shirt." He showed her the splodge of red on the hem.

"Quick, take it off and we'll run that bit under the tap. The sauce isn't dry yet, it might come out."

Eric did as he was told although he was somewhat shy about exposing his somewhat skinny torso. She looked at him and smiled. "Come on Tarzan, hand it over."

The stain came out, well almost, and after a couple of minutes with a hair dryer he was able to put the shirt on again. She smoothed it out across his shoulders with her hands.

"There you look lovely. Come on, time to go."

Her last sentence broke the spell, but it had been an intimate moment. Eric was a happy man.

The evening was brilliant. Just brilliant. They both got to do their floor spots, both did ok, and the guest artists, the Dransfields sang as only brothers can. What the Everley Brothers were to early pop records, Robin and Barry Dransfield were to English folk song. Just stunning.

It was the Dransfields that got Eric into English folk song. Some inexpert record shop owner had filed their album "Rout of the Blues" in the Blues section of the shop. Eric was no more expert; he bought the album and only when he got the record home did he realise the song Rout of the Blues referred to the recruiting campaign for an old army regiment known as the blues. He might have been upset at wasting his money, but the record just blew him away. He was an instant convert.

The club was packed. Quite a few of Eric's friends were there but he and Elaine were in their own little bubble. They sat close as if they were there all alone, both lost in the music.

When the car pulled up outside Elaine's flat, she turned in her seat towards Eric.

"Thanks, it's been really great. I won't ask you in for coffee 'cos I'm on earlies tomorrow, in at six. Working all weekend."

Eric felt momentarily deflated until she gave him a big kiss on the lips and said "We must do this again."

"OK. Next time I'll cook."

"You're on. G'night."

Eric drove home in a warm glow. He understood they weren't really a couple. Yet. But there was something about Elaine and the way they got on together. Maybe this was his longed for soul mate. It felt good. Then, as he drew up outside his flat, a chilling thought struck him. Doreen Marshall. He was supposed to see her on Monday. He needed to if he was going to find out about that package, but he couldn't go through with what Doreen wanted him for. Not now.

CHAPTER 17 - BANJO

Saturday morning brought a return to reality. Eric's thoughts of the pleasure of the previous evening were continually overwhelmed by the shadow of the Doreen problem. How the hell was he going to get in that house and look for evidence without falling into the clutches of Doreen. The delectable but predatory Doreen.

A cup of coffee in hand, he paced the floor of his living room only half listening to the radio which was banging on about the escaped prisoner. After he had walked about half a mile round and round, a plan was beginning to hatch, but he would need someone to help him. Someone utterly unscrupulous. And Eric knew just the man.

Swigging down the last of his cold coffee, he quickly dressed and slamming the flat door climbed into his creaking old motor. He didn't slam the door of the car; he thought it might fall off if he did. After the customary minute or two of cranking the starter the old engine spluttered into life and he pulled out of the car park. It was half past ten, just about the right time by his reckoning. His route took him round the back of town, past the gas works. Aah there it was, Tannery Lane. Not one of the most salubrious part of town admittedly, but it was where he knew he would find Banjo.

No-one knew how Banjo got his name, although Eric always assumed it was because he was loud and annoying. It reminded him of the old joke about the definition of a gentleman being a man who is able to play the banjo but doesn't. He drew up the car, engine coughing and spluttering, outside the grubby old lock up. He opened the door and looked inside.

"Well bless me. If it ain't me old pal Eric. Do you know, I heard that car draw up outside and I thought to myself, that engine sounds as sweet as a nut. Beautiful little motor that. Still pleased with it are we?" The man stood up wiping his hands with an oily rag.

"No, Banjo, it's a heap of junk that you did me out of seventy five quid for."

"Ooh that's a bit unfair Eric. There ain't nothing wrong with that old motor. A bargain you got. I'm a fool to meself sometimes."

"Perhaps you could explain then why it uses as much oil as petrol. I had to get out of it at the traffic lights the other day and pour some more oil in. That oil light is on and off like a Belisha beacon."

"Well you gotta expect to use a bit of oil in a vintage motor like that. Just a bit of piston ring wear that's all. I'll tell you what, leave it with me a couple of days and you'll never see that oil light come on again. I'll do you a special price."

Eric was not in the mood for bargains. "I know you Banjo, you'll just pull the bloody wires off the oil light"

"As if I'd do a thing like that to an old pal Eric. No, I got some special stuff you pour in. Repairs the worn rings in no time. Tell you what, I'll do it at cost."

"Banjo, I don't want you to touch my car and that's final. In any case as soon as I've saved up a few more quid I'm buying a proper car."

Banjo's eyes lit up. "Ah I can help you there Eric, I got a nice two tone Triumph Herald coming in next week. Near mint it is. One owner since new, little old lady only used it for going to church on Sundays. Radio, heater, the lot, and," he paused for dramatic effect, " and, it's got white walled tyres."

"Banjo, I wouldn't buy another car from you if it was a three week old Rolls Royce for fifty quid. That's not what I'm here for."

"Oh." Banjo looked disappointed. "Then what are you here for?"

"I need you to do me a favour."

Banjo shuffled his feet nervously. "Ah well, I'm a self-employed man Eric. Time is money to a business man like meself. If I goes around wastin' time doin' favours for people, I'm losin' money ain't I?"

"No money Banjo, this one's for old times' sake, it'll only take you two minutes."

Eric told Banjo what he wanted. Banjo wasn't at all pleased.

"Nah nah nah, I can't go round doin' fings like that. I mean it's probably illegal innit."

Eric looked him hard in the eye. "Not as illegal as getting a friend to write out an MOT certificate without ever having seen the car is it?"

Banjo looked affronted. "Come on Eric, it's just a formality that. My colleague, who shall remain nameless, knows that if I tell him a car is safe, then it is. It's a matter of professional trust. I tell him the car is good and he writes out the ticket."

"I wonder if that's how the law would see it Banjo. Now then why not do this simple favour for me, I'll leave the price of a pint for you behind the bar at the Red Cow, and I'll forget about how my car got its MOT. How does that sound?"

And so the agreement was made on the condition that Banjo did as asked and Eric kept schtumm about the MOT.

Eric climbed back in the car. "Don't forget now, five minutes late and the deal's off." He drove off to do some shopping. It wasn't long now until Christmas, a little something for Elaine wouldn't do any harm.

Eric was fidgety all day on Sunday. Tomorrow was a big day, first the prison and then Doreen Marshall. As he saw it, it was his last chance to find out what was going on, but he had to do it without falling into Doreen's clutches. So, to keep his mind off the problem he kept himself busy. The launderette, a bit of a clean and tidy up round the flat and some serious guitar practice. Even then his mind kept returning to Doreen. What if it all went wrong? What if Banjo let him down? What if the Mangler found out? Maybe he should forget the whole thing, make his excuses and just walk away. That would be the rational thing to do. Then Cooper could get on with whatever he was up to at the prison. No, Eric couldn't stomach that. He had developed quite a dislike of Cooper, the way he seemed to despise the lads he was supposed to be helping.

Eric decided he had to go through with it. Whatever 'it' was.

CHAPTER 18 - BACK IN THE BUSHES

Strange that after a man has got out of prison by escaping, they step up the security on getting in. Locking the stable door after the horse has bolted, in Eric's opinion. He was subjected to a pat down search and his briefcase was emptied out and closely inspected. Heads had obviously been knocked together and everything was strictly to rule and on high alert. When Eric finally made it through to the education block he found Cooper looking very agitated. "Bloody security, they're turning the place upside down. Can't think why, the bugger's already escaped. Probably half way to South America by now."

"Did you know him, this Quentin bloke?"

"Not really, he came to a couple of literacy classes that's all. Just another one of the great unwashed. They're all the same to me." Cooper was his usual disdainful self.

Eric was curious. "Do they know how he escaped?"

"In a rubbish skip they reckon. Best place for him if you ask me. Nasty piece of work he was by all accounts. Used to smash the knuckles of anyone he didn't like with a hammer. A lot of the cons in here ran in fear of him."

Jack came in with the tea. "Your lads are just coming across the yard now sir. You drink your tea and I'll let them in the room for you."

Cooper looked up sharply "Sit in with 'em Jack and keep 'em quiet," Jack nodded and moved off. "and Jack, keep 'em away from that blackboard. D'you hear? Make sure."

What was it about that blackboard stuff that Cooper was so bothered about? Eric was sure it was something important, but he couldn't figure it out. Maybe it was something coded into the French writing, a message perhaps. Yes, that could be it. He would make a note of what was written down today and work on it and the other previous messages when he got home. Meanwhile, what could he extract from Cooper?

"I was looking at your French conversation sentences last week. Students getting on well are they?"

Cooper looked uncomfortable.

"So so I suppose."

"Do you have more than one group? I was wondering why you leave the stuff on the blackboard."

"Just the one group." Cooper's answer was abrupt.

Eric pressed on. "Then why do you .. "

"Finish your tea Dolan, your lads are waiting." interrupted Cooper brusquely. He clearly wanted Eric's line of questioning closed down. A quick swig of the milky tea and Eric acquiesced and made his way to the classroom.

"Thank you Jack, I'll take over now" Jack looked relieved and scuttled out of the room leaving Eric looking at what he suddenly realised was a much depleted class. "Where is everybody? Where's Wesley and Kevin, where's what'sisname our young entrepreneur?"

"Wes and Kevin they're going out this afternoon, lucky buggers, they done their time. Asked us to tell you they're having a party in the Duke of Edinburgh tonight and you can go for a drink. Old Thunderclap Newman is in dead trouble, being questioned about assisting with the escape he is. Made a duplicate key to the bin yard they reckon and sold it to the con what escaped."

He was indeed an entrepreneur then, thought Eric. Fancy that. Old Brylcreem, well the other lads had said not to trust him. His entrepreneurial spirit had obviously got the better of him. Now he wouldn't be setting up in business outside any time soon.

He glanced at the blackboard. "Any of you guys read French?"

The boy at the back whose name Eric could never remember laughed. "Hah. Half of us can't read English." Gallows humour they call it.

Three more sentences were chalked up today.

Puis-je voir le menu

Puis-je avoir un steak bien cuit s'il vous plaît

Cette viande est froide

Just restaurant talk as far as Eric could make out. He would copy them down later. Time to get the session going.

"Let's break into two groups and have a race. This group write down ten jobs where you use hand tools, that group write down ten jobs where you provide a service to individual people."

And so it went. Once again these so called young criminals, thugs, or whatever you might call them set to the task with interest and vigour. Eric peered over the shoulders of the groups as they worked. One lad, Mick, looked up at Eric. "I wish old misery guts Cooper would do stuff like this in his lessons. We don't learn nothing with 'im. He just sits at the front reading magazines while we're supposed to be reading a sheet or doing stupid tests and all he does is shout at us when anybody speaks. Nobody likes him, he's a waste of space. "

The Education Department's suspicions confirmed then, thought Eric. He only had two more of these prison sessions to do. Then he would be asked to send in a private and confidential report. From what he had seen, it would be hard to say anything complimentary about Cecil Cooper, although Eric didn't see why he should be called on to pass judgment on another professional. He decided he would just report on things heard and said and observed without passing any opinion of his own.

It had been an enjoyable afternoon, and for a brief period Eric had been able to put aside fears about his forthcoming visit to Doreen. He was having bad premonitions about it. He was getting out of his depth and he had no idea what he would do if things didn't work out properly. His mind buzzed over and over again with contrasting propositions. What's the worst that can happen? He could end up in bed with an attractive sexy woman. Well you couldn't complain at that could you? And then have his arms broken by a twenty three stone wrestler. Mmm, that wouldn't be so nice. Banjo had better come up with the goods or he was done for.

He went home to get ready. What should he wear? Should he take a bottle of wine? Should he be early, or late maybe? No no that would ruin the timing. In the end he resorted to clean jeans and shirt, a bottle of claret and spot on timing.

Once again he parked his old banger well away from the Marshall house and walked down the lane, all the while checking his watch. He was very, very, nervous. He stood by the gate. He hesitated. There was still time to back off, make some excuse, or just send her a note saying he had thought better of it. He heard the church clock strike seven. To hell with it, here goes. He pressed the gate button.

"Eric?"

"Yes"

Click. Buzz. The gate swung open and, heart in mouth, Eric stepped inside.

She was waiting at the door when he got to the house. My God, she was done up. Dark blue eye shadow, lipstick, a choker round her neck, and a long slinky black dress. In other circumstances Eric would have thought all his birthdays had come at once. But not now. He felt sick with fear.

"I was afraid you wouldn't come." She looked as nervous as he was. She gave him a warm kiss and turned to lead him inside, holding his hand behind her back. Oh God, the dress was backless. Eric felt himself beginning to sweat. Her perfume reached him, musky and sultry. He bit his lip. Mustn't get aroused. Mustn't.

A coffee table stood in front of the sofa. Wine glasses, little bowls of finger food, from a posh delicatessen by the look of it. This was seduction food.

"Make yourself comfy, the drinks are chilling and I've got some canapés in the oven. I'll be right back." She walked through to the kitchen.

Quickly he was on his feet. "Mind if I look at the trophies in the other room?

"Help yourself, they're all labelled."

He stepped into the trophy room. Blimey, there were a lot. But that was not what he was looking for. Frantically his eyes scanned the cabinets and shelves. Yes! There it was on the top shelf. A package just like the one the Mangler had handed over to Cooper. He reached up. Bugger, it was too high. Quickly he grabbed a chair to stand on.

"You alright in there? Nearly ready. "

"Yes, I'll be right there". Eric was standing on the chair and reaching for the package. Got it. The wrapping was only loosely folded. Fingers trembling he scrabbled it open. Inside, a plain white cardboard box like the ones holding a deck of cards. He opened the end flap. Chalk? Blackboard chalk! What the hell?

"Ready sweetheart. Come and get it."

He pulled out one stick of chalk and put it in his trouser pocket.

POP!

Eric started. What was that? He very nearly fell off the chair. He jumped down.

"You do like champagne don't you?" She came into the trophy room, glasses in hand just as he had put the chair straight.

"Oh, lovely." He took his glass and she passed her arm round his, so they were interlinked.

"Here's to us."

She sipped and he gulped.

"Come on, enough of these old cups and shields. Let's go through." Simple enough words, but the way she said them they were full of . . , of . ., well, you know.

As she led him back, Eric sneaked a glance at his watch. Seven sixteen. Come on Banjo, where are they?

"Try one of these." Doreen sat him down and leaning over him she placed a canapé in his mouth. "They're supposed to be an aphrodisiac, but I don't think we'll need them. She sat on his knee and put his champagne glass to his mouth again. He sipped again. She put the glass on the table and leaned forward to kiss him.

Come *on* Banjo. Time was running out for Eric. She put her hand on his thigh as she snuggled closer. He sneaked another look at his watch. Seven eighteen. Oh god. They were going to be too late. Another kiss. Oh it was too nice. Much too nice. He was, he feared, going to have to lie back and think of England. She took his hand and placed it on her breast. Lights flashed in his head.

Hang on. Those lights were flashing in the room. Bright white lights. What the . .

Bang bang bang.   "Anyone there?   Police. Open up please." Bang bang bang.

"What the . . " Doreen looked even more startled than Eric. It seemed to take her a while to surface. "Police? What the hell do they want here? What's that light? What's going on? How did they get through the gate?" She was standing but didn't seem to know which way to turn.

"You'd better answer it."

She was still dithering. "Yes. OK. Oh Eric." She put her hand to her head and went to the front door. A copper and a WPC stood on the step."

"Don't be alarmed madam but I'm afraid we're going to have to ask you to temporarily leave the premises."

"You what?" Now she was annoyed as well as confused. "How did you get in here? This is private property. I've got a guest for, erm, the evening. What's all that light?"

"Sorry madam, we need everyone out of the house. We've received information that an escaped prisoner may be hiding in the house next door. He may be dangerous and he may try to get away through your premises. You'll be safe with us. I must ask you and your guests to leave now please."

"Quentin. This is the police. We know you are in there. We have the house surrounded with armed officers. Come out now with your hands up." The voice was coming from a loudspeaker van in the road. Three big search lights played on the next door house.

The WPC stepped into the house. If you'd like to call your guest quickly madam, we'll take you to a safe place.

We've set up facilities in the church hall. First, do you know who lives next door? Our records don't show."

Doreen looked shell shocked. "Er, it's been empty for a couple of months." She called out to Eric. "Eric. Eric. We'd better do as they say. Sorry darlin'. Eric. Eric?" Where was he? She ran to the lounge. The French door was open. "Eric." She shouted into the garden. "Eric you idiot. Eric."

Answer came there none. Just a rustling in the bushes. She looked round at the WPC. "He's gone. My guest, he's gone."

CHAPTER 19 - CONSEQUENCES OF STUPIDITY

It was cold in the bushes and Eric was in full panic mode. Why the hell did he run? He knew the police would call. He set it up after all. A quick anonymous tip off from Banjo over the phone. Easy. A knock on the door from Mr Plod and he and Doreen would probably leave for the safety of the pub. But he didn't think it would be like this. The lights, the loudspeakers, the armed police. My God, the armed police! What if they saw him running away or skulking in the bushes? They might shoot. Oh God. Oh God.

This is silly. Go back to the house. Act normal. He ran back across the lawn and jumped in through the French doors.

"Freeze. Don't move. Put your hands in the air. Slowly!"

Two men in combat gear were pointing guns at him. Real guns with bullets in.

"Oh." Eric could barely get the words out, he was so scared. "It's only me."

It took Eric a couple of minutes to convince the armed men that he was not an escaped prisoner.

"Why did you run?"

"Aah, well," Eric was thinking on his feet, "I thought I saw someone in the garden and I ran out to see and, um, got lost in the rhododendrons." Surely they wouldn't believe that.

Oh yes they would.

"Where, what did he look like, which way did he go?"

Eric was in a hole now and he kept digging. "Through the bushes, behind the garage, he was big." How big was this escapee supposed to be? Eric didn't know. "Or maybe smaller. Average, yes average that's it. It was dark I couldn't see much."

The men dashed out of the French doors, shouting into their walkie talkies. The front door of the house banged open and three more officers burst in. "Which way did they go?"

"Out there." Eric pointed to the garden. "Where shall I go?"

"Stay there, don't move. We've got guns aimed at the house." The men rushed into the garden. Eric could hear a helicopter overhead.

Eric's heart nearly stopped. This wasn't just panic, this was superpanic. He flung himself on to the sofa keeping his head below the front window. How did he get into this mess? All he wanted was to find an escape from Doreen's clutches and now he was a potential marksman's target.

After what seemed like three hours but was probably three minutes, the men returned from the garden. They looked angry and frustrated. "Tell us again what you saw. Why did you run outside?"

"I'm not sure now." Eric was trying hard to back out of his mistake. "Maybe it was a shadow from the house, or a badger or something. I'm sorry, it's probably nothing. Can I go now?" The men seemed singularly unimpressed. They took his name and address before handing him over to the WPC.

In the church hall, Doreen was pacing up and down clutching a cup of hot sweet tea when she looked up and saw him. "Eric, what the hell happened to you? Where have you been?" The tone of her voice told Eric she was more angry than concerned.

"I went out into the garden and I think they thought I was the convict. They came chasing after me. I didn't know what to say. They took my name and address."

"Oh you idiot! Why did you draw attention to yourself like that? Suppose they come back asking more questions after George gets home. How am I supposed to explain you being in the house?"

Eric hung his head. He felt so stupid. "I'm sorry; it was a dumb thing to do. You can just say I came to discuss career options for Philip. Something like that." He looked round the room. People were beginning to notice their little tiff. "Look, I think I should get off home now. This evening isn't going to work out is it?" The question was rhetorical.

"Hang on. What about me? Stuck here in this smelly old hall, while some dangerous nutter is prowling round next door to my house. You can't just abandon me. Not now." Then, noticing from Eric's reaction that abandoning her was precisely what he had in mind, her manner changed. Her whole body language in fact, and she stepped close to him, whispering. "Look darlin' why don't we go back to your place?"

Instinct is a wonderful thing. Without any forethought, without any planning, without even realising what he was saying, Eric just said, "Aah, I don't think my wife would like that."

"Your wife!?" Doreen looked gobsmacked. "You've got a wife?"

"And three kids." Eric was on a roll now. In for a penny . . . , "So my place is out of bounds, er, and I ought to be getting back."

Doreen stood open mouthed. Eric saw his chance for exit before she could respond.

"Bye then." And he was off before Doreen could utter anything except a bewildered "But, but .."

He might have felt a touch of guilt, but in reality all he felt was a wave of relief and a buzz of the excitement that comes with escape. Once outside, he realised that things weren't quite that simple. His car was at the other end of the road which was now blocked by police vehicles and a small but growing posse of press men with cameras.

"Jim Burton, Evening Chronicle." A man with a notepad stood in Eric's path. "Are you a resident? Can you say what you have seen tonight. Mr ? The reporter's pause was obviously meant for Eric to give his name.

"No, no, I'm just er, um," Eric couldn't think what he might just doing. "I'm just out asking people if they have found Jesus."

Brilliant. A master stroke. The reporter couldn't seem to get away quick enough. Eric walked off in the opposite direction from the melee and eventually found his way back to the car by describing a large semi circle through the nearby streets. Reaching in his pocket for his car keys, he felt the piece of chalk he had taken from the Mangler's trophy room. Why the hell would people be surreptitiously smuggling bits of chalk around? He supposed it was chalk and not something else. It looked like normal blackboard chalk. He took the piece and scratched it on the kerb by his feet. It was chalk. Or it wrote just like it, leaving a nice clean white mark. He shrugged and put the stick back in his pocket, climbed into in his creaking old car and drove back to his flat. His wifeless, childless flat.

He remembered he had a can of bitter in the cupboard and a bag of crisps, so he settled down with them and turned on the TV. There wasn't much to watch, just a repeat of an episode of Callan and a panorama programme about the situation in Northern Ireland. He was just about to nod off when he looked up and saw himself. He blinked. There he was sure enough, in the background behind a reporter standing in the street. The picture changed to show a couple of houses. Doreen's and the one next door.

"The escaped prisoner, Herbert Quentin is believed to be holed up inside the house. Police received an anonymous tip off at seven fifteen this evening. The building is now totally surrounded and local residents have been vacated to the nearby church hall. Shortly afterwards a man was reported as having been seen in the bushes in the garden of the next door house, although a thorough search of the area failed to find anyone. The owner of that house, Mrs Doreen Marshall is quoted as saying she is too afraid to return to her home.

"We're able to speak now to detective inspector Holmes of the local CID."

"Inspector Holmes, what's the situation now?"

"Just a few minutes ago, four of my officers forced an entry to the house where the escaped man was believed to be hiding, but unfortunately there seems to be no sign of him having been there. Whilst we are relying heavily on members of the public keeping a lookout for this man, we occasionally receive calls of a hoax nature and this may be one such. Hoax calls are a serious matter and anyone discovered making such calls with intent to deceive the police will be dealt with using the full force of the law."

Eric wasn't dozing off now. He was very wide awake. What if they somehow traced the call back to Banjo? What if Banjo talked, saying Eric had put him up to it? He felt sick. What a stupid idea this had been, all for a stick of chalk.

He rummaged in his sideboard drawer and found his phone list. Banjo's number was in there somewhere. He found it and dialled the number. No reply. What should he do? The Red Cow, that was it, Banjo was certain to be there this time of the night. It was nearly closing time but the landlord wasn't known to be too fussy about chucking out. Lock ins were pretty frequent and the police didn't seem to bother a lot about it as long as the curtains were drawn and people left quietly when they went.

Eric jumped in his old car and sped round there. Well, sped is hardly the word, the old banger had a top speed of not much more than forty five miles an hour. He might just make it before the door got locked. He pulled up in the pub yard at twenty to eleven. Just in time.

"Sorry sir, we closed ten minutes ago, people are just drinking up." The landlord didn't know Eric and only regulars got invited to a lock in.

"It's OK Dave, he's with me. Mine's a pint Eric, and a whisky chaser. Forty eight to win, that's sixteen, double sixteen."

Eric turned to see the figure gently swaying on the oche, fag in his mouth and a dart in his hand. Banjo blinked and squinted with the smoke in his eyes as he tried to aim his dart. The dart flew lazily towards the board where it hit a wire and bounced off to stick in the floor an inch from Eric's foot. Banjo threw again, his final dart sticking in the white tyre surrounding the board. "Eric you bastard, you put me right off me stroke. I was about to win a tenner off Mike."

"Banjo, we need to talk." Eric brought Banjo's drinks to the table in the corner.

"Wassa matter me ol' pal?" Banjo's speech was slurred, he had obviously supped well.

"That message you phoned the police."

"Message? Ah. Sorry me ol' pal. Been busy. Forgot all about it. Tell you what, I'll buy you a drink. Hey Dave, a double Talisker for me ol' pal wassisname here. Stick it on me tab."

"You forgot making the call? What did you tell 'em?"

Banjo blinked. His mind was working at a snail's pace. Nah, nah, I didn't tell 'em anythink. I forgot to make the call. Sorry mate, I hope it didn't cause you no bovver."

"You must have made the call you daft old git, the police were everywhere. What did you tell 'em?"

"Nah, nah, I never. I was doin' a bit of weldin' on a Ford Anglia. Lovely little motor, sage green. Do you a treat it would. Anyhow, it took a bit of a while and then, and then, well I don't remember makin' no call. Then it was too late so I come down 'ere for a couple of drinks. Sorry mate."

"Look, don't bugger me about Banjo. You must have made that call, else how did the police end up in Lacketts Lane?"

"Search me, me ol' mate. I can't remember makin' no call, honest. 'Ere, are you goin' to drink that Talisker, or do you want me to?"

Eric grabbed the whisky glass before Banjo could reach it. He took a large gulp then coughed as the spirit caught the back of his throat. "Honest is not a word I associate with you Banjo. Either you're lying to me or you're too pissed to remember what you did two hours ago."

"Tha's a bit unfair mate. I wouldn't lie to you, straight up. Look here's the bit of paper you give me with the details on. Have it back." Banjo rummaged in his trouser pockets, pulling out betting slips and sweet wrappers, some small change, a roll of fivers, a disgusting handkerchief and a cigarette lighter, but no note. "It was in 'ere before. I ain't changed me trousers or nuffink' and I ain't got no more pockets."

"You idiot Banjo, you must have dropped it somewhere. Anybody might have picked it up."

"Well that's alright then. All it said was escaped prisoner in Lacketts Lane. If somebody picked it up they would phone it in for the reward wouldn't they? Five grand I heard they was offerin'."

"What about my name and number you berk. That was on the paper. If the police got hold of that I'm in dead trouble." Eric was going hot and cold all at once. He swallowed the last of his Talisker and rose to his feet. "Banjo, if I never see you again, it'll be too bloody soon." And with that he stepped put into the cold night air and climbed into his ancient jalopy. He slammed the car door in his anger and frustration.

The door handle came off in his hand.

CHAPTER 20 - SKI RESCUE

Overnight Eric rehearsed a hundred ways in which he would try to explain to the police why his name and number was on that bit of paper. All of them were pathetic. He couldn't escape the fact that if they got hold of it, he was done for. Then there was the other thought. If Banjo didn't make the tip off phone call, then who the hell did? Whoever it was, they must be holding the bit of paper with Eric's name and number on it. Did they give it in to the police? No, wait a minute, the policeman on the telly said it was an anonymous tip off. Why would that be? Didn't Banjo say there was a reward? None of this made sense.

Brrrrrrr. Eric sat up. He reached out to stop his alarm clock, then realised he wasn't in the bedroom where the clock was. He also slowly realised that he was fully dressed and sitting in his old armchair. He wasn't sure what time he dropped off to sleep, but he seemed to remember dawn coming up. His mind was working at a snail's pace and he was shivering in the cold living room. Tuesday. It was Tuesday. Oakfield day. Oh God, he couldn't face it. He blinked, the daylight hurt his eyes. He blinked again, it was extraordinarily light outside. Stumbling to his feet he pulled back the curtain.

Snow! Deep snow! He looked over towards the main road. Nothing moving. Hey, maybe Oakfield would be closed. Sure to be. He turned on the radio and fumbled with the dial, trying to find the local radio station. Eventually he got it and heard a list of closed schools. Virtually all of them. Hoo bloody ray, they were advising people to stay at home unless their journey was essential. Would the office be open he wondered? He could walk in if it was essential, but that would probably take a good hour in this weather, and surely no customers would make it in. He decided to ring HQ after breakfast. No rush.

He had some eggs in the fridge. How about a proper breakfast for once? Normally it was a quick bowl of cereal and a panic dash out of the door. Eric was not an early riser. Groping around in the veg cupboard he found a couple of mushrooms that were still just about edible and decided on a mushroom omelette. What a luxury for a Tuesday morning. He set to work with the frying pan. Two eggs beaten up with a dash of chilli powder and the sliced mushrooms. Lovely. He plated up and sat at his wobbly pine table in the living room.

The phone rang. Strange at that time of the morning. Aah maybe it was HQ ringing round telling folks to stay at home. He felt quite cheered.

"Eric Dillon speaking. Good morning."

"Good morning Mr Dillon, this is detective sergeant John Amory from the central police station. I believe you were present at a house in Lacketts Lane last night at the time of the escaped prisoner search."

Eric's blood froze. This sounded like trouble. Why did he have to tell those stupid lies? On top of that, if that incriminating bit of paper turned up he would be in a right mess. He decided to act low key.

"Yes, I was there, but I don't think I can be of any help really."

"A colleague tells me that you saw someone in the bushes at the rear of the house you were in, and I was hoping you could give some details or a description."

"Ah, well, you see, thinking about it now, I don't think it was anything, just the wind in the bushes. I don't think I actually saw an actual person actually. It might have been my own shadow from all those floodlights. False alarm really I just, er, it was nothing. Nothing."

"I'm told that you rushed out into the garden when you saw whatever it was. Why did you do that? "

"Did I? Oh yes, er well, just, um, instinct I suppose. Silly really. I'm sorry, I would help if I could, but um, that's it really." Eric had his fingers crossed, hoping the policeman would just give up and go away.

Not yet he wouldn't.

"May I ask the reason for your visit to the premises last night? We noticed that you left the church hall rather suddenly, before we had a chance to complete our questioning."

"Oh, that, well er, it was just a social call on Mrs Marshall, I never intended to stay long, and I wanted to get back home before, um, before it snowed." Ooh that was a good one. Eric was pleased with himself.

"Strange, Mrs Marshall told me it was a business call." The copper sounded suspicious.

"Ah yes, well, business and pleasure. We were having er drink and nibbles whilst discussing, er business." Eric was wincing as he spoke; he was walking a tight rope here. The more porkies he told, the more he had to make up other stuff.

"And what business are you in Mr Dillon?"

"The Careers Service. I've been giving careers advice to her son and she, um, asked me round to, um, give some more advice. We ran out of time in the school interview."

"Hmm I see." The sergeant didn't sound at all satisfied by Eric's flimsy answers, although it seemed he had run out of things to ask.

"Well thank you for your time Mr Dillon. We may get in touch later if we need a statement."

Eric was trembling when he put down the phone. He didn't like all this. Not one little bit. A policeman asking questions about him and Doreen. Suspicions about his cock and bull story about his sortie into the garden. How did he get into this mess? That bloody Cooper bloke, it was all his fault. If it wasn't for him, Eric wouldn't be undergoing all this trauma. Right. That's it. Enough's enough. No more Doreen, no more poking about after mysterious packages, no more making up stories, just finish his stint at the prison and return to his normal boring life. As for Cooper, Eric decided his final report on the prison would just say that Cooper had no empathy with the young prisoners and little interest in improving their life chances. End of story.

The phone rang again. He very nearly didn't answer it, but curiosity proved the stronger and when he did it was HQ telling him that they had decided to close the office for the day. He looked out of the window. The snow had stopped falling now, but out on the main road the traffic, nose to tail, was moving at a snail's pace. No point in trying to go anywhere even if he did have the day off. He poked around in the kitchen cupboards, looking for something to construct a meal from. Oooh a Fray Bentos steak and kidney pie and a tin of marrowfat processed peas. Food fit for a king in Eric's book. He might even manage a portion of mash from the somewhat skanky handful of spuds in the corner cupboard. Once more the phone rang. Eric looked suspiciously at the handset. Should he answer it? He was definitely not at home to any more coppers. It rang again. Steeling himself he picked up the receiver and decided on a simple "Hello".

"Hello. Eric? Is that you?"

"Elaine! Hi, how are you?"

"Bloody frozen, our electricity is off. Are you off work too? I need somewhere to get warm, and nobody else seems to be at home."

"Yeah, I'm off all day, why don't you come over. I can't say it's toasty here but we do have a working electric fire. Oh, aah, I see a problem. How will you get here? The traffic's nearly at a standstill. No buses running."

She giggled. "I thought about that. I've got skis!"

"Skis?" Was she mad?

"Skis. My dad gave me his old ones. Proper cross country jobs. It'll only take me half an hour I reckon. I've been longing for a chance to use them."

"You what? Are you sure? Is it safe? I mean with the cars skidding about and all that."

Skis! Eric couldn't help worrying he was out of his depth here. People who had skis came from a different stratum of society from the likes of him. When he was young he never even mentioned the school skiing trips to his parents because he knew for sure they could never afford to let him go.

"Yeah, I can come across the park and down the back lane. What number is your flat?"

"Seven. Ground floor. I'll put the kettle on. Take care. See you soon."

Eric looked around his untidy flat. Oh God. Thirty minutes to clear up. He grabbed a black plastic rubbish sack and tore round the room shoving all manner of rubbish, bits of paper, bread crusts, crisp packets and beer cans into it. There was a communal rubbish bin along the walk way outside the flat. He rushed out with the bag and slipped and slid along to the bin cupboard. Good. Now just a quick blast with the vacuum cleaner and he would be presentable. He slid back along to the flat and pushed the front door. NO!!

The bloody door had slammed shut. He was locked out. Keys. He patted his jeans pockets in the forlorn hope of finding a key. Bugger!

He surveyed the scene. Door and windows were all firmly shut except the tiny little top light in the bathroom window a good seven feet above the walk way floor. He attempted a stupid little jump to reach it. Nowhere near. In desperation he looked around for something to stand on. If he could reach the little window there was an outside chance he could squeeze through. There was nothing. No boxes, no bikes leaning on the wall, no milk crates. Nothing.

Eric realised he was feeling cold. Very cold. He had on only jeans and a tee shirt, and his old carpet slippers. Time was ticking by. The plant tubs. Yes, that was it. The big plant tubs with the bay trees by the main entrance. He ran over and grabbed the edge of the first tub. God it was cold. The icy edge of the tub stuck to the skin on his frozen fingers. He gave a mighty heave. The tub was very heavy and Eric pulled really hard. Something had to give. It was Eric's feet. Smack on his back on the icy path he went. Lumps of slushy snow oozed their way under the back of his tee shirt. Struggling to his feet, he grabbed the narrow trunk of the young bay tree and heaved again. Nothing moved. Once more he tried, making a superhuman effort. This time the tree did move. Unfortunately the tub did not and once more Eric found himself lying in the snow, but this time holding an uprooted bay tree.

"Eric? Eric, is that you?"

Eric looked up to see a slender figure in full winter gear hold two ski poles.

"Elaine. Um, I've um, I'm trying to shift this tub." He was shaking his frozen hand and had begun to shiver visibly. "I've, um, locked myself out and I'm trying to reach the little bathroom window."

Anyone trying to make a good impression on a member of the opposite sex would be well advised not to look like Eric did at that point. He was beginning to turn blue and it would have been hard not to use the word pathetic in describing his appearance.

"Here take my coat. You'll freeze to death. Is that the window?" Elaine pointed to the little bathroom light. "Give me a leg up, I'm smaller than you."

Elaine took off her big ski boots and stepped into Eric's cupped hands and he hoisted her up so that she knelt on his shoulder. Had he not been freezing cold and afraid of falling over, it might have been a strangely intimate moment. She got a foothold onto the window ledge, where after a brief struggle she slipped inside the window. She opened the front door and let him in.

"Here come and get warm. How the hell did you get locked out?"

"I went out to empty the rubbish and the door slammed behind me. I don't know what I would have done if you hadn't shown up. Thanks."

"Dope." Elaine filled the kettle and lit the gas. "Tea or coffee? Go and get a jumper on. Shall we have a couple of biscuits out of this jar?"

So it was they sat by the electric fire, mugs of coffee in their hands, and eventually laughed about the ridiculousness of it all. After a while, Elaine picked up Eric's guitar and picked a few chords. "Did you know The Lord Palmerston are having a duo competition after Christmas? Do you fancy having a go to see if we could put something together?"

Did he fancy it? Did he ever! "Yeah of course, that would be really nice. What could we do?"

Well it was a good idea in principle, but putting two people with different musical backgrounds together was always problematic. All afternoon they made false starts on songs that wouldn't work out. The idea was grinding to a halt. Nothing they tried seemed to have a chance of working. Eric was getting a bit downhearted. What with being locked out and looking pathetic and then not being able to bond musically, this was beginning to look like an opportunity missed.

"You know what the answer is," she said, "we shouldn't be trying to fit me into your songs or you into mine. What we need is something new, something, well, us."

"Us". She said "us". Eric felt a flush of excitement in his temples. "Is there an us?"

Elaine paused for so long he thought she'd never speak.

"Maybe. We'll have to find out won't we?" She smiled. "I'm starving. I can't survive all day on two ginger biscuits and I seem to remember you owe me a meal. Now might be a good time to repay the debt."

Women were good at changing the subject like that, just as Eric was getting excited. He had to confess that the cupboard was nearly bare, but she seemed unexpectedly satisfied with his offer of Fray Bentos pie and tinned peas and spuds. While he opened tins in the kitchen, Elaine sat on the floor leafing through his pile of LPs, pulling out two or three. "Who the hell are all these people in these records? I've hardly heard of any of them. Who's Michael Chapman? You've got three of his."

"Put one on. You might like it."

And so she did put one on. And she did like it. They sat on the little sofa, plates on their knees eating the only slightly burned pie and lost themselves in Chapman's warm and languorous songs. They got through all three albums and by the end Elaine was cuddling up to Eric and looking very relaxed. She yawned and stretched. "It's getting late. Time I was off home."

"But you can't go out in all that snow in the dark. It's not safe. I think you ought to stay, don't you?" Eric did of course care for her safety, but it would be a lie to say that that was the main motivation behind the offer. Not that it mattered, for Elaine was too smart for him. She laughed and gave him a peck on the cheek.

"Nice try, but if you care to look out of the window, you can see that it's raining. The snow has gone. You can give me a lift in that old banger of yours. It's been really lovely Eric, but I need to get back to feed the cat." She stood up. "Come on."

"Damn. I never liked cats." Eric knew when he was beaten. He drove Elaine home and outside her place they kissed and it seemed like she meant it.

"Let's do this again soon, only this time you can let me in the door, not the bathroom window."

He watched her go up the steps and in her door and drove home feeling good. Frustrated, but good. For a few short hours he had forgotten about the mess he was in. Suddenly now he felt again the cloud hanging over him. Tomorrow he must start untangling the mess somehow.

CHAPTER 21 - A BASKET CASE

Eric hadn't fixed up an employer visit for this week. A quiet day at the office catching up on paperwork would suit him fine. He would sit in his office and keep his head down.

"Aah there you are Eric. Keeping a low profile are we?" It was Wendy. "No visits today then? You'll be missing your quota."

"Well I did have one planned but it fell through," he lied, "so I can get some other work done. Be a love and keep me clear will you? I've got masses of reports to write."

"No."

"No?"

"No. Sorry, but we need to send somebody out to a chap in Hampton Parva. Got a job vacancy but he wants a visit first. Everybody else is out at school. A bit of fresh air'll do you good. Arthur Snow, Lower Bank Farm."

"A farmer? I don't do farmers, that's Ralph's specialism. I don't see why I should do his stuff. I'm building trades, factory and handicrafts. Remember? Anyway none of my lads would go out to Hampton Parva for a job. They're town lads, all of 'em."

"Yes, I remember, but this one is handicrafts. A basket maker. Needs an apprentice."

"Basket maker? We've never had one of them. Might be interesting I suppose." Eric could do with something to take his mind off his troubles. "Tell you what, make me a coffee while I finish this batch of forms and I'll go and see him. Do we know how to find it? There's all sorts of little small holdings out that way."

Wendy supplied the coffee and the directions given to her by Mr Snow. Forty minutes later Eric was driving down the little lane to Lower Bank Farm. He winced as the old motor crunched into every pothole in the lane. Surely it wouldn't be long before the suspension gave way completely. The sooner he ditched the old banger the better.

The old lady at the cottage turned out to be Mrs Snow. She called Eric "Dearie" and led him round the back to a little bothy overlooking a straggly patch of rough grazing with a couple of piebald horses standing under a tree.

"Arthur. It's the young man from youth unemployment. There you go dearie." She opened the bothy door and Eric peered inside. All round the walls, bundles of willow cuttings stood like soldiers, a little cast iron stove in the corner showed a flickering flame through its glass window, and in the middle of the bare earth floor, next to a tin bath with willow wands in soak, sat an elderly man, legs spread and a board across his lap with a part finished basket in the middle.

"Mr Snow? Eric Dillon from the Careers Office. How d'you do."

The man looked up and took off his cap, wiping his brow. With some effort he pushed the board aside and climbed arthritically to his feet, wiping his hands on his trousers. He offered a gnarled hand.

"Aah, just the man. Glad to see yer. Have a seat."

He pulled up an old wooden box and brushed the dust off the top. Eric sat and gazed around the little hut. It might have been something out of a Thomas Hardy book. A few hand tools on an old bench in the corner, piles of willow, and old copper kettle atop the little stove, and behind the door, a pile of identical square baskets.

Arthur Snow had been making baskets for over sixty years. Big ones, small ones, baskets for bicycles, picnic hampers, baskets for dogs and cats, even for hot air balloons. All by hand, his only tools being a knife, an awl, a pair of secateurs, and an old file which he used on edge for beating down the willow wands to tighten the basket weave. While he was talking to Eric he worked on, finishing one basket and making another. Eric was spellbound. This was real, ancient, timeless skill.

Now Mr Snow was getting old and stiff. He had plenty of work, but he didn't know how much longer he could keep it up. He needed someone to pass the work on to, and he knew he would have to train someone because there were no other skilled basket makers in the county.

"I wants a keen young lad to learn up the trade. I can teach him everything. Every type of basket, and when I gets too old he can have the business, so it carries on. Folks 'll always want baskets and the machine ain't never been made what can do it. A strong young lad. Hard worker. I can't pay him much to learn but once he gets going he can earn according to what he makes. Do you reckon you could find me somebody?"

Eric wasn't sure. This was the nineteen seventies. How many young lads would consider working in an old shed with an old man for not much money? Somewhere there must have been somebody, but he warned Mr Snow it might take a while and he might have to try two or three lads before he could find one that would stick it. The old man was philosophical. He was all too aware of the way of the world, aware that in many ways he was an anachronism. His face betrayed his sadness as he shook his head.

"I know lad, I know. I just can't bear to think it won't go on. There's nothing like a proper willow basket. People always wants 'em but it seems like I'm the only one wants to make 'em. Just do your best lad. I can't ask no more."

They shook hands and Eric climbed back in his car and clattered and banged up the lane. Back on the main road, Eric could hear a knocking from the suspension. He must steel himself to have a look underneath sometime. It didn't sound good.

Back at the office, he wrote up a vacancy card for the file and had a word with Terry and Bob to see if they had any suitable lads, or girls of course. No one came to mind. They would just have to hope someone would show up.

Then it was back to his own office hidey hole and head down to assault the backlog of write ups. He didn't get far. Every few minutes he would find himself staring at a blank form, thinking about suspicious policemen and scraps of paper with his details lying in the gutter. He felt sick. The phone rang.

"Lady for you Eric, parent I think. I'll put her through."

Eric sighed." Good afternoon, Eric Dillon speaking. How can I help?"

"Who's a naughty boy then? You sly old dog. You never said you were married."

"Doreen?"

"I reckon that makes us as bad as each other. What fun."

"Doreen please don't ring me at work. People could listen in. In fact, please don't call me at all. Not any more. It's, it's not right. I made a mistake. No offence, but I can't see you again."

Doreen was not to be so easily put off. She turned on her seductive voice; pouting probably. "Come on Eric it's only a bit of fun. What's the harm? Please Eric, why don't we meet for a drink. How about after your office shuts?"

"No Doreen I can't. Goodbye Doreen."

Eric's hand was trembling as he put down the phone. "Well, that's that then." He felt a sense of relief. One problem out of the way.

After work, he had a try at problem number two. He walked the route from Banjo's place to the Red Cow kicking the leaves under the fences and peering into the gutters. That bit of paper must be somewhere. He even poked around in litter bins, looking furtively over his shoulder. Nothing. There was nothing more he could do, except hope that no-one had picked it up and read it. Logically, it seemed like someone must have done just that, otherwise how did the police get tipped off? He shivered at the thought. Maybe the police already had the note. Maybe he was being watched. He looked around, down the line of parked cars in the street. There - a man in the bus shelter, his collar turned up and his hat pulled down. Eric's blood ran cold. He turned and walked as fast as he could without running, looking over his shoulder as he turned the corner. The man was still there.

Along past a little row of shops. Who was that man standing smoking outside the chip shop? And the man in the car in the shop lay-by. Oh God, this was awful. He couldn't see any stranger without thinking they were watching him. That bloody Banjo, it was all his fault.

When he got home Elaine rang. She obviously sensed his nervousness. "You alright? You seem edgy."

Calm down Eric.

"Sorry, just a hard day at work. How about you?"

"Every day's a hard day in A&E. I need a bath and an early night. Tomorrow though I wondered if we could go to the Queen's Arms club? We could think some more about a song. Can you pick me up at half seven?"

Eric was pleased and confused at the same time. The lovely Elaine was making the running. He mused that he would never have made the first move. He would never presume to be attractive to a girl who went skiing. That was out of his class. It was clear she was in the driving seat in this relationship, but in his present state that suited him fine. He had enough other stuff to worry about without the stress of the fear of rejection if he made the approaches. Maybe she sensed the way things had to be. Or maybe she liked being in control of the pace. She was pretty independent. Whatever. It was great.

"Love to. As long as the old banger survives another day I'll be there. Enjoy your night in. See you tomorrow."

CHAPTER 22- WHEN ELAINE MET DOREEN

The Elaine situation had put a spring back into Eric's step. He was feeling more up-beat as he drove out to Red House next morning. He was ready for anything. Bring 'em on. He parked up and entered the hallowed portal to be met by Sidney Cobbold, the head teacher.

"Morning Eric, I'm afraid we're a bit at sixes and sevens this morning. Charlie Tanner has gone down with the flu. We're still trying to find out what interviews have been arranged. As far as we can tell he hasn't booked you a room either. I'm afraid we'll have to put you in the craft department office, it's all we can find. If any boys report for interview we'll send them down. Is that Ok?"

He showed Eric over to the craft block. Stepping inside, Eric stopped to look at a model steam engine in a glass case. Obviously hand built, it was a beautiful piece of work. Every tiny brass part honed and polished.

He peered closely into the glass case. "Was this built by one of your pupils Mr Cobbold? It's very impressive."

"Yes indeed it was, and believe it or not it was built by one of our less able pupils."

Eric turned to look Cobbold in the eye. Head or no head, he had to challenge that one.

"No it wasn't."

"I'm sorry?" The Head looked rather taken aback.

"This wasn't built by one of your less able pupils. This was built by one of your *more* able pupils."

"Aah, yes. See what you mean." Cobbold took the point and looked a little shamefaced. "I hadn't thought of it that way."

That was the trouble with a lot of academics and teachers. They prized ability in traditional academic subjects but failed to recognise genuine talent in other fields, particularly in engineering disciplines. The same people who espoused the values of science education and mathematics often ignored the importance of those who applied that very same science to put it to practical use. Consequently the engineering industries were crying out for high level technology talent, while science students could often see no further than medical or laboratory work.

Only two boys turned up for interview that morning. The same flu bug that had hit Charlie was doing the rounds of the pupils it seemed. Eric got back to office by lunchtime. He wasted the afternoon in idle contemplation of his planned evening out with Elaine.

"You can run, you can run, tell my friend Willie Brown"

Unjustly, the great blues player Willie Brown is more famous for being mentioned in Robert Johnson's iconic Crossroads song than for his wonderful playing. Actually Willie was perfectly good enough in his own right to manage legend status without Johnson's help. Sadly, unlike some of his contemporaries, Willie never got to enjoy the fruits of the nineteen sixties blues revival on account of the fact that he made the crucial mistake of dying of heart failure in 1952. That was one bit of bad luck. The other was that there seemed to be another blues guy called Willie Brown around at the same time as our Willie, and the sixties blues geeks couldn't make their minds up as to which Willie was which or whether they were one and the same. If it was the same one, then he had quite a life, because one or other of them was married in

1910 which would have made our Willie a married man at the age of eleven!

Then as if dying too early wasn't bad luck enough, he had strangely become better known through other people's versions of his songs than his own versions- enough to give anybody the blues, as long as they were alive, which he wasn't. A case in point was Mississippi Blues, possibly his masterpiece in which Willie managed to get his guitar to imitate the playing of blues piano. Hardly any of the keen young guitarists of Eric's generation had heard Willie's original version, but learning to play it became a sort of right of passage for aspiring young country blues pickers in the sixties largely thanks to it being featured in one or two "how to play blues guitar" books. Even Eric could make a fair stab at it although some of the rhythmic subtleties of Willie's bass lines sometimes evaded him. He never got to play it in public though, largely because he too had never heard the original and the fitting of the lyrics to the accompaniment was obscure to say the least. One he did once perform though was his version of Willie Brown's Future Blues, a prime example of the Delta blues style played in an open tuning and a heavy hand. Typically though, he couldn't resist changing the words so that he could play off the song's title by starting off "I woke up tomorrow morning." Despite his love of a relatively unpopular art form, Eric was never one to force obscure examples of it on to the general public without softening it with humour, and least of all forcing it upon a girl friend.

That evening, Eric took special care over his appearance. He had to look good for Elaine after looking so pathetic stranded in the snow last time. Clean jeans, his best casual shirt, and just in case, just on the off chance, just in case he got really really lucky, his new stripy underpants. Then at the last moment he cut himself shaving. Right on the top lip. Bugger. He couldn't seem to stop it bleeding and in the end had to resort to the old trick of sticking a tiny piece of toilet paper on it. So long as he remembered to remove it before he knocked on Elaine's door he might get away with it.

Twenty minutes later:

"What's that bit of paper on your lip?"

"Oh bugger, I forgot to take it off." Eric could have kicked himself. "Cut myself shaving. Excuse me a sec, I'll peel it off."

He availed himself of Elaine's bathroom and soaked the bit of paper in a bit of soapy water. There. Just a tiny cut underneath. Elaine watched over his shoulder, fascinated. "Is that how you do it? Glad I don't have to shave. Apart occasionally from my legs I suppose."

Eric wondered if he'd ever manage to look cool in front of Elaine.

Over at the Queens Arms it was busy. In the downstairs bar there was a noisy darts match and a lot of cheering and shouting and laughing. It didn't bother the folk club too much. They were quite capable of making their own noise, and tonight's band featured a melodeon, a banjo and a euphonium. There were no rules in folk bands, any instruments were acceptable. Eric and Elaine both did floor spots in the first half. Chalk and cheese you might say. Elaine was tuneful and relatively safe, whereas Eric's performance had a touch of anarchy about it, no doubt annoying the hell out of "straight" people like Gerald but going down well with the masses. That is if twenty seven people can be called the masses.

The half time interval was the traditional time to recharge beer glasses, so Eric left Elaine chatting to friends on the landing while he went downstairs for the drinks. It was quite a struggle to get to the bar and even harder to catch the bar man's eye to get served. Eric manoeuvred his way to the front and waived his fiver in the time honoured manner. He didn't notice the people either side of him until he felt a hand on his bum and a voice said, "Eric, well this is a surprise. Changed your mind, have you?"

"Doreen! Bloody hell what are you doing here? Have you been following me?"

"Eh, I thought you was followin' me. I'm here with George. He's in the darts team. What the blazes you doin' here?"

"In the folk club upstairs." His voice dropped to a whisper, "Look, I'm sorry, but I can't talk to you. 'Specially with your old man there."

At last the barman came to Eric and he got his beers. Grabbing them, he turned and left, bidding Doreen an apologetic goodbye. As he left the room, she followed him onto the stairway.

"Eric, Eric darlin'." He turned on the stair and looked back at her. "Please Eric, don't go like that." He turned away and looked up the stairs. Looking down at him, her expression dismayed, stood Elaine. Oh God. He started up the stairs after her, but was pulled up short.

"Oi. Doreen, where the 'ell do you think you're goin'?"

Eric looked back to see a face he hoped he would never see again. The Mangler. This could be trouble. Had he heard Doreen pleading with him? What would she say now?

"Calm down George darlin' I was only goin' to see what the singin' was like upstairs."

He looked at her with obvious suspicion. "Who was that bloke you was talkin' to at the bar?"

Eric looked away and started back up the stairs, listening hard to the conversation below.

"I don't know, just one of the singers. I was askin' him what was goin' on upstairs that's all. Look, you're back on in a minute, let's go back in the bar." And with that she let the huge man away.

That was all very well for Eric, but what would he say to Elaine? She had presumably heard Doreen call him darlin', and pleading with him not to go. How could he explain that one away? He had no idea.

He went back into the club room with his and Elaine's beers. He smiled weakly, she gave him a frosty look.

"Friend of yours?"

"Eh?"

"That woman on the stairs." The look in her eyes suggested she didn't really want to hear the answer. What should he do? Bluff his way out? Make up some story? No, he had had enough of making up stories, and Elaine was someone he never wanted to lie to. He decided on a pruned version of the truth.

He sighed. "Her name's Doreen, and I met her at work, the mum of one of my clients. You won't believe it but she seems to have a crush on me and I can't shake her off."

Elaine looked at him hard as if to say, yeah tell me another.

"It's true honest. I know it sounds crazy but it's true."

She stared at Eric for what seemed like an age. He had blown it. He knew it. He was crestfallen. Then, she laughed.

"You? Her? I don't believe it. Hah hah that's priceless. You being chased by somebody's mum. Oh Eric, who'd have thought it?"

Eric felt hugely relieved that she had obviously believed him, then on second thoughts somewhat disappointed that she thought the idea of someone fancying him so funny.

Elaine pressed on, making fun of him. "Well she's a bit of a looker, why don't you take her up on it?"

"Well for one thing, her husband is a heavy weight wrestler." She laughed and shook her head. "No, he really is." he said, "And for another, I have my eye on someone ten times nicer. Some nurse I met."

That sounded like a confession and it might have backfired, but it didn't. In fact, it appeared to hit the spot. Elaine blushed and smiled. "You old sweetie you." Then, lowering her voice in conspiratorial fashion she asked, "So what are you going to do about the delectable Doreen?"

Eric shrugged. "Just keep out of her way I suppose. I couldn't believe it when she was here tonight. Um, I ought to tell you one other thing. I told her I was married."

Elaine's eyes nearly popped out of her head. She put her hand over her mouth in shock. "You told her that?"

"With three kids."

"Aaagh! Why?"

"To get her off my back. If we see her again, you might need to pretend you're my wife."

"Hang on, do I look like someone who has had three kids?"

There was no good answer to that question. Eric decided to back off.

"OK, sorry. I'll just avoid her if I see her. None of it is my doing, honest. I don't know how to deal with it. It's all a bit embarrassing"

Oh dear. Here we go again. Eric was back to looking pathetic. It didn't matter, Elaine was smiling benignly. She loved his innocence. Of course she still didn't know about all the other stuff. He hoped she would never need to.

CHAPTER 23 - SAVING SEP

The evening ended without romantic disaster, although Elaine maintained her mastery by sending Eric home after he dropped her off. He didn't mind. Well, not too much anyway. He just felt very lucky that she had believed his story.

Next day he was back in the office and although still stressed about the police and Cooper and all that, feeling positive. That was until Wendy rang through to say that Sep was in to see him.

"Oh Sep, you told me you would stick it this time, you've let me down. Sep, I don't know how much longer we can go on like this. How can I send you to firms when you end up sacked or you've walked out after a couple of weeks?"

"It's not me Mr Dillon, honest. The job this time was good and the boss said I was doin' good as well. Then, then, well, the police came for him, so now I'm out of a job."

"The police came for him? For what?"

"Receivin' stolen goods they said. They said the fencing we was usin' was nicked. He won't be doin' no fencing for a while they reckon, so I'm back here."

The irony wasn't lost on Eric, the fencer was nicked for fencing fences. Such a shame though. Sep might have stuck this one; he looked genuinely disappointed for the first time since Eric had been dealing within him.

"Fair enough Sep, not your fault this time. The bad news though, is that we don't have much in at the moment, and definitely no fencing jobs, or outdoor jobs for that matter. Poor Sep. He looked so looked miserable.

"This was the first time I really liked to be at work, Mr Dillon. Now I'm back where I started. It don't seem fair."

Eric was stumped. He had to do something before Sep slid down the slippery slope into dependency or worse. He was a decent lad underneath it all. He just needed a father figure and a chance to learn a skill.

"Sep, you'll just have to come back next week to see if anything comes in. We've got nothing at all now for outdoor work, just stuff you're not qualified for, oh, and a job learning basket making. Nothing in your line."

"Basket making? My Dad used to know an old bloke made baskets. Arthur Snow. He was alright he was. Dead now probably. I didn't think there was anybody left doin' that."

"This vacancy *is* with Arthur Snow Sep, he's looking for somebody to teach how to do it, but he can't pay much until you can make some baskets. Not for you is it?"

"I used to watch him when I was a little nipper. I always wanted a go at it. Is he still up at the farm in Hampton Parva?"

"He is, but Sep he can't pay enough to keep you while you learn. How would you manage?"

Sep sighed. "Yeh. Old Arthur is probably as 'ard up as we are. Do you think he'd mind teaching me while I can't get a proper job?"

"I don't know Sep. He might. If you know him why don't you go and see him. Tell him I sent you. I still want you back here next week mind. We've got to get you an income somehow. Meanwhile take this form down to Social Security, you should get a bit of money now you lost your job through no fault of your own."

And so it was that young Sep, the boy who couldn't settle to anything, took the first steps towards a new life. This was nothing to do with Eric, except he happened to be the go between, but in years to come, whenever he met Sep at a country fair or the county show, he felt a real delight in seeing the wayward young lad turned into a real artisan, proud of his work and ever respectful of the kindly old man who had taught him the skill to make a living.

As for old Arthur, he poured not only his art, but also his soul into young Sep, and the two became inseparable until Arthur passed away aged ninety two, leaving Sep the very proud and deserving owner of a steady business.

Eric took no credit for this. Sometimes all the training, the industrial psychology, the educational psychology, the career development theory, and all that Eric had learned, was surpassed by a simple trick of fate. He really liked that.

CHAPTER 24 - BAD NEWS

He left work that evening feeling tired but a bit more positive. Maybe Arthur Snow and Sep would hit it off, and as for last night, the little episode with Doreen and Elaine hadn't turned out too badly. In fact it had taken a bit of weight off his shoulders. Outside in the street, the bus stop was crowded with Christmas shoppers waiting for their bus home, and others waiting for lifts from their partners or whoever. It was a popular spot for cars to pull in for that purpose. As he crossed the road deep in thought, he was distracted by a stationary car tooting its horn and flashing its headlights. He couldn't make out who the driver was through the dark windscreen and he bent to the passenger door to look inside just as the electric window rolled down.

"Doreen! Oh no. Look Doreen you've got to stop this. It can't go on."

"Get inside, quick."

"What?"

"Get inside quick, we're in trouble."

"No I can't Doreen, just leave me be."

"George is on the warpath, you could be in big trouble. Now get in quick."

"Trouble? What trouble? Look Doreen . . "

"He'll break your bloody neck if you don't do what I say, now for Christ's sake get in the bloody car and we'll go somewhere where I can tell you about it."

Eric was beginning to get that she was serious. She looked pretty desperate. He looked up and down the street. No one seemed to be watching him. Against his better judgement he climbed into the car. Before he could get his seat belt on, Doreen put her foot down hard and the car sped off into the darkened streets.

"What's this all about Doreen? I hope you're not fooling around. I've told you I don't want this to go on. Where are we going?"

"Just to park up and talk. Sit quiet for one bloody minute and I'll tell you."

She drove, somewhat expertly Eric thought, through the busy going home traffic and swung the car into the riverside car park, taking the car right to the empty far end where it was quiet. She stopped the car and turned off the ignition.

"Now, tell me true, when you was round my house looking at George's trophies, did you pinch anything?"

"Me? Of course I," he paused. "What sort of anything?"

"George is going ballistic because he says somebody's been tampering with a package he had in there. I told him I haven't seen any bloody package, but he's giving me a lot of grief over it. Now you're the only person what's been in that room, so I reckon you owe me an explanation or else I'm gonna tell him you made a visit about our Philip and you went in to look at that room."

Eric's heart sank. This was trouble. Big trouble. All for a piece of chalk. Although it seemed very likely now that the chalk wasn't chalk as we know it. Then,

"Hang on a minute. There were coppers running all over the house after that escaped bloke that night, perhaps they took something. I never took anything, I swear."

"I don't believe you Eric, them policemen was too busy doin' what they was doin' to be pokin' round in George's trophy room. Now what did you nick, was it a little badge or a shield or something? A little keepsake was it? If you give it me back, I'll say I found it behind the bookshelf or something.

Don't make me tell George about you bein' there and I might 'ave to say you was pesterin' me, and believe me Eric, you really wouldn't want that. Not unless you want to end up in A&E."

What could he say? Doreen obviously knew nothing about the packet of chalk. The Mangler must be keeping her in the dark. He knew he had to say something or she might carry out her threat.

"Really Doreen, I never lifted anything. All I can remember is picking up a bit of chalk off the floor in case it got trod into the carpet. Really, honestly, I swear, there was nothing else."

"A bit of bloody chalk? That can't be it. You're lyin' to me Eric. Now for the last time, what did you take?"

"Honest Doreen, I would tell you. George scares the living day lights out of me. I'm sorry but that's all. Only that bit of chalk."

"It can't be no bit of chalk he's worried about can it? What did you do with it?"

"Oh I, er, I put it in my pocket I think." Now he had to make up another lie. "Yeah, I remember I threw it away when I was emptying the pockets of my jeans at the launderette. Look, Doreen, have you thought it might be more than just ordinary chalk, else why would George be going ballistic?"

"What do you mean, not just ordinary chalk? What are you talking about?" Doreen was moving from plain irate, to baffled.

"Well, I don't know. Perhaps it's drugs or something."

"Drugs? George don't do drugs. He can't, not with his wrestling. Anyhow alcohol is his thing. He don't do drugs. Never has, never will."

"Well perhaps he's keeping them safe for a friend. Look, I don't know either, but supposing it is this chalk you're talking about, couldn't you just mention that you found a bit on the carpet when you were doing the vacuuming and you threw it away?"

"That's easy for you to say darlin', but I'll get it in the neck from George." There was a long pause, then she sighed and looked downhearted. "Do you reckon it is drugs then?"

Eric was beginning to feel sorry for Doreen now. "Well, I can't think of another reason he should get so upset over a piece of chalk."

"Stupid bugger, I ought to strangle 'im. He said he'd never do nothing like that." She took a deep breath to compose her thoughts. "Alright, I'll say I found some chalk and binned it. He can't really blame me for that. As long as he thinks it's only chucked away he won't have nothing to get that worried over. As long as it is the chalk he thinks he's lost. Are you sure you never nicked nothing?"

"Totally sure."

She looked at him with resignation.

"'Ere, that lady at the top of the stairs in the pub. Was that your wife? She looked a bit daggers at me."

Eric paused for thought. Should he admit he wasn't married?

"I'm sorry Doreen, I lied about that. I was scared and I wanted out."

"You mean you're not married?"

"Yes. I mean no, I'm not married and I don't have any kids either."

"You bastard." She was more hurt than angry. "And that woman on the stairs?"

"My girl friend. Sorry. Look, I never started all this. I don't want to hurt you or your feelings, but well, that's it really."

"Then you shouldn't have agreed to come round my house that night. You must have wanted to."

Eric could hardly tell her he came round purposely to look for the package. He just shrugged.

"You must have liked me Eric." She took his hand and squeezed it, but he pulled it away. Oh no, not that, he'd been here before. He opened the car door.

"I've got to go. Sorry Doreen. I hope it goes alright with George." And before she had chance to react he jumped out of the car and walked quickly down the footpath back towards the town centre.

Doreen sat for quite a while before starting the engine. At last, she took a long deep breath and although now on her own, she said out loud, "So do I bloody hope it'll be alright with George. You'll be the first to know if it don't Eric."

As she drove off, she didn't notice the car in the corner of the car park quietly pull out and follow her.

Walking over the town bridge, hands in his pockets and head down against the cold drizzle, Eric was lost in thought. There were so many questions. That chalk, could it really be made from a drug, or were drugs concealed inside? That would explain why the Mangler was so upset, because if it went astray it could be incriminating. And what about Cooper and his language classes? Was he passing on the chalk to his cons for money? Or were they getting some kind of fix from handling the chalk and the blackboard?

There was only one thing for it. He still had his sample of the chalk; he needed somehow to find out what was in it. No, he thought, he didn't know how to do that, short of someone ingesting it, or maybe a junkie would recognise the taste or smell. No, don't go there. Too risky. The other alternative of course would be to turn it over to the police, but how would he do that without deepening the mess he was already in? They might ask too many questions and might find out about him arranging the anonymous escaped prisoner tip off. Whose stupid idea was that? His.

Eric stopped off for fish and chips on the way home. He wasn't in the mood for shopping and cooking. After his meeting with Doreen, he needed someone to talk to, but there would be no chance of seeing Elaine tonight, or even of a phone chat, because she was at work. Briefly he imagined he might inflict some minor injury on himself, or feign chest pains and roll up at A &E to see her, but he didn't think that would go down too well.

He sat at his dining table eating the fish and chips straight from the wrapping paper and staring at the wall. What the hell would happen next? As sure as hell something would. The phone would ring and it would be the police accusing him of giving false information, or the Mangler ready to beat him up after finding out it was him who took the chalk, or worse, for having a liaison with his wife.

He went into the bedroom and picking up his jeans from the floor, rummaged in his pocket for the stick of chalk. Then taking it back to the table he stood it on its end like a candle and stared at it while he finished his chips. It had to be drugs. Why else would it be smuggled around like that?

He picked up the chalk stick and examined it. To him it looked like any other stick of schoolroom chalk, a thin yellow coating over a chalky white middle. The yellow was just to keep the dust down wasn't it? He rubbed his finger over the end of the stick and looked at the thin layer of white on his fingers. Gingerly he touched the tip of his tongue on his finger. It tasted of nothing. No clue there then. Maybe he would go into some strange hallucinogenic state in a minute.

Oh, God, he hadn't thought of that. Maybe he would have a bad trip and jump off the roof or something. Maybe he would become an instant addict. Alcohol apart, Eric was a scaredy cat when it came to substance abuse.

Nervously, he checked himself out. He didn't feel addicted. In fact he didn't feel anything. He spat onto the chip paper to get rid of the tiny amount of powder on his tongue and licked his lips clean. It was then he noticed a numbing sensation on his lips. Not much, but it was definitely there. Better be careful. He went to the kitchen and tore off a piece of plastic cling film, then carefully used it to pick up and wrap the chalk. He wanted rid of it. This chalk spelled trouble, Eric wasn't used to having to conceal illegal substances. It could be incriminating and that wouldn't be fair because he wasn't a criminal, unless you called the theft of a piece of chalk a crime. He wanted it out of the flat, but he wasn't ready yet to throw it clean away.

He decided to leave the chalk hidden outside somewhere. Somewhere away from the flat. Somewhere no one would see him hiding it, or retrieving it later if need be. He decided on the little alley way where he cut through to the local off licence. That was dark and secluded and there were piles of dead leaves under the bushes. Come to think of it, a visit to the "offie" wouldn't go amiss while he was at it. He was all out of cans of beer. Putting on his coat he left the flat, walked across the car park and onto the path that led to the alley. At the alley's entrance he turned to look around, trying (but failing) not to look surreptitious as he checked no one was watching him. There was no one about except some bloke sitting in a car reading the paper. Probably waiting for someone, and anyway the bloke couldn't see into the alley from there. Hiding the chalk was a simple matter. Eric just dropped it into the dead leaves under a bush and kicked over the leaves to ensure the chalk was covered.

Returning from the offie to the flat with his four cans of bitter, two bags of crisps, a bar of Old Jamaica rum and raisin chocolate, (comfort food), and a copy of the local paper, he noticed the bloke was still in the car reading his own paper. Hmm. Probably nothing. Nothing at all. Eric was by now beginning to recognise, and cope with, his own paranoia.

Opening a can of the bitter, Eric sat down and opened the local rag. His eyes popped when he saw the front page. VICIOUS ESCAPEE STILL AT LARGE . According to the article, the man Quentin was still believed to be hiding somewhere in the locality. The Police, it said, were following up several leads and searches were continuing in properties throughout the area. Then came the bit which made the hairs stand up on his neck. "Extra undercover officers had been drafted into the area to carry out investigations amongst former associates of Quentin."

Why would they say that? Why would they give the game away like that? Eric couldn't work it out. Unless, he thought, they were trying to close down any activity to support or hide Quentin. That might drive him out into the open. Very clever. He smiled. Eric liked clever people, or at least he liked clever ideas. So maybe they had people watching Quentin's former contacts. "Oh," He sat bolt upright as he realised the implications. "God, that might include me!" He rushed to the kitchen window and looked out into the car park. Where was that bloke in the car, reading the paper? He squinted his eyes to see out into the dark. The car was gone.

CHAPTER 25 - UPSETTING GERALD

Saturday morning dawned misty moisty. Eric was up early to get the flat straight. Elaine was coming round after lunch to have a go at a working out a joint song. As soon as he was on his feet, he checked the car park. No, whoever that man was, he was there no more.

Elaine, carrying her guitar, came round at two and they had a great afternoon, talking, laughing and singing. They even decided on a song to sing together. He liked Bob Dylan and she liked Joan Baez, so they decided on Its All Over Now Baby Blue which both Dylan and Baez had recorded. Actually, by the time they had worked out the chords and she had found a harmony line, it didn't sound too bad.

"Hey, that sounded pretty good. We should make it the first track on our album. We could be the next Sonny and Cher."

She laughed. "That'll be the day."

"No I don't do Buddy Holly songs."

"Well that's because you're not a brown eyed handsome man."

"No, that's a Chuck Berry song"

And that's roughly how the conversation went until they ran out of puns and jokes and got hungry. In reality, what he was pretty hungry for was Elaine, but at that moment her appetite was more for food, so he capitulated and retired to the kitchen to make a curry. She came in to give a hand with chopping onions, standing at the work surface by the window.

"Who's that bloke in that black Nissan? He was there when I came in."

Eric flinched, the knife missed the onion but found his finger tip.

"Ow, ow."

"What?" She looked up.

"I cut my finger." He stuck is finger in his mouth to catch the blood. He looked out of the window. Oh God it looked like that man in the car last night. Maybe they *were* watching him.

"Here, show it to the nurse." Elaine examined his finger tip which had sustained a tiny cut, barely a scratch really. "Hmm, this is a job for an A&E specialist. I think if we act quickly we can save the arm. Do you have any plasters."

Of course he hadn't. Did this woman know nothing about single men? Single men don't think to buy stuff like that.

"No, you'll have to rip off my shirt and tear it into strips to make bandages. Oh I feel faint, I think I need the kiss of life." He sank into a chair in mock collapse.

"Huh, what you need sir, is a bit of iodine or something. Something that will sting like hell when I put it on. I'll just look in my bag." She had the measure of him.

"Ah, well, actually nurse I suddenly feel a lot better. See the blood has stopped already."

She laughed and gave him a little kiss. "I thought that might do the trick. Anyway, you didn't answer my question. Who's the bloke outside in the car?"

Eric looked out again thoughtfully, "Dunno." He stared at the car a moment longer, then said, "Probably some simple reason. Gawd knows. How hot do you like your curry?"

The dinner was good, and afterwards they sat together on the sofa, feeling replete.

Elaine gave Eric a thank you kiss for dinner. "That was lovely, so you can cook a bit after all. Arts Centre club tonight. Shall we go?"

"Um, well we could I suppose, or we could stay in and I could transport you to heights of connubial bliss." Wow that was brave, although it was said more in hope than expectation. He knew full well how she would take it.

"In your dreams."

"How did you know that?"

She laughed and gave him a playful whack over the head with the folded newspaper.

"Come on, our public awaits. I'll drive tonight."

Gathering up their instruments they headed off out of the flat. The man in the car was still there. Eric stared at him to make it obvious he had noticed him, but when they drove off the man made no attempt to follow. Maybe he was watching someone else.

They didn't perform 'Baby Blue' that evening. That needed a fair bit more work and anyway they wanted to keep their powder dry for the competition at The Lord Palmerston. Nevertheless, people were beginning to notice the budding relationship twixt the two of them. Cravat man Gerald in particular was appalled.

"Hello Elaine, enjoyed your set as usual. Lovely, really lovely, well done." Gerald had a good line in condescension. "A word in your ear though. Just a bit of friendly advice from an admirer of your, um, of your , um, work. A lot of people, myself included, think you're a great talent. You could really go far with your voice and sensitivity, but I'm concerned that people will, um, well, fail to take you seriously if you allow yourself to be associated with, um, with shall we say, less credible performers like Eric. I mean I know he's a harmless enough chap, but you could, um, well you know what I mean."

Elaine kept a straight face. "Well thank you for that Gerald. I appreciate your concern. However, I don't have any great musical ambitions, so I'm not worried about being seen with Eric, especially as he is so dishy. Bye. Oh, love the cravat by the way."

She returned to Eric and made a great show of giving him a hug and a kiss in clear view of Gerald.

"Gerald thinks you're bad for my career."

"What, nursing?"

"No, as the next Joan Baez I think. He warned me off you. You're holding me back. Dragging me down." She smiled.

"Well, he's got me bang to rights. Guilty as charged. I suppose we're finished then."

"Well, I think I should fulfil my contractual obligations to you vis a vis The Lord Palmerston competition, before I ditch you and go off to my new career in Nashville, don't you?"

"Absolutely, otherwise I'll sue you for every penny you have. You'll be ruined."

"Gerald thinks I already am, hanging around with you."

Eric looked across at Gerald. "He's right. How can I compete with a man like that. I don't even own a cravat."

"Thank God", she kissed him yet again. In public! Cravat or no, Eric was ten feet tall.

As they drove homewards, Eric had another attempt at advancing his case for a more intimate relationship.

"You're not going to dump me off at my cold lonely flat are you? I make a very good breakfast, and we could get on with our practice in the morning if I stayed at yours. I'll even go out to get the milk and the paper."

"OK."

"What?!" Eric nearly jumped out of his seat.

"OK, you can sleep on the sofa."

"On the sofa?" he said with exaggerated despair.

"It's a very nice sofa, and I've got plenty of blankets. Now do you want me to drive to mine or to your's?"

"Will you tuck me in, and give me a goodnight kiss?"

"Alright, I'm good at tucking in. I'm a nurse."

And so that's what happened. Slow progress Eric, but progress nonetheless.

In spite of his offer to make breakfast, she was up first on Sunday morning. He woke to find her making coffee in the kitchen. He pulled on his jeans and wandered in.

"Oh that's disappointing; I hoped you'd still be in your nightie."

She smiled and gave him a warm hug. "Oh Eric, I really like you, but can we do this at my pace? I've been caught out before, and now I need to be sure before jumping in the deep end."

He hugged her back. "OK but remember I'm a good swimmer especially in the deep end."

Over breakfast they talked of this and that until he remembered something he meant to ask her. "Aah, you're a nurse aren't you?"

"You know I am. Oh that reminds me, I'm back on shift at six tonight. Four nights on, so I won't be able to see you until Thursday. Anyway why did you bring up the nurse thing?"

"Ah yes, well, do you know anything about drugs?"

"Course I do. Do you mean medicines, or the crap that brings in a lot of our patients on a Saturday night?"

He took a swig of coffee. "The latter probably. What might it be if there was a white powder that makes your lips numb if you dab it on them?"

"Sounds like cocaine to me, why do you ask?"

"Cocaine?"

"Yes, probably. Is this something one of your clients got caught with?"

"Er, something like that. Can't say much. Prison matter. Somebody suspected of smuggling it in. Not one of my lads, although," he looked over his shoulder as if checking to see if they were being watched, "they have tried to get me to smuggle in a tube of Smarties."

"Smarties eh. Dangerous stuff, the pink ones are highly addictive. I've had an overdose myself occasionally."

The day was good. A walk by the river, a shared lunch and a bit more song practice. She dropped him off at the flat on her way to work.

"Thanks Elaine it's been great."

"Me too. Have a good week. See you Thursday."

He watched as she drove off. Would it be a good week? He doubted it. Tomorrow he was back to the prison. "So," he mused, "Cocaine eh? "

Cooper couldn't be left to get away with that.

CHAPTER 26 – THE CAT AMONGST THE PIGEONS

Next morning, despite a disturbed night, Eric rose especially early. He had made his mind up. All night he had been mulling over what to do, weighing up all the risks and all the possible outcomes, good and bad. It was time to bite the bullet. Be decisive for once. Do it now before you change your mind.

He drove to the public phone box by the local shops. It was early and no one was about. Donning a pair of woolly gloves, he pulled out a clean handkerchief. He got a pile of coins ready for the call and dialled the police station. With the hanky over the mouthpiece just like in the films he asked for CID and told the man that Cecil Cooper the Education Officer at the local prison was supplying cocaine to inmates concealed in sticks of blackboard chalk which he got from George Marshall the wrestler. Before they could ask any questions in return, he put down the phone, left the phone box and drove away. He was shaking like a leaf.

What would happen now was anybody's guess. Nature, or the police force rather, would have to take its course. What he must do, he decided, was just to follow his normal work routine, same as usual, and that meant going into prison that afternoon.

The morning seemed to drag on forever. At his office he could concentrate on nothing. He pretended he was preparing his education material for the afternoon, but in reality he looked out of his window across the back roofs of the shops and offices and chewed his pencil. Pretty soon now, all hell would be let loose, assuming of course that the police took his call seriously. If they didn't, well, he had a second plan. He would send them his stick of chalk, then they'd have to take notice.

Lunch time came and Eric's stomach was churning but it wasn't with hunger, it was pure nerves. And so the time came to climb in his scruffy vehicle and drive around town to the prison. All was quiet when he arrived. There was Cooper's Mercedes shining in the little car park. Eric drove his old banger alongside as it shuddered to a halt. He climbed out and walked to the little steel door set into the much larger big prison gate.

"Afternoon Mr Dillon, back to see your lads are you? Got your pass?" The man behind the thick glass reception window looked relaxed. Well, obviously, nothing had happened yet.

Eric was going to have to work hard to appear calm and normal when he got to the education block. He sat alone in the visitors' waiting room flipping through old copies of Woman's Weekly and Autocar feeling more nervous than he did at a visit to the dentist. He was about to face the man he had shopped, not that Cooper knew that.

The wait was agonising, Eric wanted to get the face to face meeting over with and to get into the comforting company of his group of lads. At least they felt the same about Cooper as he did. They were mostly only petty criminals, just kids who had not been shown the right way to live. They meant no real harm to other people. Despite their upbringing in a harsh environment, they were not so cynical as the calculating, grasping, unsympathetic fraud that was Cecil Cooper.

Eventually an escort officer showed up and led Eric through the depressing series of locked gates to the education block office. Cooper was there, having a spring clean by the look of it. There were piles of books on the chairs and a black plastic sack stuffed with trash to dump. Jack the trusty was dusting the bookshelves while Cooper himself appeared to be going through piles of papers, tearing most of them up and feeding them into the black sack.

Eric knocked on the open door. "Afternoon."

"Oh, it's you Dolan. Forgot it was your day. Just having a clear out. This place is a bloody pig sty. Move those books if you want to sit down. How about some tea Jack? Is this your last week Dolan?"

"No, I've got one more after this."

He looked on with concern. All this tidying up wasn't good if the police came in looking for the chalk. He looked around to see if he could spot it. It was nowhere to be seen. Cooper looked like he was being thorough in his clear up. Eric made a space to sit down.

"Why the big clear up?"

Cooper wiped his brow and sat on the edge of the desk. "Education inspectors coming in a couple of weeks. Bloody waste of time, just before Christmas and all. I don't know why they can't leave us alone to get on with it. This is not a bloody school, it's a classroom in a nick. We're not educating the little darlings of the middle classes, all our students have rejected school long before they got here. They only come to classes to get out of their stinking cells. I don't know what these inspectors think we're supposed to achieve with this lot, but when half of the buggers can't read and write, we won't be dishing out many diplomas at the end of the year."

Eric said nothing. Strangely, he was glad to hear Cooper talk like that because it made him feel a whole lot better about shopping him to the police. As far as he was concerned the sooner he was exposed and got rid of, the better.

After the customary insipid cup of tea from Jack, Eric's class arrived and he went in to join them. He decided this week to find out if the lads had remembered anything he had told them over the past few weeks. Hopefully he would prove Cooper wrong. A teacher might set a test or an exam at this point, but Eric had a better idea.

"Right gentlemen, form yourselves into two teams, we're going to have a quiz. Sit this side if your birthday is an odd number, that side if it's even. Decide on your team names, thirty seconds." The lads shuffled into position and started the inevitable arguments about team names while Eric turned to the board to set out a score sheet. It took a few seconds before he realised the significance of what he saw. The blackboard was squeaky clean. Totally, uniformly black. No French sentences, no dust in the grooved lip at the bottom, and a fresh clean cloth for use as a wiper. No one was going to find any cocaine here.

"Bugger. Oh sorry lads, just remembered something I forgot." He suddenly realised he had sworn in front of the group.

"Ha ha, I told you he swore in real life." Billy, a goofy boy who always sat at the front obviously enjoyed Eric's slip. The lads in the class used their extensive repertoire of profanities very freely, but usually Eric chose to remain professional.

Eric continued cursing under his breath as he set out the board in two columns.

"Team names then. What about this side? "

"Muggers"

"Yeh and we'll be Druggers."

"Very funny, but it might not be good to have that on the board if any high ups pay us a visit. Come on, let's have something legal. I tell you what, how about Ferraris and Maseratis."

"What's them" Big Wayne obviously didn't follow luxury sports car makes.

"Cars, you dumbo. Yeh, we'll be Ferraris. I know a bloke nicked one of them once."

"Where is he now?"

"C block I think."

"OK lads that'll do. Right first question coming up. First team to raise a hand gets a go at answering. What kind of firm would employ a hod carrier?"

And so it went. The lads got quite competitive and Eric was pleased that they remembered some things he had told them about employee rights, and local industries. After half an hour the Ferraris were marginally in the lead.

"Right, don't put your hands up for this next one until you've got three answers. Give me three occupations where you work with animals."

"Pigs."

"Yes Wayne, pigs are animals." Eric had learned you had to be patient with Wayne.

"No, pigs. Pigs. Outside." Wayne was pointing over Eric's shoulder through the glass partition.

Eric turned to look. Policemen four or five of them clustered round Cooper's office door. The lads were on their feet. "There's that bastard Hopkins what nicked our Barry.", "And old fish face Turner, what's he doin' in 'ere?"

"Quiet lads. Who's the bloke in the brown suit?" Could this be it? Had they come to look for the chalk?

"That's the governor, Stanway. And there's that detective bloke, Amory."

Amory. That rang a bell in Eric's head but he couldn't immediately place the name. The Governor knocked on the classroom door and stepped in.

"Sorry to interrupt you Mr, er..."

"Dillon. I'm giving a careers lesson."

"Ah yes, Mr Dillon. Well I'm sorry but I'm going to have to ask you to stop now. We're conducting a, um, a, um, security exercise. If you would like to wait here a moment, an officer will take these prisoners back to their cells, then I'll get you escorted out."

Eric looked through the glass where Cooper appeared to be remonstrating with two police officers. The lads in the class were on their feet getting a good look too.

"Wossgoinon? What's old Cooper been up to?"

A prison officer appeared at the door. "Quiet you lot. Now, single file straight out of the block. Quick as you like, go."

The lads filed out, still gawping at the scene outside Cooper's office. Eric stayed put as instructed and watched proceedings. Cooper, escorted by two officers followed the lads out of the block, and a prison officer and what looked like a plain clothes policeman went into the office. The governor, looking somewhat harassed, returned to the classroom and spoke again to Eric. "Mr, er, . ."

"Dillon"

"Ah yes, I thought our Mr Cooper said your name was Dolan. Anyway, what I wanted to say was I'm sorry about all this but we do occasionally have these unannounced security exercises. Nothing to get concerned about, but I'd be grateful if you don't mention it outside of these four walls. People misconstrue things so easily you know. Ah, here's your escort now. So glad to have met you. Goodbye."

Eric didn't think he was misconstruing anything. This was the big one alright. The governor was sweating visibly as he showed him to the door.

It didn't seem worth going back to the office, and anyway, Eric wouldn't have been able to concentrate. It could all be coincidence of course. After all, the governor said they do carry out random security checks. No, they wouldn't call in the police for those would they? There were four or five police cars in the prison car park when Eric got out. A van too, with dogs. Dogs! Surely they would find any drugs Cooper hadn't managed to get rid of.

Eric was puzzled. All that cleaning up of the office and the washed down blackboard. Could Cooper have known the fuzz was coming? How could he? Unless someone at the police station had tipped him off. Bloody hell, it didn't bear thinking about.

His thoughts turned to Doreen's house. Were they searching that too? Surely, they must be. They have to hit all these places at once to avoid people warning each other. "Only one thing for it", he thought, "drive round and see." He started up his old jalopy and pulled out into the traffic. The town roads were always choc a bloc at that time of day with all the mums picking up their little darlings from school. It took ages to reach Lacketts Lane. He parked in the next road and walked round to take a peek. The late afternoon sun was sinking fast and all Eric could see were silhouettes. My God. Yes, there they were! Three police cars and a van. A copper was standing outside keeping passers by at bay, so Eric held back in the distance. How long, he wondered, before the press got hold of the story. This was no place for him to be seen. He felt the sudden urge to put some serious distance between himself and all this, so he headed back to the car and high tailed it home.

CHAPTER TWENTY SEVEN

BUMP IN THE NIGHT

There was no way Eric wanted to sit at home that evening dreading the ringing of his phone, so he grabbed his old guitar and headed out to the Science Lab folk club. He got there early and sat in the corner tuning up and wondering what to sing.

"Ah, good evening Eric, no Elaine tonight?"

"Oh hello Gerald. Sadly, no." Eric tried to look forlorn.

Gerald on the other hand, looked at first triumphant, then he composed himself and trying hard to look earnest said, "Ah well never mind old chap, these things never last. I didn't like to say anything, but I didn't think she was really your type if you know what I mean. Still got that same old guitar I see. I just got myself a Yamaha FG140. Pretty decent."

"Yes, not bad those, once they're played in a bit. I'll look forward to hearing it."

He was enjoying this. Not only did Gerald not know that things were going swimmingly with Elaine, but he obviously didn't appreciate the value of Eric's vintage guitar either.

Actually despite his nerve wracked day, and the lack of Elaine, he had a pretty good evening. He felt safe in the Science Lab Social Club. On home ground. No chance of Doreen and the Mangler turning up for a darts match here. Mitch, the club organiser was also generous to Eric, putting him on third in the second half of the evening, with the audience nicely warmed up but not too lubricated. Perhaps not the best time for a blues number, but probably the best spot of the night. So he treated them to a rendering of his favourite wartime song, Bloody Orkney, a song by servicemen stationed up there in World War Two. Much to Gerald's dismay, every noun and every adjective in the song is preceded by the qualifier *Bloody*

Always a favourite that one, and it went down very well with everyone, except of course Gerald. So Eric was feeling pretty good when he climbed into the car for the short journey home. The troubles of the day had receded somewhat. Now that the chalk business was in the hands of the police, perhaps it was the beginning of the end of the whole episode as far as he was concerned. Even his crumbling old motor car was sounding in tune tonight. That was until he turned into the lane leading to his block of flats.

The drain in the road had never been right. After the council resurfaced the road it lay a good three inches below the new Tarmac topping. Eric had got good at tweaking the steering wheel so that the old banger straddled the hole, but tonight he wasn't concentrating and, bang, the front offside wheel took a mighty whack as it dropped into the hole. Straight away, he noticed the difference in the steering and as he pulled into his car parking area hear could hear a loud knocking underneath the car. Coming to a halt, he climbed out and peered underneath, but it was too dark to see anything. "Bugger!" Eric's voice rang out clearly across the midnight car park. It didn't look like he'd be driving anywhere tomorrow.

Next morning he got up early and went out with a mat to lay on to look underneath the car. Eric knew nothing about cars but he knew that the front wheel suspension ought to be connected to the rest of the car somehow. Sliding on his back under the car, he could see the problem. It would be hard not to as it was an inch from his face. He could see where the sub frame or the chassis or whatever you called it had rusted right through so that the gubbins that held the suspension in place had come right out. This was nothing that Eric could fix, but it looked expensive. It might even be terminal.

He went back inside and made a call.

"Banjo? It's Eric. That bloody old heap of rust you sold me has finally fallen to bits. No I can't drive it round to your's, the bloody front wheel is hanging off. Yes, hanging off. The suspension's ripped away from the frame. Whaddya mean next week? I can't go without a car for a week, I've got schools to drive to. Look mate, you still owe me one for that phone call cock up. I need it fixed ASAP."

Eric didn't know whether to believe Banjo's promise to get it sorted in a day or so, but he had little choice. He certainly didn't have enough cash to take the vehicle to a "proper" garage, and anyway, once they saw it they would probably condemn it and refuse to have anything to do with it. He wouldn't have been surprised to hear the vehicle referred to as a death trap.

CHAPTER 28 - A DAY TO TRY TO FORGET

It took two buses to get out to Oakfield, and the morning was a tough one. First up was Sunil, a cheery Indian lad whose father insisted his son should become a doctor or a lawyer despite the poor boy struggling to pass his two O levels. He seemed to think that he just needed to stay on and on at school until he would eventually get high A level grades. Several years if need be. And the reason to choose those careers? Well they were good jobs. No thought of Sunil's interests or aptitude or ability. Eric knew this wasn't a case to be solved in one hit. He did what he could to broaden the range of careers to consider and made a mental note to see the lad without his dad next time.

Next up was one of those nightmare interviews. It didn't happen very often, but every now and then Eric came across a lad with absolutely no discernible interests or aptitudes. No hobbies, no favourite pastimes, about the same at all subjects at school, and no idea at all of even the broadest category of career that might interest him. Every question Eric answered was met with a shrug or a "Don't know". The lad would probably turn out to be Prime Minister, but for now, Eric would get Lennie to recruit him for help in the school careers library to expose him to some ideas.

Next up, an interview Eric would afterwards try to forget, but never ever would. Jamie Wootton. He recognised the surname and smiled. "Are you the brother of Steven that I interviewed a year or two back?"

"Yes"

"I remember him well. Nice lad. Bright. What's he doing now?"

Jamie paused and then said "He's dead."

"Dead?" Eric blanched. "What? How?"

"He shot himself. In the garden shed." Jamie's matter of fact answer hit Eric like a baseball bat. What do you say next when you get a reply like that out of the blue? He was dismayed and appalled. At first he regretted asking the question, but then realised that it was a good job he had, for young Jamie couldn't possibly be unaffected by it, so it was bound to be relevant. Nevertheless, getting back on track in the interview was a delicate matter. He had to carry on though. Jamie had his own life to live.

"Oh Jamie, I'm so sorry. I didn't know. I liked him; I remember him so well. "He paused, "To tell you the truth that's shaken me up a bit," Eric meant it. Deep breath. "but today is about you. You have twice the reason now to have a good life. Let's see if we can get you off to a flying start. Are you alright to carry on?"

Jamie's eyes were wet with tears, but he nodded bravely. "Yes. Thanks." He smiled as if to comfort Eric, and in a strange way, it did.

One of the good things Eric had learned through his work, was to be a good listener. There were often times in an interview when the best thing to do was to keep silent and wait for the interviewee to say what was in their mind. After a long enough pause, a hidden truth would so often come out. At moments like that you could reach the real person behind the facade, and that's when the real work would start. Jamie didn't reveal any more about his brother, but he revealed so much about his motivation in life now.

Jamie was a good boy, just like his poor brother. It came as no surprise that he wanted to be a psychiatric nurse. Eric spared no efforts in doing whatever he could to help this young man on his way.

Eric was shattered come lunch time, but it was a good shattered. It was good to be reminded that what he was doing was helping young people to discover themselves and to see where their lives might lead. Sometimes he could steer them away from mistakes. Sometimes he could open their eyes to new possibilities, and sometimes he could ease the path to their goals. Sometimes. He couldn't win 'em all, but now and again it all came together and he knew again why he was doing the job.

Just a couple more interviews in the afternoon, then he made his way back to the office. Thankfully, the waiting room was all quiet. Eric could get some notes written up.

"Ah there you are Eric. Lady rang for you. Familiar voice, but didn't say who she was. Left this number."

Wendy handed Eric the bit of paper with the number. It wasn't a number he recognised. Better ring it anyway. He walked the long corridor to his office and slumped wearily into his chair. He picked up the phone and dialled.

"Hello." The voice was indistinct.

"Hello, I was asked to ring this number. This is Eric Dillon from the . . "

"Oh Eric, thank God."

"Doreen? Doreen? Is that you? Why are you crying?"

"Oh Eric, he hit me. He hit me Eric, and I walked out." She was sobbing.

"The police came and he was livid after. They searched the place but they never found nothin'. "

"Doreen where are you?"

"At a friend's house. Listen sweetheart, he knows about you and me. He's been having me followed, you too probably. Eric, he thinks it's you what told the police. He'll come for you Eric. Oh sweetheart I'm so sorry." He could hear that she was in floods of tears.

"Where are you now? Are you safe?" Eric felt his heart thumping. All he could think was to try not to panic. Must think straight.

"I'm ok, George don't know where I am. I'm in Basingstoke."

"Basingstoke? Basingstoke? What in Christ's name are you doing all the way out there?"

"Well that's why I'm here. He won't never look for me here. My cousin Linda let me have her flat what she keeps when she's working up this way. She lives in Torquay. George don't know about the flat. Anyway, look, you need to do something about George. He'll come looking for you Eric."

"He told you that?"

"No, but I heard him on the phone to one of his mates after the police left. He was livid. Bloke called Cecil. Sounds like they both reckon you got them into trouble. What have you been up to Eric?" She sounded angry now. "Is it about that bloody chalk?"

"Bloody hell. Where are they now?"

"I don't bloody know do I? I'm in Basingstoke remember. Why don't you come down here with me? You'll be safe here."

Eric could hardly breathe. He had pains in his chest and he was sweating. Bloody police, why didn't they find anything?

"I can't just run away Doreen. There's my job, my flat, and my," he hesitated, "my girl friend, and anyway my car's bust."

"You don't know what he's like Eric. He'd think nothing of breaking your arms. He'll put you in 'ospital. You can't let him get you, just phone in a sicky for a couple of days and come down to Basingstoke on the train. We'll work out something. We gotta help each other out Eric."

Eric felt doomed. Violent retribution or a couple of days in Basingstoke. He didn't know which was worse. He sat in silence desperately thinking while he could hear Doreen sobbing over the phone. It was, he supposed, true that he needed to hide while he worked out what he should do, and Elaine was on shift until Thursday. He sighed a big, deep sigh.

"Alright I'll come this evening, just for a day or so. And listen Doreen, no hanky panky, this is strictly business. How do I get there?"

"Change trains at Reading, there's one every hour. I'll pick you up at the station, say seven o'clock?"

Eric looked at the office clock. Work finished in an hour. He made an excuse about feeling unwell and left, hurrying back to the flat to pick up a toothbrush and a change of clothes and headed for the station, keeping to the back streets and pulling the hood of his duffle coat as far over his head as it would go. He was a complete bag of nerves. Every time a car passed, he turned away, hunched over as if lighting a cigarette. He glanced nervously at every middle aged man that appeared on the street, frantically looking for escape routes in case one of them was after him.

Doreen was at Basingstoke station as promised. She flashed the car lights as he stepped out of the entrance. He climbed in the car and looked over at her. "Why are you wearing dark glasses and that head scarf?" His anxiety came welling back. "I thought you said we'd be safe here."

At first she hesitated, then slowly and deliberately she removed first her headscarf and then her shades.

"Jesus Christ Doreen, did he do that to you?" Eric shuddered as he looked at the swollen bruises on her cheek and the eye all puffed up and half closed.

"Just a slap he called it. That's when I walked out. Miserable bastard. I bet you any money if he knew where I was he'd be round here all tearful, beggin' me to come home. Not this time I ain't. He blames you for all this. If he catches up with you, he'll put you in hospital, no messin'." She replaced her shades and scarf. "No good talking here, let's get to the flat. Have you had anything to eat?"

Eric was normally good at remembering routes, but Basingstoke had him bamboozled in minutes. One roundabout followed another and another until he had lost all sense of direction. Maybe it was a good place to hide after all.

The flat was drab and uninviting and not very warm. He gazed out of the window at the bare trees edging the residents' car park while Doreen knocked up a cheese sandwich. Safe and anonymous it might be, but he couldn't stay here forever. Poor Doreen, what would she do? The thought of all the trouble he had caused was weighing heavily on him. Whatever he did now, he owed it to her to somehow straighten things out. Thinking about her situation brought him close to tears.

"Doreen, I'm so sorry all this has happened. It's all my fault. Once this mess is sorted I'll make it up to you."

"Nah, forget it sweetheart." Although she was obviously shaken by the events of the last twenty four hours, she appeared philosophical. "This split with George has been a long time coming. Ever since he took up wrestling he ain't been the same. It really changed him. Why do you think I been chasing other men? Anyway it was me what started it by getting you to come round. Soon as George calms down I'm asking him for a divorce. I made me mind up. Me and

Philip'll go and live down Torquay near my cousin. I quite fancy that."

"Oh God, Philip. I'd forgotten about him. Where is he? Is he safe?"

"Oh don't worry about Philip, he's used to us having rows. He keeps his head down, and anyway, George dotes on him. Pound to a penny George'll send him to his sisters to live for now. He'll be alright there. Proper spoilt I expect. It's not him I'm worried about, it's you. George and that Cecil bloke ain't gonna forget what they think you done. Sooner or later they'll catch up with you. Then what'll you do?"

Eric didn't reply. What could he say? He had no answer. It was true, the inevitability of having to face the Mangler and Cooper at sometime had to be faced up to. He slumped in an armchair, his head in his hands. He wasn't up to this. This was way out of his league. If only the police had found the stuff, then the two of them would presumably be safely banged up, "helping the police with their enquiries".

He bit into his cheese sandwich. It tasted like cardboard, although in truth it was probably Eric's dry mouth rather than the cheese that was at fault. "Is there anything to drink?"

"Tea or coffee?" said Doreen.

"I don't suppose you've got anything stronger? I need to settle my nerves."

Doreen walked over to a corner cabinet and peered inside. "Only some Tia Maria and a bottle of Retsina."

"Retsina? What's that?" Eric knowledge of booze didn't stretch much beyond beer and claret.

"Ain't you never been to Greece sweetheart? That's all they drink over there. It's the Greek idea of wine."

No, he had never been to Greece, or anywhere continental for that matter except a disastrous camping holiday as a student when an old Dormobile van he and his mates had bought together broke down so often they had to abandon it in Belgium.

Doreen found a couple of wine glasses and opened the bottle. Eric took a sizeable gulp and nearly choked as he fought not to spit it out. "Bloody hell it's ghastly." He held out the glass for a refill. "Top me up. I'll drink anything right now as long as it's alcoholic."

They finished off the Retsina and started on the Tia Maria. Eric started to calm down a bit. He looked at Doreen with her poor battered face and gave an ironic smile. "Oh God Doreen, how did we get to this?" He paused. "What's more, how the bloody hell do we get out of it?"

"I'll be alright sweetheart, it's you what's got the biggest problem right now. What are you gonna do about George and that other bloke?"

Eric sighed and shook his head, then sitting up and squinting his eyes as though formulating a fresh thought, said, "Well it seems to me I can't avoid him forever, so if I have to confront him, it might as well be on my terms rather than his."

"What do you mean?"

"I haven't got a clue Doreen, except I need to think up some way where I can come out on top. Obviously I can't beat him physically, but is there any other way I can stop him? Is there anything he's afraid of ?"

"Who, George? You must be joking, he ain't afraid of nothing."

"Everybody is afraid of something Doreen. Even George." Eric peered into his empty glass. Pour us another glass of that coffee hooch, it steadies my nerves."

After a few more glasses of the liqueur, Eric's nerves got so steady, he couldn't move.

CHAPTER 29 - A DECISION

He awoke cold and stiff next morning with a thumping head, and still in the armchair. The empty Tia Maria bottle lay on the floor alongside. He staggered to his feet, holding his head, then shuffled out to the bathroom and rummaged in the wall cabinet, hunting for an aspirin. No aspirin, but he found a little bottle of paracetamol, and swallowed three tablets, washing them down by drinking direct from the cold tap. Shutting the cabinet door he caught sight of his face in the mirror. Ugh, it wasn't a pretty sight. Maybe a bottle of Retsina followed by a whole bottle of coffee liqueur wasn't such a good idea after all.

Eric splashed cold water on his face, then slouched back towards the kitchen where he searched the fridge and cupboards for something he could eat. Nothing. He felt awful. The noise of the banging shut of the cupboard doors was hurting his head. Wait, there was another banging. He tried to focus. What was it? Then he realised it was the flat's front door. Someone was trying to get in.

Eric flew into instant panic mode. Bugger, how the hell had they found him? What should he do? He was trapped. If that was the Mangler outside, there was no escape. The window, what about the window? He opened it and looked out at the drop to the path below. Too high, he'd break his neck if he jumped. The banging on the front door was getting louder as if someone was beating it with their fists. Maybe if he tied some sheets together he could climb down them to escape. His heart was beating so hard it was as loud as the banging on the door.

"Eric!"

He froze.

"Eric. Open up Eric, it's freezin' out here."

The voice was coming through the letter box. It was Doreen's voice.

"What the . . .?" Eric was slow to catch on.

Bang bang. "Eric, let me in."

He felt a wave of relief wash over him. Then he just felt stupid. He opened the front door to see Doreen standing there with a bag of groceries. He stood back while she carried the bag through to the kitchen.

"I thought I'd never wake you up. Didn't you hear me banging? 'Ere, why is that window open, you'll lose all the heat in the flat."

"Oh, I just, um, needed some fresh air." He shut and fastened the window. "How long have you been up?"

"Well it is half past ten darlin'. Mind you, I didn't drink all that alcohol last night."

Eric looked at the empty bottle. "I didn't drink all that surely."

"Well, I had one to start with, then you finished off the bottle. Feelin' a bit delicate this morning are we? I'll put the kettle on. Fancy a croissant? Still hot from the bakers."

Eric had never eaten a croissant. He peered at them. They smelled of hot butter.

"I think I'll give 'em a miss. A bit greasy for me at the moment."

He settled for her next offer of white toast and jam, and after a cup of tea and a slice of the toast he began to feel marginally more human. The paracetamol had begun to dull the thumping in his head. Doreen kept pouring him glasses of orange juice which eventually revived him enough to hold a conversation.

"I don't suppose I came up with any good ideas last night did I? I don't remember much after I started on that bloody bottle."

"Sorry love, you wasn't saying much at all. I been thinkin' though." She lit a cigarette and took a long drag. "About that what you said about George bein' afraid of anything."

"Oh. And?"

Doreen looked out the window. "It's a nice sunny frosty day out there. How about a walk through the park? You need a bit of fresh air to clear your brain sweetheart."

Eric thought she was probably right. "Good idea, just let me freshen up first." He picked up his jacket from the floor and found his toothbrush in the inside pocket.

He felt better after a wash and a comb through his hair which, being fashionably long was a right mess after a night in an armchair.

The park was only a short stroll from the flat. There was nobody much about, just a couple of dog walkers. Their arms linked, Eric and Doreen walked along an alley of bare trees, kicking at the frosty leaves on the ground.

"So you were saying? About George."

"Oh yeah. Well, it ain't much, but I ain't never seen him scared of nothin', but that day the police come round, he was proper frightened. If I hadn't been there he would really 'ave panicked. And after they went, when he was on to that Cecil bloke on the phone, he was in a right state."

"Mmm. They didn't find anything though did they?"

"No, but you could tell they was still sure he was up to no good. I got the feelin' they thought they was on to something big. Just because they never found nothin' they didn't treat him like an innocent man. Know what I mean? He's still scared they're on to 'im."

"But he's your husband Doreen. You don't want him banged up. I don't like what he's doing but even if I could pin anything on him, I don't want to break up your marriage do I?"

"I told you Eric, I'm finished with him. This ain't the first time he's knocked me about, and in any case, I don't 'old with drugs. If he's been helpin' supply drugs to the poor bastards what takes 'em then he deserves whatever he gets."

He could see that she meant it. Not that it was all that much help. Even if George was terrified of being caught by the police, Eric didn't see how he could use that in self defence against the undoubted talents of the champion wrestler. It would appear that the cops didn't have enough on George to make an arrest.

"Doreen, how come the police didn't find anything when they came to the house? What had he done with the chalk?"

"Ooh after that bit went missin', he got proper anxious like I told you. He give that room a deep clean, top to bottom."

"What do you suppose he did with any more chalk he had?"

She shrugged. "Gawd knows. Chucked it away I expect."

Eric scratched his head. "I don't think he'd chuck it away, it must have been worth a few bob. He must have stashed it away somewhere safer. Where would he do that do you think?"

She had no idea, and anyway it was getting cold walking round the park, so they headed back towards the flat, their arms still linked.

"This is nice." She gave his arm a little squeeze.

"What is?"

"You and me together like this. We got the place to ourselves back at the flat. Nobody knows we're here, we should make the most of it." She was putting on that voice again, but this time Eric was determined not to succumb.

"Now then Doreen, I'm a happily married man with six kids. Remember? And anyway, I'm a sick man, off work for a couple of days."

She laughed, "No you ain't. Anyway you said it was three kids last time. Are you serious about this girl friend then?"

He hesitated, then, "Yeah, I suppose I am."

Back at the flat, the worst of his hangover seemed to have passed. In the kitchen he tipped out the bag of groceries Doreen had bought. Clever girl, she had bought a packet of crumpets. Just what the doctor ordered. He toasted three each which they ate in a leisurely fashion washed down with cups of tea.

"Doreen, I'm not being antisocial, but I'm going to sit quiet now and have a think." Had he been Sherlock Holmes he would have smoked a pipe full of opium or played the violin, but to his eternal regret he had never learned the violin, so he didn't. Instead, he just plonked himself in an armchair, closed his eyes and let his imagination run through a few scenarios. It must have been nearly two hours before he surfaced.

"Well?" She said

"Well what?"

"You know very well what. Have you thought of what to do?"

He nodded. "I have."

"Well?"

"Well what?"

"I'm gonna thump you in a minute. What is it you are going to do?"

"I dunno. Ok. I do, but I don't know how it will play out, and it's best if you don't know."

"Eric!" She was exasperated. "I thought we was in this together."

He sighed. "Very well then. I'm going back home, back to work and to get on with life as", he paused, "huh, normal."

"Then?"

"Then nothing. I'll just deal with things as they happen."

"Eric you're crazy. They'll catch you and do you in. Haven't you been listening to me?"

He shrugged. "I know, I know, but I can't see any alternative, and I can't just hide away. I'm going back. Something'll turn up." It was easy to say, but in truth Eric felt beaten. He knew he would just have to let fate take its course. Life had to go on, and he had had enough of all this cloak and dagger stuff. What would happen would happen and in a couple of weeks it would be behind him.

Doreen's continued pleading did nothing to change his mind. With a heavy heart and a sinking stomach he made ready to catch the four o'clock train. "Can you take me to the station Doreen? I'm sorry I can't stay on but my mind's made up."

For a minute she just stared out of the window, then she turned, took a deep breath, and said, "Well then, I might as well do the same. I'm going back as well. I'll drive you home."

"No, don't be daft, you're safe here. I'll be alright."

"No Eric, you're right. You can't keep running away from things. You have to face up to them in the end, and I'm dealing with George face to face. I'm not going back with him, but I'm not running away. Come on, let's get it over with. Help me clear up this place. I ain't got much to pack."

He didn't argue. He could see she meant it. In twenty minutes they were on the road.

Eric was back home by tea time. He'd persuaded Doreen to drop him half a mile from home. The last thing he needed was to be seen getting out of her car. He walked back the rest of the way looking nervously over his shoulder as he picked his way through local footpaths and alleyways. Arriving at the car park outside his flat, he studied the parked cars carefully before emerging from the alleyway. Only when he was sure that it was safe did he run across to his flat and scramble inside. Quickly he bolted the front door and breathing heavily he leant against it while he gathered himself. Should he switch the lights on? It would advertise his presence. He opted for the table lamp in the sitting room and kept the curtains drawn. He found himself creeping around like a cat burglar. Surely he couldn't go on like this. Not indefinitely anyway. He picked up the junk mail from the doormat and wandered into the kitchen to rummage for food. As he suspected, the cupboard was bare, unless something could be knocked up from spaghetti and tomato ketchup. He needed comfort food. The flat was cold and gloomy. What day was it? Wednesday. Bugger, the one night when there was no folk club to hide in.

He decided on a visit to the chippy then an evening in the safety of the Arts Centre bar. It was unlikely that Cooper or the Mangler would find him there, he'd never seen them there anyway and besides, it was likely he would find a friendly face there to chat to. It was a popular spot with the local folkies, and they kept a blinding pint of Brakspears Special.

In the event, he did find someone to chat to, which would have been very nice had it not been Gerald. "Still," he thought "any port in a storm . . " Gerald even gave Eric a lift home at closing time. Maybe he wasn't all bad after all.

It was all quiet when he arrived back home. He climbed straight into his cold bed and surprisingly, dropped off immediately to sleep. Whilst he had plenty of worries to keep him awake, his nervous exhaustion overcame them. Not to mention the small matter of the effect of four pints of Brakspears and two hours listening to the thoughts of Chairman Gerald.

CHAPTER 30 - CAR FIXED, CAR BROKE

Next morning, Eric couldn't face going in to work. He was still feeling very stressed and anyway his old car was still out of action. Deciding that getting the old banger sorted was his top priority, he gave Banjo a call. Catching him at home was easy. As long as he phoned before ten thirty, Banjo was always still in bed.

"Morning Banjo, what's happening about the front suspension on my car. I need to get back on the road."

Banjo was his usual mendacious self. "Eric me old pal. I had me hand on the phone to call you. Front wishbone attachment wasn't it? To tell you the truth Eric, I got people queuing down the street with jobs at the minute. I'd like to help you but it might be some time, unless if course you can afford to pay for, shall we call it, my express service. I might fit you in ahead of another customer but that would risk me losing that job so naturally I'd have to charge a bit more."

"No way Banjo. If I wanted to pay a bit more I'd go to a proper garage wouldn't I? Don't forget you still owe me one. What I said about that MOT still holds, remember."

"Eric, Eric, don't be like that." Banjo tried hard to sound hurt. "I thought we was mates. Look, I'll tell you what I'll do for you, although I'm a fool to meself for doin' it. I'll put you straight on to Igor. He sometimes helps me out with welding jobs. Just say I sent you and he'll do you a lovely job cheap. He's got a little place in that track that goes behind the Council tip. Know where I mean? I think he's flogging Christmas trees down there at the minute, but he'll weld that bit up for you while you wait if you tell him it's for me. Nice bloke Igor. Russian he is. He don't speak English too good but he can weld brilliant and he won't charge you hardly nothing."

Eric sighed. "Alright, I'll give him a go, but if he does a bad job or overcharges me I'm holding you responsible Banjo. Down behind the tip you say?"

"Yeah. Oh by the way I forgot to tell you"

"Tell me what?"

"That note we lost."

"That note you lost you mean. What about it?"

"Oh I found it in my overalls the next day, and then I remembered I did make that call. Funny how you forget things and then some little thing brings it back again ain't it?"

Eric nearly exploded. "Banjo you, you . .", he was struggling to find a word bad enough. "Why didn't you say you stupid stupid . . ", no word was sufficiently disgusting "I've been worried sick, you, you . . Doh." He just slammed the phone down in exasperation.

He wasted the next fifteen minutes pacing up and down mentally going over what he should have said to Banjo. He had rarely felt so angry. Then it slowly dawned on him that he should be relieved that no one else had found the note and no one knew about his hoax call plot. Eventually he calmed down and got on with his day promising himself that if he ever saw Banjo again he would bust his nose.

So it was that Eric coaxed the engine of his rust heap into action, and with the steering wobbling alarmingly he cautiously piloted the car round the back roads and past the tip. He very nearly abandoned the trip when he saw the pot holes in the ash track, but he could see the XMAS TREES CHEEP sign just up ahead so he pressed on for the remaining hundred yards and pulled into the gateway. There were piles of trees right and left and up ahead through a thick pall of smoke, a clearing with two men sitting in front of a brazier burning tree trimmings. One of the men rose slowly to his feet and strolled over to the car.

"Good mornink sir. You after nice tree yes? I do you good one cheap."

"Ah, well, no, I don't need a tree. Are you Igor? Banjo sent me round and said you could do a bit of welding for me."

"Banjo? Banjo send you. Well he gotta cheek, he still owe me money. He not a honest man."

Eric shrugged sympathetically. "I know what you mean Igor, he owes me too, but this job is for me and I'll give you cash as soon as you finish. It's this car, the suspension has come away from the chassis, can you fix it?"

Igor dropped to the floor and on his back crawled underneath the car to survey the damage. There was a bit of banging and the front wheel wobbled. He emerged from underneath and struggled to his feet.

"You got much petrol in the car?"

"Petrol? Well, no it's nearly on empty. Why?"

"I do it now for four quid cash. You sit by fire, keep warm." He called over to the other man. "Frank. Frank, get mattress."

Frank shambled off to the shed at the back of the yard while Eric took his place by the brazier, coughing as the thick smoke bit his lungs. Igor climbed on the back of an old lorry and dragged off a pile of ancient looking welding gear. Then through the smoke Frank emerged dragging a large but filthy double bed mattress and manoeuvred it so it lay alongside the stricken car. Both men then walked to the other side of the vehicle and before Eric could object, they squatted and heaved the car over on to its side on the mattress. Now Eric understood the question about the petrol! He walked forward and took his first good look at the underside of his car. It was not a pretty sight. What underseal remained was cracked and damp looking and Eric could see flaky rust patches in an uncountable number of spots. So much for Banjo's description of the car as being sound as a bell.

"Banjo sell you this car? He bloody crook." Igor wasn't far off the mark there.

Frank wandered off to the shed and came back with a couple of small steel plates. These he clamped either side of the place where the chassis fixing had failed and Igor deftly welded them in place. A big power drill came off the lorry and made alarmingly short work of drilling a hole through the plates to take the suspension bolt. The two men wrestled the suspension into place and bolted it through, they walked round and hefted the car back on its feet and that was that. Barely fifteen minutes from start to finish.

"Are you sure that doesn't hurt the car, rolling it over like that?" Eric enquired.

"We do it all time. Maybe little scratch, but on old car like this no matter. Four quid." Igor held out his hand for the money. "Is good job, strong. Car safe now."

Eric could hardly believe what he had just seen, but it did look like the job would hold. He counted out four pound notes and handed them over.

"You want nice Christmas tree? I do you good one cheap. These little ones only one pound fifty."

Eric declined politely, he wasn't into Christmas decorations at the flat.

"You nice man, I do this one for a pound. Give it your girl friend."

Hmmm, that was an idea, Elaine was back home this evening. "OK then, a pound."

Frank threw the tree on the back seat of the car, the three men shook hands and Eric drove off through the smoke. The car felt good. Well, less bad at any rate. He considered whether he ought to report into work for the rest of the day, but he knew that schools were well into Christmas plays and whatnot and didn't have time for careers work and his office was less busy as youths trudged the shops looking for cheap perfume for their mums rather than go looking for work. The notion of returning to his flat however, wasn't at all attractive to Eric. It was probably one of the few places where the Mangler might track him down. Instead he drove out of town intending to take a walk along by the river somewhere. Passing a little plant nursery he noticed they were selling those plants with the red and green leaves everybody gets at Christmas. That would be another nice thing for Elaine, so he stopped off and eventually came back out bearing what he now knew was called a poinsettia and some tinsel and a few decorations for the little tree. Strange how it made him feel good buying things for someone else.

Elaine would probably be home and rested now after her shifts, so he drove over to her place. She opened the door to see Eric with a tree in one hand, the plant in the other and a plastic bag of decorations gripped in his teeth.

"Nerry Christmas." It was hard to speak properly with a bag in his teeth.

She seemed pleased to see him. "Eric, I've been ringing you for days, where have you been? Are these for me?"

He stepped inside and she relieved him of the bag, planting a kiss where it had been.

"I'm off now until Christmas Day."

"Christmas Day? You've got to work on Christmas Day?"

"Well someone has to be there to fix all the kids with their fingers stuck in new bike wheels and Grandads who stepped on a bit of Lego and fell over, not to mention the usual drunks. Anyway, where have you been?"

Mmmm, what should Eric tell her? Not everything obviously. It was all too scary, and he didn't suppose that she would be impressed by the fact that he had been with Doreen. Unable to lie to her, he decided on a doctored version of the truth.

"Basingstoke."

"Basingstoke?" She laughed. "Blimey, what in heaven's name took you there??"

"Oh, just something I had to do for a client. Anyway there are worse places than Basingstoke although frankly I can't bring one to mind just at the minute." He deftly changed the topic. "Shall we put this tree up? Look I brought tinsel and everything. There's even a little fairy for the top."

A neat change of subject, and it worked. They set to on the tree and made a fine job of it. Together with the poinsettia, it suddenly made the Christmas season arrive, then and there.

"Tea? Or would you like a Christmassy drink? I've got a bottle of Tia Maria in the cupboard."

"Oh, I'm up to here in Tia Maria, had a whole bottle of it the other night, I'll stick to tea."

She laughed. "Oh yeah. I bet you've never even tasted it."

"Straight up. I drank it to wash away the taste of the bottle of retsina I had first."

"Retsina? Now I know you're kidding." She put the kettle on. He thought how neat it was to hide the truth by telling it.

When she came back with the tea, complete with a couple of chocolate wafers, she said "It's Thursday. Queens Arms tonight. Shall we?"

"Oh, um," the Queens Arms was where the Mangler had seen him, "um, er". Eric wasn't exactly looking keen.

"Oh come on Eric. I've been in A&E all week, it'd be good to get out. Tell you what, you drive, and you can stay over tonight. I bet your flat is freezing if you've been away. You'll be nice and warm here on the sofa."

"I'm sorry. Yes, you're right. It'd do us both good. Let's do it. As to the sofa, you're right, it is nice and warm, and you could join me tonight if you like."

"I'll pretend I never heard that."

"Spoil sport."

At least he would be safe at Elaine's, they didn't know where she lived.

They arrived early at the pub and found a good spot in the car park. After climbing out of the car Elaine took her guitar case from the back seat and turned to grab Eric's arm but he was gone. She just caught a glimpse of him scuttling through the pub door. When she got into the club room after struggling up the steep stairs with the case she didn't seem too pleased.

"Well thanks for giving me a hand. What's the rush? We're the first ones here. Are you going down to get the drinks?"

"The drinks, ah yes. If I give you the money can you go and get them? I'm going to, er, put the chairs out. Nice to give them a hand setting out the room." Elaine looked at him through furrowed eyebrows. Something about the way he said it made her suspicious.

"Eric."

"What?"

"Why are you acting strange? You scuttled in here like a frightened rabbit, and now you don't want to go downstairs."

"Ah that, yes, um, well," he was buying thinking time, " it's just that, um,"

"It's that Doreen woman isn't it? She was here when we came before and you're scared of her. Is that it?"

It wasn't Doreen he was scared of, it was her old man, but Elaine had dreamt up a good excuse so he used it.

"No, not scared exactly, but I'd rather not bump into her, so if you could go and get the drinks. Look here's a quid, do the honours would you?"

Elaine gave way and went off to get the drinks while Eric peered through the curtains to see if he could recognise Doreen's car, or worse still, the Mangler's or Cooper's. All clear so far. He put out a few rows of chairs and felt better when folkies started arriving and the general hubbub began. Actually it was a pretty good evening. Everyone was in fine voice and although he didn't have his guitar, he was persuaded to do a spot which allowed him to indulge in one of his occasional monologues. He had a small collection of these in his repertoire, the one he chose that night being an old music hall one about Little Nell, whose mother's numerous husbands all met untimely but comical deaths.

No-one would call it poetical, but the punters liked it, all except of course Gerald. Anyway, it lifted Eric's spirits and Elaine did a good spot too, although in a more serious vein. By the end of the evening Eric was feeling relaxed and content. Whatever might happen over the coming days, he was alright tonight and he was going home with Elaine. The club wound up at about ten past eleven and they made their way down the stairs as the rest of the pub was turning out. Some of the customers from downstairs were pretty rowdy, but it manifested itself only in tuneless singing and laughter.

Elaine climbed into the passenger seat and Eric put her guitar on the back seat and climbed in to drive.

"Oi. Oi you. I want a word wiv you."

The shout came from the pub door as a huge figure came running out. Eric didn't need to look twice to recognise the shape of the figure. He only knew one man that big. The Mangler.

He slammed the car door and turned the ignition key. The old banger's battery wasn't good at the best of times, but on these cold December nights it really struggled to turn over the engine. The starter motor made a slow grinding sound as it made its feeble attempts to bring the engine to life.

"Eric, who's that man? Why is he shouting at us? Eric?"

Eric wasn't listening. He was frantically turning the ignition switch and working the pull out choke button. The monstrous man was impeded in his dash across the car park by other cars pulling out to leave, but he reached the old car and grabbed Elaine's door handle just as the engine spluttered into life. Eric graunched the lever into first gear and put his foot down. The car lurched forward and there was a loud bang as the door handle broke off in the Mangler's hand. Foot still hard to the floor, Eric shot straight in front of two other cars waiting to get out, and headed out into the road.

Cars right and left were honking their horns. "Eric, your lights. You haven't got your lights on." Too right he hadn't, his old car battery would never have turned the engine over with them on. He reached forward and flicked the switch and the dim yellowish headlights picked out the cats eyes in the road, but not a lot else.

Elaine meanwhile was getting hot under the collar. "Eric, who was that man? What's this about? That man broke the door handle off. Why are you driving like a maniac? Eric? I'm frightened."

Eric was squinting into his rear view mirror, watching the headlights of the cars behind them. One set of lights was overtaking others and coming closer at speed.

"Oh God, he's chasing."

"Who is he? Tell me Eric." Elaine was shouting now.

"George Marshall, Doreen's husband. He thinks we've been having an affair. Hold tight." The car's gearbox screamed as Eric changed down from flat out in top gear. "Sorry, the brakes are useless, this works better." The car decelerated rapidly as Eric swung right into a side road. There was a bang as Elaine's door flung open under the centrifugal force of the turn and she screamed

"Let me out, stop Eric, you'll kill us both."

He swung the car violently left at the next corner and Elaine's door slammed shut.

"We haven't Elaine."

"What?"

"Been having an affair. Me and Doreen, honest. He's mad 'cos she's leaving him. Bugger, he's still behind us."

"It's no good Eric you can't out run him in this old heap. You'll have to stop and talk to him. I'll back you up."

"Are you mad? He'll kill me. You saw the size of him. He's a professional wrestler for God's sake."

"He's a what?" Elaine was aghast. "Put your foot down!"

"My foot is down. This is top speed."

She looked at the speedometer. Fifty three miles an hour. The noise was incredible. The engine and gearbox were screaming like a racing car and it seemed as though every part of the old banger was shaking itself to bits. She could see the engine temperature gauge was already into the red and climbing.

The car behind was nearly up with them. Eric hunched over the steering wheel just as the car reached the arched railway bridge. There was an almighty thump as the car hit the bridge hump and both their heads hit the car roof. Reaching the apex of the bridge, the car briefly took to the air before landing with a crash. Another loud clunk sounded at the rear of the car and a piece of the vehicle parted company with the rest.

"I think that was the bumper. Are you alright?"

"No I'm not bloody alright, I'm bloody terrified. Aaagh."

She screamed as from behind came yet another almighty bang. Eric peered into the mirror. The steel bumper bar bouncing down the road collided with the windscreen of the chasing car which swerved violently and smashed into the Give Way sign at the foot of the bridge.

"Stop Eric. Let me out." Elaine's voice came across as an order, not a request.

"Oh Elaine, don't get out. We're OK now, he's stopped. Let's go home. I can explain everything." Eric was distraught, her whole demeanour had changed. He had never seen her like this. She was fuming. He feared this was the end of their relationship.

"Stop and let me out. He might be hurt. I'm going back to see." That wasn't a request, it was an order. She virtually spat out the words.

The car drew to a halt and before Eric could reason with her, she was running back to the bridge. He could hear the horn of the other car continuously blaring as steam hissed from the vehicle's radiator. Reaching the car, she flung open the door and reached inside. The horn stopped blaring and the car's headlights were extinguished as she turned off the ignition key.

"Come here Eric." She shouted down the road as he stood by his broken car, seemingly paralysed with fear and confusion.

"Eric, come here. Now."

He did as he was ordered, and arriving at the car he saw the huge man slumped over the steering wheel.

"Is he, is he . .?"

"No he's not dead, but his breathing is weak and he's out cold. I don't think his neck's broken. Help me get him out, then I can see to him properly. My God he's enormous."

Getting a limp twenty three stone giant out from behind a steering wheel is a non trivial task. They heaved and struggled for several minutes before he lay on the side of the road while Elaine checked his pulse and his breathing.

"I don't like the look of him. Go and find a phone box Eric and get an ambulance. We need to get him to A&E pronto."

The bridge ran over the platform of a railway halt. Eric realised that there ought to be a phone box outside the platform exit and he ran off to find it.

"Emergency, what service do you require?"

"Ambulance, we need an ambulance, there's been a car crash. A man unconscious."

"Then you'll need Police as well. Where is the incident?"

Eric went numb as a great weight descended upon him. The police would be coming and he'd have to explain how all this happened. This was the worst day of his life. The crash, the police, and on top of all that, Elaine. Surely she would dump him now.

When he got back Elaine was giving the man artificial respiration.

"I think we might have saved him. Come on ambulance where are you?"

She knew the ambulance drivers when they arrived. The big man was stirring, but not properly conscious. They stretchered him into the ambulance and she climbed in after. She looked at Eric with emotionless eyes.

"You'll have to stay and deal with the police."

The ambulance doors closed and they drove off leaving Eric standing cold, shivering and wretched in the road as the air horns and flashing lights of the police cars announced their arrival.

CHAPTER 31 - A CHAT WITH THE POLICE

"You alright sir? Is this your car?" The policeman shone his torch into Marshall's car as Eric stood alongside.

"I'm OK, a bit shaken though. This one belongs to him just gone in the ambulance. Mine is the one down the road." The policeman followed Eric's gaze to where the distressed vehicle sat rather lopsidedly under the street lamp by the railway bridge. The rear left wheel had punctured.

"And this is yours I take it." The PC bent down and picked up the chrome bumper, examining the brackets which had broken off the car. "These brackets didn't take much breaking with all that rust. Car got an MoT has it sir?"

The hairs on Eric's neck stood up. That bloody MoT. As if he wasn't in enough trouble. He decided to play dumb.

"Yes it had a new MoT when I bought the car a few months ago."

The PC stood up slowly. He was not a young man, but by the looks of him he was no old fool either. Eric could feel the copper weighing him up, looking first at him and then his pathetic vehicle.

"Let's go and have a look at your vehicle then shall we sir." They started walking towards the old car. "Would you like to tell me exactly what happened tonight?"

"Well, we hit the hump of this bridge with a bit of a bang and the bumper fell off and bounced into the car behind."

"We, sir?" The copper looked around for whoever the other half of the 'we' might be."

"Me and my girl friend. She's a nurse. A&E as it happens. She was looking after the injured guy and she's gone off in the ambulance with him."

"Hmm, we'll need to speak to her later as a witness. Now let's have a look at your motor." He did a quick tour of the outside of the vehicle, peering underneath and examining the place where the bumper used to be attached.

"You say you bought this car not long ago sir? Was it in this condition then? I hope you didn't pay much for it. It looks like a scrapper to me. The look on his face implied a vague disgust at the state of Eric's vehicle.

"It's all I could afford. Seventy five quid I paid for it. With an MoT like I said."

"Well I would suggest you choose more carefully in future sir. MoT or no MoT, this car doesn't look roadworthy to me. Where did you buy it from? Not a proper main dealer I'll tell you that!"

"No, just a bloke I met in the pub. I was desperate to get some wheels and he got it for me for cash."

The policeman tutted and shook his head.

"Hmmm, now you say the bumper fell off when you hit the bridge hump. What speed were you doing at the time?

Eric thought for a moment and decided he should tell the truth because they would ask Elaine later anyway.

"About fifty."

"Fifty? Are you sure it wasn't any faster? You must have hit this hump with one hell of a bang. I would have thought sixty more like it."

Eric gave a hollow laugh. "If you can get sixty out of this old heap, you can have it. Fifty or so is flat out."

The policeman didn't seem all that amused. "I don't think I would have this car under any circumstance sir. So, you say you were doing fifty miles per hour. Are you aware we are in a thirty limit?"

"I had no choice. I was trying to get away from the other car, he was chasing me. I was afraid."

The old PC's eyebrows rose. "Chasing you sir?"

"He tried to attack me outside the Queen's Arms, in the car park. He's a huge bloke, a wrestler, he might have killed me. So I drove off and he chased."

"Hold on a minute, let's get this straight. You know the other driver?"

"Yes, his name's George Marshall, he's a wrestler."

"What, the Mangler? That George Marshall?"

"Yes, that George Marshall, and he wanted to beat me up."

The PC gave a long low whistle. "Blimey." You don't want to go tangling with the likes of him sir. He looked back up the road to see other police cars arriving. "It sounds like we need a long chat down at the station. Have you had any alcohol today?"

"Only a pint in the pub."

The PC pulled a plastic bag from out of his pocket.

"Hmm, ever used one of these before?"

"If that's a breathalyser, then no."

The constable showed Eric what to do and they went through all the huffing and puffing followed by an agonising pause while they waited to see if the crystals changed colour.

"Oooh, nearly."

"What do you mean? Nearly in or nearly out?" Eric was for the first time in his life regretting finishing off his pint.

The constable shone his torch at the crystals and examined them again. Eric held his breath.

"No."

"No what?"

"No you haven't exceeded the limit, but I reckon you were close. Looks like it's your lucky day sir."

"Huh, if this is a lucky day, I wouldn't want an unlucky one."

The constable told Eric to wait while he went off to talk to the other police who had just arrived. His mind was in a whirl. He stood in the cold dark street, shivering. He was obviously in all sorts of trouble, but in a strange way he was relieved. Maybe now was the time to unburden himself, to get it off his chest. The problem was, would they believe him? As to his car, he hoped it was a write off. He didn't care if he never saw it again. What should he say about Banjo and the MoT though? Assuming they followed that up of course. He decided he'd cross that bridge when he came to it.

Half an hour later Eric was drinking a welcome cup of tea in the unwelcoming surroundings of the Police station interview room. The old PC came in carrying a note pad.

"Right sir, let's see if we can get to the bottom of this. Where shall we start? How about with our wrestler friend, how have you been upsetting him? Oh, I just heard from the hospital by the way. You'll be glad to know he's not badly hurt so you don't have to worry about old George. Just a bit of concussion, I reckon he's been hurt worse in the ring many a time. So what was it? His missus was it? What's her name? Doreen if I remember right. Been playing away with you has she?"

All these questions were making Eric angry.

"Look, get this straight. I have not been having a, a, a relationship with Doreen Marshall, although I suspect

George Marshall might think I have. I met Mrs Marshall in the course of my work. I interviewed her son at school. I'm a careers officer. Subsequently she invited me to her house to offer further careers guidance. So that's how I know her."

"You sure there isn't more to it than that?" the PC looked sceptical. "If not, why does old George want to give you a good hiding then?"

Eric hesitated. This was it. This was the moment when he had to decide whether to tell all he knew, and probably get into deeper trouble, or to play dumb. He took a deep breath.

"He thinks I shopped him to the police."

"To us? What for?" Now the policeman looked very interested indeed. Then he obviously recalled more about Marshall.

"Aah, I heard we'd had a tip off about him but it came to nothing. Is that it? Another bloke too, works at the prison. What makes you think he thinks it was you what shopped him?"

"Because he knows I was round his house and some drugs went missing. Cocaine I think. And because I know Cecil Cooper the guy at the prison."

"Hang on, hang on." The PC was beginning to get serious now. "You're telling me you know Marshall and that fella at the prison?" This was turning from a routine traffic incident into something much more interesting. "I think I'd better get somebody from CID in on this. You sit tight sir, I'll be right back."

It was ten minutes before he returned. Ten long minutes during which Eric had to decide how much to say. He decided on candour, to tell the true story. It was the only way. The door opened and the PC came in with another much taller man who was not in uniform. They sat opposite

Eric at the table, and the new guy laid out a notebook and pencil.

"Good evening sir. I'm detective sergeant John Amory. I understand you have an interesting story to tell."

Amory, Amory. Where had Eric heard that name before? Oh God, yes, he was the one that phoned after the escaped prisoner raid at Doreen's House. Oh heck, Eric had forgotten about that. He couldn't admit to setting up a false lead could he? That would be a criminal offence, he might end up in prison himself. Maybe he would tell the truth but not the whole truth, so help him God.

"Now then sir," Amory began, "let's start with the easy bits. Can you tell me your full name and address?"

Eric's worst fears were soon realised when he gave his details.

"Dillon? Just a minute. Are you the Eric Dillon I spoke to about the raid on the Marshall's place looking for the escapee?" He looked at the PC. "Is there more to this than meets the eye?"

When he turned back to Eric, his face had hardened. "It seems to me Eric that things are not so simple as you are trying to make out. Now you don't want me to charge you with obstructing the police on the course of our enquiries do you, so perhaps we'd better start at the beginning, and let's have the whole story, not just the bits you think might get you off the hook."

So Eric did just that. He went right back to his job at the prison, the instructions from Jock McNeish the auditor, his visit to Doreen's house and her attempt to seduce him, the incident in the garden when he saw the package handover, Cooper's car, the blackboard stuff in the classroom, his next visit to Doreen when the police came in, the box of chalk, the lot. Everything that is except for two things. The tip off phone call from Banjo and the trip to Basingstoke.

DS Amory was scribbling notes furiously. He didn't interrupt or ask questions during Eric's tale, preferring to let him get it all out. Only when Eric finished did he make any comment.

"If you don't mind me saying so Eric, you've been a very silly boy. You've been messing around in things that should be left to the professionals, and now look what a mess you're in. A wrecked car and a couple of very nasty pieces of work wanting to do you serious harm. As to this auditor chap, what's his name, McNeish, he ought to know better. We'll be having a word with him.

"One thing bothers me though. That night we broke in the house looking for the escaped prisoner. I can't figure out how that fits in. That tip off we got, was that anything to do with you?"

Eric feigned surprise. "Don't be daft," said Eric, "how could I? I was in the house. Why would I want to be found there? That's why I ran into the garden when your lot came in."

"So it wasn't you who tipped us off? "

"Me? Absolutely not."

"And this business with Mrs Marshall. Were you having an affair?"

"No. I told you, I only went to look for the package. I had to pretend to Doreen that I was up for a bit of, well, you know."

"And if we hadn't have burst in? What then? What did you plan to do, lie back and think of England?"

"Well" Eric lied, "I hadn't really thought it through. I suppose I was going to say I felt ill or something. I don't know. Anyway, if I couldn't think of an excuse, there's worse things happen at sea."

Amory laughed. "Well there is that I suppose." then changing the subject, "So it was you that rang in about Marshall and Cooper, and you did that anonymously because?"

"Because I'd had enough and I wanted shot of the whole business and I didn't want to be sitting here answering a load of questions like this. Look, I've told you all I know. When can I go?"

Amory shook his head and tutted. "Oh if it were only that simple Eric. I mean speeding, driving an unsafe vehicle, wasting police time, withholding information, there's a lot of stuff to deal with unless . . "

"Unless what?"

"Unless you can help us nail Marshall and Cooper. If you could do that then I dare say we wouldn't need to pursue your other misdemeanours, ain't that right PC Wootton?"

The PC, silent up until now, said "Well these are serious matters, but I imagine that we just might be able to deal with it via a caution. Given that is, the requisite amount of cooperation from Mr Dillon here."

Eric's heart sank. He didn't like the sound of this. All he wanted was to walk out of the cop shop and back to his old life and to try to patch up things with Elaine. He didn't need more cloak and dagger stuff.

"Cigarette Eric?" Now the detective was obviously switching to Mr Nice Guy mode. Eric spotted it a mile off, not that it made any difference.

"No, I don't smoke. Look, what is it you want?"

Amory lowered his voice and leaned forward. "Well Eric, it's like this. As it happens, I'm inclined to believe your story, well, most of it anyway. We've had our suspicions about Marshall for a little while now, and Cooper too for that matter, although we never linked the two. Trouble is, we've got no hard evidence. We found nothing when we did the searches. We need some help to nick these bastards Eric."

"Well don't look at me," said Eric "my cover's blown. Cooper and Marshall both want my head kicked in, remember."

"Don't you worry about them Eric. After tonight's little episode they'll want things to cool off a bit. No, what we want is evidence from inside the prison. And, a bit of that chalk would come in handy. You said you saw some in Marshall's house. What happened to it Eric?"

"Aah well I can help you there, I took a piece of it and had it at home for a bit, then I got nervous and hid it under the bushes near my house. I suppose it might still be there, it's in a plastic bag. I dabbed a little bit of it on my lips and they went numb, that's how I thought it was cocaine. Not that I have ever taken cocaine, but my girl friend who is a nurse said that's probably what it was."

"OK Eric, good start, we'll give you a lift home when we've finished and you can show us. Of course we'll need a signed statement from you saying where and when you picked up the chalk in the first place and about the package handover you saw in the lane. You understand if we nail these guys, you're going to have to testify in court."

Eric gulped a "Yes", then said "A pity you never found anything when you searched their places. I reckon Marshall got the wind up after losing that bit of chalk and got rid of his, and then tipped off Cooper to do the same."

Amory nodded. "Well thanks to your little episode tonight we've got Marshall's car now, so we'll be having a good look over that while it's in our possession. You never know we might find traces of something. As to how you can help us further, we'll have a think and get back to you. Now let's get your statement about what you saw and found and we'll get you home and have a look for that bit of chalk."

So that's what they did. The chalk was still there alright, much to Eric's relief as it corroborated his story and gained him a tiny bit of sympathy from Amory. It was well after one in the morning by the time he got back inside his freezing cold flat. He should have been relieved but he slumped into a chair with his head in his hands. Filled with pessimism over his chances with Elaine after tonight's events, he marvelled at his own ability to cock things up. Well, he decided, it was no good trying to ring her at this time of night, and anyway he suspected she might not be speaking to him after what had happened. Then there was his car, or what was left of it. The police said they had pushed it into a side road for him to collect tomorrow. God knows how he was going to get back out there. On foot he supposed. He didn't think asking Elaine for a lift was a good idea this soon. Depressed, cold, hungry, and exhausted, he climbed into bed and fell into a fitful sleep.

CHAPTER 32 - A DAY FOR REGRETS

Eric rose early, still feeling tired but not capable of further sleep. He had a lot to do today. The first thing was to get out to his damaged car and get it disposed of. He had no desire to keep it. Apart from the fact that it was a dangerous heap of rust, it would now hold too many bad memories for him.

A bus got him to within half a mile of the bridge where the car had crashed and he walked the rest, head down and muttering curses to himself as he trudged through the cold morning streets. When he arrived, the first thing he noticed was that Marshall's car had already been removed by the police. Eric's old banger sat lop sidedly in a layby. He opened the boot and prodded at the spare wheel tyre. A miracle! It seemed to have enough air in it to withstand a short drive.

Squatting on the cold damp kerb he gingerly attached the car's jack, hoping it wouldn't collapse the car's rusty sill. Puffing and straining at the stiff old jack handle he wound the car off the ground and removed the punctured wheel, skinning his cold knuckles as he did it. The spare wheel went on easily enough just as the jack gave way and the car dropped with a bang. A rusty hole had appeared in the sill, but Eric couldn't give a damn. As long as he could drive it away he just didn't care.

The wheel nuts nipped up tight, he unlocked the door and climbed in to the driver's seat. He crossed his fingers. "Now you old wreck, for one last time, please please start." He turned the key and the engine groaned over once before stopping with a clunk. "Bastard." Eric shouted. He thumped the dashboard in despair. Well there was nothing for it, he would have to bump start it. Climbing out, he opened the driver's window so he could steer the car while he put his shoulder to the door pillar and pushed. Slowly the old banger pulled out on to the road and started to lurch down the gentle slope and eventually it gained enough speed for Eric to jump in. It wasn't a long hill so he reckoned he only had one chance to do the bump start. He pulled out the choke, pumped the accelerator and waited for the speedo to show ten miles an hour. Foot on the clutch, into gear, ignition on. Please please start. There was a give way sign at the bottom of the hill, so it was now or never. He lifted his clutch foot and shouted "Just do it you old heap of junk." The old jalopy must have taken pity on him one last time, for after a series of lurches the engine came to life, albeit misfiring badly.

Eric knew just where to take the car. The streets were still largely empty in the early morning as he drove to the old lockup where Banjo plied his dubious trade. Banjo of course would still be tucked up in bed, which suited Eric nicely. He placed the old car sideways on in front of the lockup door. There was an old street atlas in the door pocket of the car. He tore out a blank page from inside the front cover and scribbled on it. ALL YOURS BANJO. I HAVE NO FURTHER USE FOR THIS HEAP OF JUNK. LOVE, ERIC.

Placing the note on the dashboard, Eric took the ignition key and dropped it down the drain in the corner of the yard, then strode back to the car where he let down all four tyres. For the first time that day he felt good. Then, a mere ten seconds later he felt guilty. Eric was no good at recrimination. He walked over and peered down the drain grid. The key was nowhere to be seen. "Oh well, done it now." He shrugged and took one last look into the car in case there was anything in the pockets worth retrieving. His eye caught something red under the passenger seat. Reaching in, he pulled out Elaine's handbag. He stared at it, deep in thought. No choice really. She would be needing it. He was scared to see her again so soon, he doubted very much that she would have calmed down yet, but he knew he would have to get the bag to her today. He took a deep breath and walked out of the yard and over the road to the bus stop.

By the time he got to Elaine's it was a quarter to ten. She would be up and about, and he knew she was not working today. He looked at the red bag. It would go through the letter box. He could just post it and run off. A minute went by as he stood there wondering what to do, then another, then another. Then in a fleeting moment of decisiveness he pressed the door bell button. Almost immediately he regretted it, but that was too late. He could still post the bag and run, but he decided to stand his ground. A light came on in the hall and the door lock rattled. Eric's heart was in his mouth. The door opened and there stood Elaine. Eric thought she looked lovely, but her eyes betrayed a coolness and perhaps a sadness.

Eric managed a faint smile as he held out the handbag. "You left this in the car. I thought you would be needing it." She took the bag, giving him an emotionless "Thank you." and made to close the door.

"Elaine, I'm so sorry. I know you're upset but, but," Good start to the sentence Eric, but the rest evaded him. He didn't want her to close that door so he blurted out anything to keep her there. "I just got rid of the car. For good. I spent half the night with the police. Explaining everything. I'm sorry you got involved. We got chased because, because,"

"Because what Eric?" Elaine's tone was that of a teacher asking why he hadn't handed in his essay. She began to close the door.

"Because I'm helping the police catch some criminals. Marshall is one of them. It's nothing to do with Doreen. I'm sorry Elaine, I couldn't tell you." He rattled out the words as fast as he could before she could get the door shut. "It's something I got involved in through my work at the prison. Please, I'm sorry. I can explain now. "

She looked hard into Eric's eyes as if searching for the truth. Whether the truth was there or not she couldn't tell but there certainly was a pleading.

"You'd better come in. You look frozen."

There was no smile, but Eric detected a faint softening, and he didn't need asking twice. He stepped inside, still exuding deference and humility. He sat at the table while she made him coffee and a couple of slices of toast.

"I suppose you haven't eaten." she said as she put the toast in front of him. "What did you do with the car?"

"I dumped it round at Banjo's."

"What's Banjo's?"

"Banjo's the guy who sold me the car. He ripped me off when he sold it to me, so I thought it was only fair he should have the job of disposing of it."

"What did he say?"

"He doesn't know yet. Probably still in bed. I just left it at his garage with a note. He'll be alright, he owes me one." Eric sipped his coffee. "Look, I think I ought to tell you how all this business with the Marshall's happened. Then you'll see .. " Once again he couldn't find the end to his sentence. "Then you'll see. . ."

As if to help out Elaine interrupted. "Marshall is still in hospital but he's alright. There's a policeman by his bed. I guessed there was something going on. Are you in danger?" Her concern was guarded, Eric didn't take too much comfort from it.

"The police don't think so. I'm not so sure. Look Elaine, I made some silly mistakes, but I've only been trying to stop some bad people doing bad things. Can I tell you the whole story? Then you might see how last night happened."

Eric couldn't read Elaine's face. She still wasn't giving her feelings away, save those of conditional disapproval and suspicion. She sighed.

"OK try me."

And so he started right at the beginning. His time at the prison, the animosity between Cooper and the lads, the meeting with McNeish and all that followed. He even spilled the beans about his trip to Basingstoke which drew the first smile from Elaine.

"You mean you really did drink all that retsina and Tia Maria?"

"I wouldn't lie to you Elaine." Except by omission, because once again he left out the bit about the police tip off to interrupt his meeting with Doreen.

"This Doreen, what's she like?"

He wondered what to say. Come to think of it, he wondered what he really did think of Doreen. He thought for a minute then somehow his subconscious spoke out for itself.

"Actually she's alright. Just not fulfilled I suppose. As long as you can keep out of her clutches, she's a good person I reckon."

"And did you? Fall into her clutches I mean." Elaine made a bad job of concealing her anxiety as she asked the question. Eric smiled.

"If I'm perfectly honest," he paused, "and truthful," he paused again as if to tease Elaine, "No I bloody well didn't." Then he took on a more earnest tone, and looking her straight in the eye he said, "My affections lay elsewhere."

Elaine sat back in her chair. "Oh Eric, you are an idiot. I mean I know you mean well but you really shouldn't have done what you did. Now look at the mess you're in. And as for me, you could have killed me last night, and afterwards I could have happily strangled you."

"And now?" Eric looked sheepish as he waited for Elaine's verdict.

She turned her face from him and gazed blankly out of the window.

"I don't know. I want a happy and carefree relationship Eric, not all this stress and drama. This is going to drag on for months by the look of it. I've got enough stress of my own at work without adding yours to it."

He couldn't think of anything to say. They both sat in silence for several minutes, and then, she said "What are you going to do? About not having a car I mean."

"Oh, it's been coming for a while, so I've already got an appointment at the bank to get a loan to buy another one." Then suddenly, "Blimey what day is it? Friday, it's today! The appointment is today." He looked at his watch. "Sorry I have to go, the appointment is at twelve in town."

This wasn't what he wanted, having to rush off before he had cleared things with Elaine.

"Can I call you later?" he asked.

She stared at her feet. "I don't know. I need time Eric. I think I'll go home to my parents for the weekend. I'll call you when I'm back maybe."

"Maybe" didn't sound good. His heart sank. He struggled to find something to say, but he couldn't.

"OK. But I'll be ready and waiting." He took another glance at his watch. "I have to go. I'll let myself out." He walked to the door and turned to say, "Thanks for listening Elaine." She gave a faint smile in recognition of his gratitude. He closed the door and stepped out.

The bank manager took Eric by surprise. Eric expected suspicious and officious, but instead he got affable and understanding. He walked out with an agreement to borrow two hundred and fifty quid to be paid back at twenty five a month. Despite his difficult morning he felt a bit cheered. Until that is, he looked at the small ads in the local rag. There were plenty of cars for that money, but phrases like 'scruffy but a good runner' 'needs MoT' and 'suit DIY mechanic' and such like seemed to be the norm at that price.

Sam Larner wasn't an old blues singer, he was a Norfolk fisherman, so why was Eric's singing so influenced by him? Well of course there was that whole roots music thing that Eric liked so much – going back to where it all started, but it was more than that. People described Sam's singing performances as "electrifying". He was not just any old singer, but a man who could make you stop and listen, a storyteller who could have you hanging on every word. When he told tales of storms at sea you could feel the fear. When he sang his fishing songs you could taste the salt. Having left school to become a fisherman at the age of twelve, he was not an educated man. Anyone who smiled at the unwitting malapropisms in some of his historical ballads knew that.

But the real reason Eric as so influenced by Sam was that they had things in common. Like Sam, Eric came from the English rural working class. Sam reminded him of the old men in his own childhood village, his own roots. So when Eric sang Sam's songs, he somehow knew how to do it and it worked. Sam might not have known it but he had technique. The intensity of his delivery was rivetting, the way in which he would interrupt himself in mid song to explain a phrase, and above all, the way he used his own authentic voice and accent rather than some notion of correctness.

Just like the old blues men, Sam was discovered by the collectors when he was an old man. He cut his first record when he was eighty two. Then in 1967 the BBC Midlands Home Service dedicated four fifteen minute programmes exclusively to Sam and his songs. Not bad for a Norfolk fisherman.

The one from Sam that Eric liked to sing was Napoleon's Dream in which Bonaparte himself recalls his finest hours. No-one knows who wrote the song, but whoever it was used the most outrageously vivid language. Sam of course had learned the song from the aural tradition, and being Sam might not have understood all the words. *"I scarce had reclined on the pillow"* became *"I scarce had declined"* and *"By the dark deeds of treachery I have been sold"* turned into *"By the dark deeds of tragedy"* and so on. Eric made damn sure he kept the mistakes in when he sang it, which was what he did when he presented himself on stage at The Lord Palmerston on Friday night. Singing stuff like that was a good distraction from his problems. Of course there were the inevitable questions from friends about the whereabouts of Elaine. He just answered, "Oh, home visiting her parents".

If Friday night cheered Eric up, it didn't last long. He spent all of Saturday finding his way to two people selling Ford Escorts both of which were a big disappointment. On top of that, there was no word from Elaine, not that he really expected any.

CHAPTER 33 - BATTLE TO BATTLE

Saturday night at the Arts Centre was to be the last of their folk club nights before Christmas. There would be mulled wine and mince pies, Christmas carols and a visit from the local Mummers group to do their traditional play about death and resurrection. It was a forty minute walk from Eric's flat, but worth the effort if it would lift his spirits. The first thing that faced him when he entered the door didn't help.

"Hello Eric. No Elaine tonight? You look a bit down in the dumps old chap."

The friend's words of sympathy didn't tally at all with his expression, which appeared to be one of smug satisfaction. Eric ignored it and made for the bar for a pint of Old Ale, the strongest they had and the first of a planned many that night.

The place was humming and the bar was full of revellers, most of whom had come for the disco running in the dance studio. Thankfully the folk club was in the cellar, well away from the thump thump of the sound system and the ghastly flickering of the strobe lights. Eric headed quickly for the cellar stairs and another world where it smelled of the mulled wine spices and the carols were already under way. Over in the dark corner stood a motley group of forbidding looking gents clad from head to foot in multicoloured rag strips and carrying wooden swords and shields, alongside them, sporting a bright yellow dish mop wig, a bearded man in a tail suit and top hat and last of all Father Christmas himself. That'd be the mummers then.

Eric had seen numerous mumming plays over the years. So many in fact that he could recite the better part of the whole script of the play, which was traditional, and largely unchanged since Victorian times when groups of farm hands dressed up in disguise and toured the big houses of the village to perform the play in exchange for a slice of pie and a flagon of cider. The mummers play predated the singing of Christmas carols by generations, and was based not on the Christian tradition of Christmas but the old yule celebration of the winter solstice. The plays might vary from village to village, but they all had the same plot based on death and resurrection symbolising the dying of the old year and the birth of the new.

The carol singing came to a natural break and someone put a mince pie and a plastic cup of mulled wine in Eric's hands. The scratch band of two fiddles, two concertinas and a tuba struck up a cacophonous tune and the first rag coated man strode onto the tiny stage swirling his sword to clear space for the action

Room, brave gallants, room

Unto this court I do resort

To show some sport

This merry Christmas time

Activity of youth, activity of age

The like of which has not been seen on any stage

And if you don't believe what I now say

Walk in Father Christmas and clear the way

So the old man himself comes in with:

In comes I old Father Christmas, welcome or welcome not

I hope old Father Christmas shall never be forgot

For Christmas comes but once a year

And when it does, it brings good cheer

Mince pies, plum pudding, who likes these better than Old Father Christmas

I've travelled a great many miles both far and near

And now I travelled here to drink a cup of your strong beer.

Then in a feat of considerable daring the actor strode over to the table where a large man sat nursing his pint, grabbed the man's full glass and in one draught swallowed the whole lot. The large man tried hard to look amused but signally failed in the attempt. The audience on the other hand thought the whole thing wonderful. One of these days that trick would backfire, but tonight they got away with it. The actor licked his lips, burped and then continued.

Now in this room there shall be fought

The most terrible battle that was ever seen

Twixt King George

(loud cheers)

And my four sons

(even louder boos)

So scrimp Jack, scrimp Jack I say

And walk in Noble Captain with King George in his way

And so the mysterious and magical play continued with the comic choreography of swordfights between George and Noble Captain, Bold Slasher, Turkish Knight and little Johnny Jack in turn, their bodies lying strewn about the cellar room floor. Well that was the death then, but what about the resurrection?

The distraught Father Christmas turned to the crowd and pleaded

Is there a doctor that might be found

Who can cure my four sons lying bleeding on the ground?

Then from the back of the room a loud cry of

Oh Yes

and the top hatted and yellow haired doctor, complete with medical bag burst onto the scene, milking the crowds enthusiasm for all he was worth

There is indeed a Doctor what might be found

Who can cure your four sons lying on the ground

Doctor Doctor What can you cure?

asks Father Christmas, and at this point the audience having seen the play every year since God knows when, gleefully join in with the traditional lines

I can cure the sick of any ill

The itch, the stitch, the palsy and the gout

The pains within and the pains without.

The doctor rummaged in his medical bag pulling out various novelty items, a stirrup pump, a bloody saw, some women's underwear, and a large pill about the size of a shoe polish tin. Waving the pill high in the air he called out

Bring me any old woman

Three scores and ten years old

Without a tooth in her head

One that's been dead ten years

Buried eleven

And in the grave thirteen

If she can rise up and crack one of these anti bilious pills

I will maintain her forever

There being no volunteers, the Doctor then drew his piece de resistance from the bag - a bottle of Guinness, waving it around for all to see

I've a bottle by my side

It's what I call the doctor's pride

Drop one drop on the skull bones of their heads

And one drop on the very touchbones of their hearts

It will strike through their bodies and bring them back to life again

Then with great relish, the doctor crouched low over the unfortunate actors and took great pleasure in emptying the Guinness bottle over their spluttering faces

And so it shall be as never before

Rise up you gallants and fight no more

The play was obviously going well judging from the cheering and laughing from the audience. Now soaked in beer, the dead men one by one rose from the floor and embraced Father Christmas. Then as the final twist to the story the old man turned to King George with the traditional cry of

So King George

Battle, to battle on thee I play

To see which of us on this ground shall lay

as George replied

Battle, to battle on thee I cry

To see which upon this floor shall lie.

And so commenced the final sword battle with the audience taking sides and cheering on their favourite. Of course everyone knew the outcome, and sure enough, after a fierce fight poor old King George lay slain as Father Christmas closed with

Now you see what I have done

I've killed King George who slew my four sons

A cup of strong ale will make us merry and sing

And then another to make the rafters ring.

So God Save the King

Merry Christmas

The play finished to huge applause as a tray of pints was brought out to the mummers who downed the lot in seconds.

"Well that beats Away in a Manger any day" said the bloke next to Eric. Eric didn't hear him; he was half way out of the door to beat the interval queue at the bar.

The bar upstairs was packed, mostly with people attending the disco, but also revellers getting tanked up before going off to parties. Eric entered the melee and worked his way towards the front, already trying to catch the eye of Sid the barman. Two lads were leaning on the bar in front of him, holding full drinks but not moving away to make space.

"'Scuse me gents, I'm dying of thirst here."

The lads turned to see who it was.

"Yo, Dillon, How you doin' mate?"

Eric did a double take. "Kevin, Wesley. Good to see you. How's life on the outside then? Going straight I hope."

Wesley, smiled coyly, "Yeah man, we ain't never going back in there. You still doin' the lessons then? I heard that old ratbag Cooper got a fright from the Police. Here, what are you drinking? This one's on me."

"Oh that's nice, thanks Wesley. Pint of Brakspears Old please mate. Yes Cooper got searched but they never pinned anything on him. I'm back in on Monday."

Wesley got Eric's drink and the three of them retired to wicker chairs in the garden room. Kevin was the first to speak after they had settled. He raised his glass.

"Cheers mate. I used to like it when you come in. Not like that bastard Cooper, we all 'ated him. If I had my chance I'd bust his nose."

"Me and all." said Wesley "He's the one what ought to be locked up. I reckon he's more crooked than most of the cons in there, and spiteful with it. He'd fit anybody up if they got in 'is way. I reckon that's what 'appened to old Thunderclap. He knew too much about somethin'. I wouldn't be surprised if it was Cooper what 'elped that bloke escape, then he pinned it on Newman."

Eric nodded. "Who? Oh old Brylcreem. Well you don't surprise me. I never liked Cooper the way he treated you lads," he paused and looked over his shoulder before continuing in hushed tones "and now he's after me 'cos he thinks it was me that tipped off the police about him in some shady dealing. I'm pretty scared about it to tell you the truth."

Wesley's eyes widened. "Shady dealing? What kind of shady dealing?"

Eric took a sip of his beer. "I'm not sure," he lied, "but it's obviously something where he's making money out of the cons in the prison. "

"The devious bastard." exclaimed Kevin. "Here, how come he never tried it on us lads?"

"Well I dunno, but I did hear him say once that you lads couldn't be trusted to keep your mouths shut. He had no time for you lot, I can tell you. Very unfair I thought."

"Very bloody typical if you ask me." said Wesley, "He's a five star git that bloke. I'd like to get my hands on him. How come he thought you'd called the police in?"

"Search me" said Eric "Maybe 'cos I kept asking him too many questions about what he was up to with the senior cons. I was only curious. Anyway now him and some other bloke are after me. The other feller chased me in his car the other night. He nearly got me, except he hit a lamp post first. Huge bloke, a wrestler they said he was. Local man apparently."

"Not wassisname, Mangler Marshall? Jesus, you don't want to mess with him," said Wesley, "Is Cooper mixed up with him then?"

"Apparently so, if that's his name." Eric drained his glass. "Another drink lads? My round."

Eric went off for the drinks leaving Wesley and Kevin deep in conversation. The queue at the bar was horrendous and it was a good ten minutes before he returned with the drinks.

"We been thinkin' " said Kevin, "if you gets any more trouble from that bastard Cooper, you ought to give us a shout. We wouldn't mind an excuse to rough him up a bit, all in the interests of defending an innocent man. Know what I mean?"

Eric smiled ruefully. "Well that's very thoughtful of you lads but I think you ought to be keeping out of trouble right now." He looked at his watch. Ten to ten, the second half of the folk night would be starting. "I think I'll have to love you and leave you lads, I need to get back to the party."

"You up with that lot in the recital room then? I thought that was a posh private do judging by the motors in the car park."

"Nah, not me," said Eric, fully appreciating that not thinking him to be posh was fair comment, "I'm down in the cellar. Folk Club Christmas party." And with that he shook hands with Wesley and Kevin and headed through the crowded bar towards the cellar stairs.

En route he decided to detour via the Gents toilets to make himself comfortable for the next session. Pint of Old in hand he crossed the landing and elbowed open the door of the facilities. Inside the toilets some thoughtful architect or interior designer had conveniently placed a shelf upon which users could lodge their beer glass while performing their ablutions. Eric put his pint down next to a large glass of whisky and looked over towards the urinals to see who its owner might be. Standing with his back to him and wearing a dinner jacket and sporting a shock of white hair was a strangely familiar figure. Glancing over to the mirror Eric got a sideways look at the man. For a second he stood frozen in shock then just as the man zipped up his flies and turned Eric leapt into the nearest cubicle and slammed the door shut. Cooper. It was Cooper!

What the hell was he doing at the Arts Centre? At that posh do upstairs he supposed. Eric was fairly sure the man hadn't spotted him. He put his ear to the door and listened. He heard the rush of the taps and the rumble of the roller towel, but despite a long pause, he didn't hear Cooper leave the room. Heart still thumping from the shock, Eric climbed silently onto the loo seat and peeked over the cubicle door. Cooper was still there alright, bending over the wash basin shelf. What was he up to? He could hear scraping. Eric strained to get a better view, standing on tip toes.

The white haired man was leaning over the basin shelf and holding a rolled up pound note. And there, on the shelf, in clear view, was a stick of chalk. Eric gasped. Cooper, hearing the sound, turned just as Eric's foot slipped from the loo seat and he fell crashing to the floor. "Aaaaghh!" The pain in his ankle was intense.

Cooper, realising he had been seen preparing his cocaine, pocketed the chalk and dashed out of the door. Eric staggered to his feet and exited the cubicle limping heavily. Without stopping to think, he followed Cooper out into the lobby to see him running up the stairs towards the recital room party. He stood and watched as Cooper reached the landing where a group of dinner jacketed revellers were having a smoke. Unable to quickly get into the party because of the crowd round the door, Cooper looked over his shoulder and down the stairs to where Eric was standing, open mouthed.

Too late, Eric turned his face away, but it was clear from Cooper's expression that he had recognised him. Both men stood stock still as if in a freeze frame, both thinking what this meant. Then the spell was broken in the worst possible way, for out of the recital room door came a large man. A very large man. None other than George Marshall, the Mangler.

Eric didn't wait to see the exchange between the men on the landing. He just made for the cellar bar stairs as fast as his stinging ankle would let him. Gingerly he put his foot on the first step down and his ankle gave way beneath him. The brick steps were steep and Eric hit every one as he rolled head over heels down the stairs then crashed into the heavy wooden door at the bottom bursting it open and tipping him into the crowded folk club where he lay barely conscious.

The assembled throng had been well into the chorus of the Boars Head Carol

Caput apri defero

Laudens reddens domino

a chorus which everyone knew although few knew what it meant. Anyway, they fell silent when Eric made his spectacular entrance. One girl screamed and a few more gasped as he lay on the red tiled floor groaning, a large gash on the side of his head. Barely had the crowd come to their senses when there was a second deafening bang as the door burst open once more to reveal the stupendous towering figure of George Mangler Marshall closely followed by the creepy figure of the rat Cooper.

The crowd around Eric's stricken body backed off in terror as the Mangler bent forward and grabbed Eric's collar and his husky voice growled "You're coming wiv us sunshine." Eric was in no position to resist. It felt like he had already broken half the bones in his body and in all likelihood the Mangler was about to break the other half. Without any expectation of success he let out a feeble "Help!"

Then, from the midst of the crowd a figure appeared which made the big man stop in confusion. He blinked at the rag coated and masked figure before him as it cried out

"Battle to battle on thee I call to see who on this ground shall fall"

The Mangler, clearly confused, looked around the room as four more rag coated figures emerged to face him, each armed with a sword and shield.

"What the f .."

"Battle to battle on thee I play to see who on this ground shall lay" shouted the mummers in unison, and then they leapt upon the huge wrestler whacking him over the head with their wooden swords. He backed off for a few seconds unsuccessfully shielding his cranium against the rain of blows from the rag coated men. Completely taken aback by this sudden attack, he stood shaking his muzzy head. The crowd was braying, women screaming and his head was hurting. He couldn't work out what was going on. What was happening? Where was he? The room started to spin and the sounds of the affray told him he was once again in the wrestling ring, his opponent taunting him. Instinct took over. Drawing himself up to his full six feet eight inches he let out a terrifying roar and with one sweep of his mighty arm he laid three of the mummers flat out and advanced menacingly towards the others. More women were screaming and running for the fire escape closely followed by their men folk as the big man stood in the middle of the floor like King Kong baring his teeth as if to dare anyone to approach.

Eric, racked with pain had managed to get onto his feet, and while the Mangler's back was turned he shoved Cooper out of the way and hobbled up the stairs into the concourse. When he reached the top of the steps he looked back to see Cooper in hot pursuit. There was no chance that Eric could outrun him for more than a few seconds. He looked around for a place of refuge and saw his only option, the dance studio, where the disco was in full swing. Before the bouncers on the door could react he plunged through the door then almost plunged out again as the pulsating noise and the room heat hit him. Inside it was packed and mostly pitch dark save for the flashing of strobe lights and some sort of coloured light projection against the far wall. Looking over his shoulder he pushed himself deep into the crowd, wincing with pain as shoulders and elbows of the dancers dug into his bruised ribs and people stepped on his throbbing ankle. He made his way through to the little stage where the DJ worked his turntables and looked back again at the entrance doorway to see the silhouette of Cooper as he entered the room. The Mangler would not be far behind he supposed.

Actually, he supposed wrongly. Back in the cellar bar, big George was swaying on his feet, he couldn't work out where he was and his head hurt. The mummers, sensing his confused condition once more advanced towards him. He waved his arms to swat them away, just like King Kong on the Empire State Building swatting away the attacking aircraft. Then just like the mighty gorilla, his eyes rolled back and with a tumultuous crash he fell to the ground.

CHAPTER 34 - A NUTTING WE WILL GO

In the disco Eric was desperately looking out for his pursuers. Were it not for the darkness and the flashing lights he might have been able to keep away from them, but he could see nothing. They could be anywhere. The heat was intense in the room and he was already sweating profusely. The throbbing of the music matched the throbbing of his head and he was beginning to hyperventilate. Any minute now he might feel the hand on his shoulder. He looked around at the faces of the people dancing near him, each one as if in a trance, in a world of their own and conscious only of the beat of the music. No good looking to them for help. Then in a flash of the strobe lights, he picked out the white hair of Cecil Cooper working his way through the melee directly towards him.

Eric was not generally a decisive person, or an impulsive one, so his next move was totally out of character. He had an idea.

Cooper was nearly upon him but instead of fleeing or hiding from the nasty man Eric made sure their eyes met before he plunged back into the crowd moving left and right through the dancers, working his way round the room whilst ensuring that his pursuer was following. Managing to stay just a few steps ahead, Eric weaved this way and that until the good luck he was looking for came his way. Almost back at the entrance, he slapped a young dancer on the back. The young dancer looked round. It was Wesley. Cupping his hands over Wesley's ears he shouted against the deafening volume of the dance music. "Look behind me. It's Cooper after me. Now's your chance mate."

Wesley looked past Eric to see the advancing Cooper and his eyes narrowed. He quickly turned to where Kevin was bopping a couple of feet away and alerted him. Eric took a further pace and then turned to face Cooper who walked straight into the trap.

Only once before had Eric watched somebody being nutted. Back then it had amazed him how a mere nod of a forehead into someone's face could do so much damage. This time it was even more spectacular. A stereo nutting! With sublime co-ordination, wonderfully visually enhanced by the slow motion effect produced by a flashing strobe light, the foreheads of Kevin and Wesley homed in on Cooper's head. One smashed his horn rimmed glasses into his face and the other caught him beautifully on the left temple. Even over the deafening disco beat Eric heard the crack. Cooper crumpled like a rag doll and fell to the ground unconscious.

Eric looked around. Where was Marshall? He looked back to see Wesley and Kevin but they had melted anonymously into the dance crowd. He looked down at the limp figure of Cooper. Quite suddenly the music stopped and the bright house lights came on as Eric looked up to see that he was standing at the centre of an empty circle and being stared at by everyone on its circumference. Just like the Mangler and the now semi-conscious Cooper, Eric's head hurt. He looked around again as the disco bouncers pushed their way through towards the scene of the incident. The lights hurt his eyes, he was sweating and he felt sick, his head began to swim. The first bouncer arrived just as Eric swooned and collapsed in a heap on top of the comatose Cooper.

Fifteen minutes later Eric opened his eyes and saw the inside of an ambulance.

"Hello mate, back in the world are we?" The ambulance man smiled. "Looks like you've had an exciting night. How do you feel?"

Eric tried to sit up but winced in pain and fell back on the bed.

"Where does it hurt mate?"

"Um, um, head, arms, ankle, ribs, shoulder, pretty much everywhere really. I fell down stairs."

"Yeah I heard. I don't think anything's broken though. Nasty sprain on that ankle and you'll probably need a couple of stitches for that head wound, oh and you might have cracked a rib or two. Try not to laugh. We'll take you in for the night just to check you out, then it'll just be a matter of taking it easy till the bruises go."

Eric didn't feel like laughing and said so.

The ambulance man said "Well, you're better off than the other two they just took in. One of them has a nasty broken nose and the other one, the big fella is delirious. Bad concussion. They tell me he's had it a time or two before."

Eric sat up again. "Ow my head. Marshall concussed? How did that happen?"

"Apparently some acting troupe set about him with wooden swords when he was trying to do you in. Never heard the like. What had you done to upset him?"

"It's a long story" said Eric. "Where is he now?"

"A & E by now mate, same place as you and the white haired fella are going. You'll probably end up in adjacent beds."

"What? No, they can't. I mean, they mustn't. They'll kill me." Eric's voice rose in panic.

"Not in their condition they won't. Anyhow they're sending a PC to keep watch and to find out what happened. Apparently when they went through the white haired bloke's pockets to find out who he was, they found what looks like cocaine. Thousands of pounds worth they reckon, made up like sticks of chalk. Amazing. Hey up, here we are."

The ambulance swung in to the bay outside A & E. The doors opened to reveal a trolley, two nurses and a policeman.

The trolley paused in reception while the ambulance driver gave details of Eric's condition to one of the nurses. Eric looked around the waiting room. A little toddler with a roughly wrapped bandage round a finger sat quietly sobbing on his mother's knee. Two drunken youths sat opposite. One was nursing a cut lip and a black eye. The other sat reading a copy of Womans Weekly.

Eric didn't have to wait long, probably because of his police escort he not only jumped the queue but was moved into a single room rather than the usual curtained off cubicle. The doctor who came in looked uncomfortable at having a Constable present, but did a thorough job of poking and prodding at Eric's injuries and shining lights in his eyes. A pain killing injection and a bandaged ankle later, Eric was wheeled off to X Ray to have his ribs photographed.

Three ribs were cracked as it turned out. Eric asked what the treatment was, fully expecting to be bound in bandages or a plaster cast. No such luck. With cracked ribs they just leave the body to get on with it and tell you to try not to cough or sneeze.

"Have you got anybody at home to look after you?" asked the doctor. When he said that he hadn't, they decided to keep him in overnight to make sure he didn't have delayed concussion. The nurse who came to settle him down looked at his clipboard and said, "You wouldn't be the Eric Dillon who's been going out with a nurse called Elaine would you?"

"Yes that's me."

"Does she know you're here?"

"Er, no. She's gone home to her mum's."

"Ooh we ought to let her know. I expect we've got the phone number, next of kin and all that. Do you want me to?"

Eric hesitated. What should he do? She would probably be angry that he had got into more trouble.

"No, best not trouble her. I'll be fine. Just a few bruises."

The nurse looked across towards the policeman and then bent to whisper in Eric's ear. "Are you, um, are you in trouble?"

"Me? No. I'm the victim of an attack. I suppose he's here to keep me safe." Eric was not at all sure that was true, but that was the impression he wanted to give.

"Safe? What from?"

"Oh I've been helping the police catch some criminals, so the baddies have been after me. I'm safe enough though 'cos those two others they just brought in are the ones who were after me."

"Blimey, did you do that to them? They're in a bad way."

Now there was a chance. Eric could paint himself as quite the action hero here. He was tempted to pretend that he'd dealt with them single handed, but then he decided he'd never get away with it.

"No. Some friends came to my rescue."

"Excuse me nurse." It was the policeman. "If you've quite finished with Mr Dillon now, we'd like to get a preliminary statement from him." He was obviously uncomfortable with all the whispering.

Eric gave a rough picture of what had happened that evening, making sure that the PC knew that he was working with Amory the detective. He didn't actually say that he was working under cover, but he couldn't resist the temptation to give that impression. The PC was duly impressed and Eric began to feel a bit like James Bond.

The nurse came back to oust the policeman, saying that Eric needed rest and tucked him in for the night. It was true. Eric was really knackered and the pain killers had made him drowsy. He fell asleep almost immediately.

CHAPTER 35 - A GOOD SAMARITAN

Next morning he awoke really early, aching all over and with a splitting headache. Any euphoria he had felt last night as a result of all the excitement had now worn right off. He was in pain, he had no one at home to cosset him, no car, and probably no girl friend. Christmas was coming and it looked like being a really crap one. In short, he was depressed. It was all quiet in his little room. He could just make out the occasional form passing the frosted window between him and the ward outside. He could make out two females in conversation. Nurses no doubt. Then there was a knock on the door and one of them came in.

"How are ya darlin'"

Eric blinked as his eyes tried to focus on her face in the darkened room.

"Doreen. Bloody Nora what are you doing here?"

"I was in seeing George and I heard you was here, so I said I was a friend and they let me in. My God you don't look too good darlin'. Did George do that to you?"

"No. No he didn't. I fell down the stairs running away from him and Cooper. Nearly broke me neck. Silly really." He tried to laugh and then winced in pain as his nerves round his cracked ribs shot their messages to his brain. "Ooh, Ow. How's George? He'll be even madder at me now."

"I don't think so darlin', he can't remember nothing. He hardly knew who I was. He's had that many concussions, what with his wrestling, and that car crash he had, that they reckon he might never get it all back. I reckon he won't remember nothing about you. They told me he'll have to give up his work or next time he could be knocked out for good."

"Oh, that's er, I mean, I wouldn't wish that on him." Eric tried not to show how relieved he was.

"Doreen smiled. "No darlin'. Lucky for you though ain't it. So is your girlfriend taking you home to look after you now then? You need somebody to."

"Aah, well, no, um, she can't."

"Can't? Why ever not. Didn't you say she was a nurse?"

"Well, yes, but she's not around at the moment. Gone home to see her mum in Cheltenham." He was going to leave it at that, but then he found himself continuing with "and I'm not sure where she and I stand right now. She was in the car when George chased me and crashed, and she got upset 'cos I was into all this trouble and she couldn't see an end to it." Eric was embarrassed to blurt it out, but Doreen was remarkably understanding.

"Hmm well I know how she feels, but I reckon you might be out of the woods now, what with George having lost his memory and they tell me that Cooper bloke got caught bang to rights with a pocket full of cocaine. So you won't be seeing him on the street for quite a while. Why don't you give her a ring?"

Eric shook his head. "No I can't do that. I might be out of trouble but I'm still in a pathetic mess. Look at me."

Doreen was adamant. "Well somebody's got to get you home and fed and watered. I suppose it'll have to be me then. When are they letting you out?"

"Um, today I suppose, but you can't do it Doreen, what about George?"

"Oh, they'll be keeping him in for a few days yet. I need something to take my mind off it. I'll run you home and get you settled. Mop your fevered brow and all that. We got to get you on the mend ASAP, it'll be Christmas in a few days."

Eric's further protestations fell on deaf ears and after being checked out by the doctor, later that morning he was discharged into the tender care of Doreen.

His flat was freezing cold when they arrived and the cupboards were bare. Doreen surveyed the rooms, tutting at the general untidiness while she gathered empty tea cups and picked up litter. "Typical man's pad, this needs a woman's touch. Where's your central heating switch?"

Eric gave a hollow laugh then gasped as his ribs reminded him of their fractures. "There isn't one. Just the electric bar fire in the big room and a fan heater in the bedroom."

"Blimey, that's not enough this time of year. I got an electric radiator at home, I'll fetch it later. Now you get into bed and I'll go and get some food from them shops we just passed. Then I'll give this place a spruce up. She looked around the room. You need some nice cushions and a rug on that floor. I got some in the spare room at home I'll bring them and all. Anything particular you want to eat?"

Eric shrugged and then said "Ouch."

Doreen laughed. "You'll have to watch them ribs Eric. No laughing, sneezing, and coughing or shrugging either by the look of it. I'll get us some stuff to make sandwiches and then for dinner I'll do us a nice casserole. How about that?"

Eric smiled. "You're so sweet Doreen. Thanks for this, it's really good of you."

"Yeah," she said, "It is ain't it. See you later darlin'."

That evening Eric was warm, cosy and well fed in his never more tidy and homely flat. Doreen had worked wonders. She had even set up the telly in his bedroom before she went off to visit George in hospital. He was just dozing off when she returned.

"You didn't need to come back." He said, although he was pleased to see her, especially as she brought him in a mug of hot chocolate and some biscuits.

"How's George?"

"Aah bless him, he's like a little boy, all confused but it seems to have knocked all the anger out of him. He's more like the George I used to have before he took up that bloody wrestling."

"What was his job before?" asked Eric.

"Painter and decorator, and before that he was in the Army. He made a lot more money at the wrestling. I suppose he might go back to decorating now, although thinking about it I don't want him up ladders in his condition."

Eric raised an eyebrow. "I thought you were leaving him. Have you changed your mind?" he said.

"We'll see. If I get my old George back then that might be nice." She smiled wistfully.

Eric sipped his hot chocolate. "Ooh that's lovely, thanks ever so much. I don't know how I'd have managed without you today, but you'd better get off home. You need rest as well."

"I'm not going home with you laid up like this." she said, putting on her matron voice. "I'll sleep on your sofa. You'll need your breakfast in the morning and I'll do you a nice hot bath. I brought my night things specially." She noticed a look of apprehension on Eric's face. "Don't worry sweetheart, I won't come in and molest you in the middle of the night. We don't want you breaking no more ribs. I brought some special embrocation George uses when he gets knocked about, which is most weeks. We'll rub it on them strains and bruises in the morning. Help you feel a lot better."

That night Eric slept like a baby. It was nine in the morning when Doreen came in wrapped in a dressing gown and carrying tea and toast on a tray. Where did that come from? He didn't own a tray.

"Mornin' sweetheart, a nice bit of breakfast for you. Sit up and I'll plump your pillow."

Eric yawned and then did as he was told although such movement was still painful.

"Ooh ow, ouch. Thanks Doreen."

She chuckled at his antics. "Typical man, can't stand a bit of pain. I'll run you a nice hot bath, I brought some Radox, that should help. Then we'll rub on a bit of George's embrocation. You'll feel a lot better in an hour or two. I'll pop over the 'ospital this afternoon to see George then I'll come back and get you some dinner."

"Oh there's no need Doreen. You've done more than enough already. I can manage, really. You ought to be getting home instead of looking after me." Much as he loved being looked after, he felt embarrassed that she was devoting so much time and effort on his behalf.

"No, I'm enjoying it Eric, it's too quiet at home, what with George bein' in 'ospital and Philip still being at Marge's, George's sister that is. Now don't let your tea get cold. I'll go and start that bath."

CHAPTER 36 - DISASTER

The bath was lovely. He lay and soaked until the water temperature had dropped to tepid then a hauled himself out and wrapped a towel round his hips before stepping out into the little hall. Just as he did so, there was a knock on the front door. He called out "I'll get it." and shuffled over and opened it up.

"Elaine! I didn't expect to see you. I thought you were still at your mum's." He was a bit taken aback by her unexpected arrival.

"I got a call from my friend Karen who works in A & E. She told me what happened to you and so, well," she hesitated as though reluctant to say what came next, "I was worried about you."

"Oh," he said, "you needn't, I'm, that is to say, I'm er,"

"Can I come in? It's freezing on this doorstep."

"Oh, yes of course. Um," This was awkward. How was he going to explain the presence of Doreen. "Come in. Um, I'd better explain, er, "

She walked through to the big room taking off her scarf. "Explain?" On entering the room, she stopped and did a double take on seeing the rug and the cushions and the general tidiness. "What the .." Then from the bedroom came the voice of Doreen.

"Come on sweetheart. The bed's ready, I need your body in here."

The words came like an ice pick in Elaine's head. For a moment she stood open mouthed, then with a look that turned Eric to stone she turned without speaking and ran from the room and the flat. He tried to follow, but his towel fell from his waist and caught his feet. By the time he limped to the door, she was already driving out of the car park.

Doreen emerged from the bedroom, a bottle of embrocation in her hand. "What was that? I heard the door slam." She looked at Eric standing naked with his head in his hands. "Ooh I say! Nice birthday suit." Then, finally, she took in his expression of despair. "What is it sweetheart? What just happened?"

His voice was trembling. "Elaine. It was Elaine. She just came in to see me then she heard you in the bedroom and jumped to the wrong conclusion and, and she just ran out before I could say anything." He punched the door frame in frustration. "Ouch, ow. What can I do? She'll never believe me." He looked over to Doreen and then, suddenly aware of his nakedness, turned away and retrieved his towel from the floor.

"Oh darlin' I'm sorry." Her sympathy seemed genuine. "Don't worry love. We'll put her straight. It's just a silly mistake. You ain't done nothin' wrong."

Eric was in despair. He climbed onto the sofa, curled into a ball and put a cushion over his head. His bruised body ached all over but it was in his mind that he had the real pain. He was emotionally exhausted and at the end of his tether. It was all too much.

"Oh Doreen, what am I going to do?" he said, fighting back tears.

She sat beside him and put her hand on his shoulder. Instinctively she knew that this wasn't the time for platitudes, so she just gently stroked his back in a gesture of comfort.

They sat that way for a good fifteen minutes, then she took the initiative. "Come on darlin, let's get them muscles rubbed, then I'll make us a nice hot drink and we'll work out what to do. It'll be alright, you'll see."

Eric felt no such optimism, but he consented to the rub down. Whatever it was she rubbed on burned deeply into his muscles. He bore the pain and discomfort as though accepting punishment for some misdeed, as if he were a monk accepting flagellation to purge his sins. Doreen's healing hands slowly smoothed away his pains and he drifted off into a deep sleep.

When he awoke he was alone. He sat up and rubbed his eyes, then reached for his watch on the bedside cupboard. Underneath it he saw a scribbled note.

"Hope you had a good sleep. I'm off to see George. Back later. D."

He smiled. Good old Doreen. Who'd have thought she'd turn out to be such a good egg. He swung his legs over the side of the bed and noticed how much less his body hurt. He sniffed and wrinkled his nose in disgust. That liniment or whatever it was might be effective but it smelled awful. He began to suspect it was stuff they used on horses. Nevertheless he decided not to wash it off yet. It might still be working its magic.

Over at the hospital Doreen sat by George's bed, feeding him grapes. He was making progress but the doctor said he should stay for another day or two. With multiple concussions patients could have a sudden bleed or swelling and have a relapse. George smiled and held her hand. "How long have I been here Doreen?"

"Couple of days. Can you remember what happened George?"

He shook his head. "What was it? Wrestling? I ain't doin' it no more babe. I've had enough." He thought for a minute. "What day is it?" He thought longer. "Doreen I can't remember. I can't even remember what month it is. Have we been on our holidays yet?"

"Don't you worry my love. You ain't missed nothin' important. You just relax. We'll have a good long holiday when we get you home."

The cubicle curtain pulled back as a nurse came in to check George's pulse and temperature. Doreen pulled her chair back from the bed and watched. An idea dawned on her.

" 'scuse me love. I hope you don't mind me asking but do you know a nurse called Elaine, works in A & E?"

The nurse looked up. "Elaine, yes. Are you a friend of her's?"

Doreen made the attempt to sound as though it was a very casual enquiry. "Sort of. More a friend of a friend really, only he's been trying to contact her. Something to do with er, the folk club but she's been away or something. Do you happen to know when she's back on duty?"

"I think she's on the Christmas Day shift. I don't think she's back on before then. Her boy friend had an accident. I think she might have gone over to look after him so she might not be at home. Sorry I can't help more but anyway we're not supposed to give contact details of staff."

"No, no, course not. Thanks anyway, I'll pass it on."

Doreen wasn't sure why she had asked the question at all, and what she might do with the information now she had it. All she knew was that she felt guilty about what had happened back at the flat. Somehow she felt she owed it to him to sort out the mess.

Back at the flat Eric was up to his old habit of pacing up and down, going over and over in his mind what he should have done and what he could do to put things right. Elaine had to understand the simple truth that Doreen was only there like a big sister looking after her little brother. The problem was, she would never believe him or Doreen. If they were having an intimate relationship, they would want to cover it up wouldn't they? What had really happened would just sound like a cock and bull story, and a poor one at that. Maybe he should make up a more plausible story, fiction less strange than truth. No, he was in enough trouble already and with his luck it would only backfire.

He was still pacing up and down when Doreen returned bearing cakes. "Custard doughnuts alright? It's all I could get."

Eric's eyes lit up. "Are you kidding? If you asked me to name a cake I like more, I couldn't. Doreen you're a wonder."

She passed him one. It lasted barely ten seconds, slipping down Eric's gullet without touching the sides. "Any more? That was orgasmic, I could eat a dozen."

"Steady on Eric, you'll get indigestion. Why not try actually chewing this next one." She gave him his second doughnut and while he was preoccupied with it she said "I been thinkin' "

"What about?" said Eric trying not to spit cake all over her.

"Maybe I should talk to your Elaine and explain. I mean it's all perfectly innocent ain't it, and let's face it, if I was still after you I'd hardly help you out getting back with her would I?"

Eric shook his head. Thanks, but no, I still don't think she'd believe you and anyway I doubt she'd even let you speak to her. What it really needs is somebody else to tell her the truth. Somebody who isn't necessarily on my or your side. You know, a sort of neutral party. And then of course, we'd have to convince them first. I can't see that happening." He sighed. "She'll probably end up with bloody Gerald."

"Who's Gerald?

"Oh some berk at the folk club, always hanging round Elaine and trying to put her off me. Toffee nosed bloke, wears a cravat and cavalry twill trousers and sensible shoes. You know the type. Bloody Telegraph reader I expect. He's into stocks and shares or some such.

"Well he don't sound her type."

"Hmm, well he doesn't get in the messes that I do, and he's got money I expect. It'd just be my luck if she went off with him."

He looked at Doreen who seemed to be lost in thought. "Have you been listening to a word I've been saying Doreen?"

"Yeh," she said absent mindedly, "What day is it?"

"Monday. I usually go down the Science Lab folk club but I'm not up to it. I'm having an early night."

"OK sweetheart. I'll pop on your casserole then I think I'll head home and get it ready for when they let George out." She had the casserole all ready, so she just switched on the oven and put it in. "Should be ready in about an hour. Take care and see you soon." She gave him a peck on the cheek and let herself out.

CHAPTER 37 - GENIUS

Down at the Science Lab club Gerald was tuning his guitar. He didn't at first notice the attractive and rather sophisticated woman who came in and stood at the back. Even Eric would hardly have recognised her had he been there. Quite where she had learned to look so casually classy was a mystery but she sure did. She might have been wearing slacks and a sweater but they, and she, looked like something from a Jaeger advert. She spent the first half of the evening quietly observing. Gerald was of course easy to spot, Eric's description fitted perfectly. With the skill that comes with years of practice of catching men's eyes Doreen unobtrusively made sure she kept in his eye line, and did her best to look alluring, so when half time came he was more than pleased when she approached him.

"Hi, I really liked that song you did. Did you write it yourself?" Eric might not have recognised Doreen's voice either, she was putting on her posh but sexy voice.

"Thank you, but no, it's a traditional song. Victorian probably." Gerald smiled condescendingly.

"Oh, well it was lovely anyway. I don't know anything about folk music, this is the first time I've been to something like this. Are you a professional singer? You're good enough." She thought such flagrant flattery might be too obvious but Gerald was plenty vain enough to fall for it.

"Goodness no. I mean I probably could, but it doesn't pay at all well compared with my profession."

"Oh, what's that?" she asked, trying to look fascinated.

"Investment banking" he replied, then quickly added "not as boring as it sounds."

"Boring? Investment banking? It makes the world go round doesn't it? That's what the Telegraph says anyway, and they're usually right." She raised her previously drained glass to her lips then said "Oh I seem to be empty."

Gerald rose to the occasion precisely as required. "Let me get you a refill. What would you like?"

"Thanks, a dry sherry would be lovely." She hated dry sherry but needs must. She feared her favourite rum and blackcurrant wouldn't have fitted the image. When he returned with the drinks she led him through to the easy chairs in the lounge bar where they could sit and talk.

"So," he said, "what brings you to the folk club?"

"Curiosity really. Some chap I had to attend to today suggested I might like it. He's a regular apparently, a bit pathetic actually. I think I came along to humour him. Silly really. Then I saw you sing and, well, I can see the art in it."

"A regular you say?"

"Yah." she was really getting into character now, on the point of overdoing it almost. "Chap called Eric, not really our sort if you know what I mean. Had some sort of contre temps with a wrestler would you believe, petty criminal apparently. Anyway he was running away from this wrestler brute and fell down some stairs. Then he got involved in a fight in a disco and passed out. Covered in bruises. I don't work regularly now but I trained as an osteopath and my number's still in the book, so if anyone calls I often do a little bit to keep my hand in. Treated him this morning at his dreadful council flat. He just needed a healing massage really. In my experience that class of person can't stay out of trouble. Police involved too apparently."

"Eric?" Gerald smiled a little too gleefully, "Not Eric Dillon?"

Doreen resisted the temptation to tell Gerald not to be so cheerful about it and instead gave a little laugh.

"Yah, that's him. Better not say anything to anyone though. Patient confidentiality and all that."

She looked at her watch. "Golly, I ought to be going, got to collect Piers off the ten thirty flight from Glasgow."

Gerald tried not to look crest fallen. "Piers?"

"My husband, been up there on business." She stood up and offered her hand. "Well it's been lovely talking to you, er, "

"Gerald" he said.

"Lavinia" she said. Well it was her granny's name. And with that she took her leave, hoping she had done enough while silently congratulating herself on her act. "Doreen that was bloody brilliant." she told herself. "You should have been an actress."

Gerald was in two minds. On the one hand he was disappointed that his relationship with Lavinia had been so brief but on the other hand he had some good ammunition to put down Eric in Elaine's eyes. Worth the price of a dry sherry he thought. Then he noticed that she hadn't drunk it. "Waste not want not" he thought, and downed it in one.

Eric woke feeling depressed. It was gone ten o'clock and the room was cold. Today there was no Doreen to bring in a nice cup of tea. At least the liniment had done a good job and his aches and pains were easing. He could go in to work, but he wasn't ready to face it. Besides, he still hadn't got a car. Slowly he dragged himself out of bed and shambled into the kitchen. At least Doreen had left that clean and tidy. He lit the gas under the kettle and shuffled drowsily into the hall to see what joys the postman had brought. Picking up the envelopes he leafed through them, working out their contents from the envelopes; his pay slip from work, the electricity bill, and a Christmas card with his brother's writing on the envelope. A right miserable Christmas this was going to be.

He turned to return to the kitchen and a rap on the door knocker made him jump. He almost didn't bother to open it, then decided he should. If it was Jehovah's Witnesses he would bust them on the nose. Wearily he opened up and peered round the edge of the door.

"Eric, I'm so so sorry."

"Elaine??" He blinked in confusion. What was going on? He stood transfixed and frowning in disbelief.

She looked concerned at his state. "Can I come in?"

"Er, yes." He stepped back and she entered the hall, then flung her arms round his neck pressing her cheek against his."

"Ow, ouch" His neck still hurt.

Elaine pulled back and looked sadly over his bruised form. "Oh poor you. I'm so sorry I doubted you. I feel so guilty now I know."

"Know what?" Eric was still dazed, but his heart was beating fast. This seemed to be good but he couldn't understand it. He proceeded warily.

"About the osteopath. I didn't know, I thought," she hesitated, fearing what she would have to say, "I thought it was that Doreen."

He looked blank.

"In, in the bedroom when I came in. She said something about, about, well I got the wrong impression. I didn't know you were just having a massage. I shouldn't have jumped to the wrong conclusion and ran out like that. I'm so sorry."

Eric was still puzzled.

"How, I mean who .."

"That creepy Gerald rang me up, gloating about how you'd got in with the wrong lot and how you were in all sorts of trouble. Apparently he ran in to the osteopath lady or whatever she was who was doing your massage and she told him. Sneaky bitch, I wouldn't hire her again if I were you. She should be struck off. Anyway that's when I realised I'd got it wrong."

Eric was aghast. "No, well, I certainly won't, um, use her again." He tried not to smile. That lady could have been only one person.

"Oh poor you Eric, you look shattered. Hop back into bed and I'll get you some breakfast and a hot drink." She pouted "Oh Eric, can you forgive me? I've been so hard on you."

Somehow he resisted the temptation to play on her guilt. "No you haven't. I've been stupid. I deserved it. Anyhow it's all finished now. I'm hanging up my detective's hat and going back to finding jobs for the boys."

She kissed him, and it was the best three seconds of his life so far. She went into the kitchen to make breakfast. "Hey this kitchen looks tidy." she called out, "How come this place has had a spruce up, and who brought those cushions and that rug?"

"Oh, someone I know through work. She took pity on me. Nice lady, you'd like her." Well, he thought, it was all true wasn't it? Elaine raised one eyebrow. "Not another one chasing you is she?"

He smiled and shook his head. "No. I think she's happy with her old man." He began humming one of old Skip James's happier songs. It goes by the name of *I'm So Glad*.

THE END

39019417R10145

Made in the USA
Charleston, SC
23 February 2015